PLANESRUNNER

IAN McDONALD

PLANESRUNNER

an imprint of Prometheus Books
Amherst, NY

Published 2011 by Pyr®, an imprint of Prometheus Books

Cover illustration © John Picacio
Jacket design by Grace M. Conti-Zilsberger

Inquiries should be addressed to
Pyr
59 John Glenn Drive
Amherst, New York 14228–2119
VOICE: 716–691–0133
FAX: 716–691–0137
WWW.PYRSF.COM

15 14 13 12 11   5 4 3 2 1

Library of Congress Cataloging-in-Publication Data Pending

ISBN 978–1–61614–541–5
ISBN 978–1–61614–542–2 (e-book)

Printed in the United States of America

To Enid, as ever.

Author's Note: There is a Palari dictionary at the back of this book.

1

The car was black. Black body shell, black wheels, black bumpers, black windows. The rain sat on its shiny skin like drops of black oil. A black car on a black night. Everett Singh zipped his jacket up to his chin and flipped up his hood against the cold wind and watched the black car crawl behind his dad, pedalling his bicycle up the Mall. It was a bad bike night. Tree branches lashed and beat. Wind is the cyclist's enemy. The Institute for Contemporary Arts' nonreligious seasonal decorations flapped and rattled. Everett had noticed that every year when Hackney Council put up their Winterval lanterns, a storm would arrive and blow them down again. He had suggested that they put them up a week later. They hadn't even acknowledged his email. This year the storm blew as it blew every year and the decorations were scattered the length of the High Street. Everett Singh noticed things like that: patterns, behaviours, connections, and coincidences.

That was how Everett noticed the car. It hadn't pulled out to skim aggressively past Tejendra on his bike. It kept a slow, steady pace behind him. London cars didn't do that, not with bikes, certainly not on a cold wet Monday night on a rainy Mall ten days before Christmas. His dad wouldn't have noticed it. Once Tejendra got going on his bike, he didn't notice anything. Tejendra had started biking after the split with Everett's mum. He said it was quicker, he had less of a carbon footprint, and it kept him fit. Everett reported this to Divorcedads.com. The site had started as a well-meaning web space where "kids could network about the pain of parental split-up." The kids arrived and turned it into a forum for swapping embarrassing dad stories. The opinion of the forum was that buying a full-suspension mountain bike for four thousand pounds when the steepest thing you ever rode over was a speed bump was typical of dads when they split up. Slipped-nott wondered why he couldn't have bought a Porsche like everyone else. *Because my dad's not like everyone else*, Everett commented back.

Other dads named their sons after footballers or relatives or people on television. Tejendra named his after a dead scientist. Other dads took their sons to Pizza Express after the football. Tejendra created "cuisine nights" at his new apartment. After every Tottenham home game, he and Everett would cook a feast from a different country. Tejendra liked cooking Thai. Everett was good at Mexican. And other dads took their sons to laser quest or karting or surf lessons. Tejendra took Everett to lectures at the Institute for Contemporary Arts on nanotechnology and freaky economics and what would happen when the oil ran out. It was cool with Everett Singh. Different was never boring.

Here came Tejendra, pushing up the Mall, head down into the wind and the rain, in full fluorescents and flashers and reflectors and Lycra with the big black German car behind him. Punjabi dads should not wear Lycra, Everett thought. He put up his arm to wave. The glow-tubes he'd knotted through the cuffs traced bright curves in the air. Tejendra looked up, waved, wobbled. He was a terrible cyclist. He was almost going backwards in the wind howling down from Constitution Hill. Why didn't the black car go round him? It couldn't have been doing more than ten kilometres per hour. There it went now. It pulled out with a deep roar, then cut in across Tejendra and stopped. Tejendra veered, braked, almost fell.

"Dad!" Everett shouted.

Three men got out of the car. They were dressed in long dark coats. Everett could see Tejendra was about to yell at them. The men were very quick and very sure. One of them wrenched Tejendra's right arm behind his back. A second bundled him into the backseat. The third man picked up the fallen bicycle, opened the boot and threw it in. Doors slammed shut, the black car pulled back into traffic. Very quick, very sure. Everett stood stunned, his arm still raised to wave. He was not sure he could believe what he had seen. The black car accelerated towards him. Everett stepped back under the arcade along the front of the ICA. The glow tubes, the stupid glow tubes, were like a lighthouse. Everett pulled out his phone. The car swept past him. Tejendra was a patch of fluorescent yellow behind the darkened windows. Everett stepped out and shot a photograph, two photographs, three, four. He kept shooting until the black car vanished into the traffic wheeling around the Victoria Memorial.

Something. He must do something. But Everett couldn't move. This must be what shock felt like. Posttraumatic stress. So many actions he could take. He imagined himself running after the black car, running at full pelt up the rainy Mall, tailing the black car through the rush hour. He could never catch it. It had too much of a lead. The city was too big. He couldn't run that far, that long, that fast. Maybe he could stop a taxi, tell it to follow that car. Tejendra had told him once that every taxi driver longed to be told that. Even if he could ever track the black car through the London traffic, what did he think he could do against three big men who had lifted his father as lightly as a kitten? That was comics stuff. There were no superheroes. He could ask the people huddling under umbrellas, collars turned up, arriving for a public talk on nanotechnology: *Did you see that? Did you?* He could ask the door staff in their smart shirts. They were too busy meeting and greeting. They wouldn't have seen anything. Even if they had, what could they do? So many wrong actions, but what was the right thing, the one right thing? In the end there was one right thing to do. He hit three nines on his phone.

"Hello? Police? My name's Everett Singh. I'm at the ICA on the Mall. My dad has just been kidnapped."

2

The police station stank. It had been redecorated, and the smell of industrial high-durability silk finish paint had worked through every part of it from front desk to the interview room. Everett wouldn't smell anything else for days. Already it was making his head spin. But that might also have been the bad strip-lighting, the too-hot radiator, the deadly dry air conditioning, the chair that caught him in the back of the knee and cut off his circulation so that his legs were buzzing with pins and needles: any one of the dozens of things about a police station that the police never think might unsettle ordinary people.

"Could I have some water, please?"

"Of course, Everett."

There were two police, a man and a woman. The woman was a Family Liaison Officer and did all the talking. She was meant to be friendly, empathetic, nonthreatening. Everett guessed she was maybe thirty; a little chubby, with over-straightened dyed blonde hair that made her face look big. She looks like a male comedian playing a woman police officer, Everett thought. She'd told Everett her name, but he'd never been any good at names. Leah, Leanne, Leona—something like that. Police shouldn't give you their first names.

The man who took down notes was the exact opposite of Leah-Leanne-Leona. He had sunken cheeks and a moustache like police wore in cop shows back in the '70s, the kind Tejendra watched on Channel Dave. He looked tired, as if nothing could ever surprise him again but he had to be ready for that time when the world might throw something new and hard at him. He was D. S. Milligan. Everett liked that. Leah-Leanne-Leona answered Everett's request, but Moustache Milligan fetched the water from the cooler in the corner of the room.

"So, Everett, the Institute of Contemporary Arts?" Leah-Leanne-Leona made it sound like the freakiest, most perverse place a dad could take a son; bordering on child abuse.

"It's his dad's idea," Everett's mum said. First Everett phoned the police; second he phoned home. It had been bad. At first she wouldn't believe him. Kidnapped, on the Mall, on a Monday night, in the middle of the rush hour. He was making it up, attention seeking—that sort of thing didn't/couldn't happen. Not on the Mall. Not ten days before Christmas.

"Mum, I saw them take him."

Then he was being malicious, getting at her. I know you blame me for your dad, Everett. He's not coming back. We have to get on with it. We have to get the family right, look after ourselves. I know how you feel. Don't you think I'm feeling things too?

"No. Mum, listen. It's not about feeling things. I saw them take him, on the Mall, in a big black Audi. Bike and everything."

The worst was when he said he was in Belgravia police station. That made her voice go tight. And short. And sharp. The way it did when she wanted to make him feel bad. The shame. Had he no self-respect? He was no different from those Virdi boys. They were never out of police stations. God alone knew where she was going to find a lawyer this time of night. Maybe Milos. He was always good for a favour.

"Mum. Mum. Listen. I don't need a lawyer. I'm making a statement. That's all. They can't do anything unless you're there."

It had taken her an hour and a half to crawl in from Stokie and an hour grumbling about the parking and the congestion charge and having to leave Victory-Rose with Mrs. Singh. That old crow Ajeet always put bad ideas into the girl's head. And this place stank of paint. She found Everett sitting on a bench thumbing through Facebook on his smartphone and eating a Twix from the vending machine. The desk sergeant had bought him a coffee. As Everett had expected, it was bad and weak. Laura Singh sat down beside him and talked very low and fast because she would be ashamed if the desk sergeant overheard. She wanted Everett to know she didn't blame him. At all. Typical of his father. Typical to land Everett in trouble and not be there.

"Mum . . ."

"Mrs. Singh?"

"Braiden." When had she started calling herself that? Family Liaison Officer Leah-Leanne-Leona introduced herself and led them down the corridors that looked as if they had been painted with sweat to the reeking interview room.

"We go to talks at the ICA," Everett said, looking Leah-Leanne-Leona in the eye. His palms were flat on the table. "Experimental economics, the coming singularity, nanotechnology. Big ideas. They have Nobel Prize winners."

Leah-Leanne-Leona's eyes glazed, but Everett saw that Moustache Milligan had spelled nanotechnology correctly in his notes.

"Okay, Everett. It's good you still have something you can share with your dad. Guy-stuff is good. So, your dad would meet you outside the ICA after work."

"He was coming over from Imperial College."

"He's a scientist," Everett's mum said. Every answer she jumped in ahead of Everett, as if a wrong or careless response from him would be all the evidence the police needed to call social services and take Everett and little sister Victory-Rose into care.

"He's a theoretical physicist," Everett said. Moustache Milligan raised an eyebrow. Everett had always wished he could do that.

"What kind of physics?" Moustache Milligan asked. Leah-Leanne-Leona flared her nostrils. She did the talking here.

"Quantum theory. The Everett Many Worlds Theory. Hugh Everett, he developed it. I'm named after him: Everett Singh. The multiverse, parallel universes, all that, you know?" Everett Singh saw that Moustache Milligan had written *Non-nuke* on his notepad beside the word *physicist?* "What does that mean?" Everett asked. "Non-nuke."

Moustache Milligan looked embarrassed.

"You know what the current security situation's like. If your dad had been a nuclear physicist, that could be an issue."

"You mean, if he could build atom bombs."

"We have to consider all kinds of threats."

"But if he doesn't build atom bombs, if he's just a quantum physicist, then he's not a threat. He's not so important."

"Everett!" Laura hissed. But Everett was angry and tired of not being taken seriously. Whether it was Belgravia Police Station or the IT room of Bourne Green Community Academy, it was always always always the same. Mock the Geek. He hadn't asked for any of this. All he'd done was go to listen to a lecture with his dad. Everett knew better than to expect the world to be fair, but it might occasionally cut him a break.

"Do you know what the Many Worlds Theory is?" Everett said. He leaned forward across the table. Previous occupants had doodled stars and spirals and cubes and the names of football clubs on the peeling plastic. "Every time the smallest least tiniest thing happens, the universe branches. There's a universe where it happened, and a universe where it didn't. Every second, every microsecond every day, there are new universes splitting off from this one. For every possible event in history, there's a universe, out there somewhere, right beside this one." Everett lifted a finger and drew a line through the air. "A billion universes, just there now. Every possible universe is out there somewhere. This isn't something someone made up, this is a proper physical theory. That's what physics means: real, solid, actual. Does that sound not so important to you? It sounds to me like the biggest thing there is."

"That's very interesting, Everett." Leah-Leanne-Leona's tea mug had a badly rendered picture of a fat tabby cat on its back waving its paws. I CAN HAZ TEE, said the fat cat.

"Everett, don't waste their time; they don't want to know," Laura said. "It's not relevant."

"Well, they had some reason for kidnapping him," Everett said.

"This is what we're trying to establish, Everett," Leah-Leanne-Leona said. "Did anyone else see this car and the three men?"

The power went out of Everett. The policewoman had found the valve to his anger, and it had all hissed out of him.

"No," Everett Singh whispered.

"What was that, Everett?"

"That was a no."

He should have asked the ICA staff, the people going in to the talk, the dog walkers and the bad weather joggers, *Did you see that, did you?* But you don't think of things like that when your dad is on his bike one minute and the next lifted off and thrown into the back of a big black Audi.

"I've got photographs on my phone," Everett said. "Here, I can get them up." A few swipes with his finger and he had them. Tippy tap, up they came one at a time. Crazy angles, tail-lights blurred. Unless you knew what you were looking for you wouldn't recognize them for snapshots of a kidnapping. The police looked unimpressed. Everett halted at one clear, steady shot where the inside of the black car was momentarily lit up by oncoming headlights.

"See that bit of yellow in the middle of the back window? That's my dad." Everett stroked the picture down to the registration plate. He opened up the magnification. The resolution of these little touchphone cameras was rubbish, but at highest magnification there was just enough detail to read the letters and numbers. "There's something you could check."

"We could run this through image enhancement," Detective Sergeant Milligan said.

"We'd need to keep your phone," Leah-Leanne-Leona said. "Just for a day or two."

"I don't want to give it you," Everett said.

"Everett, let them have it," Laura said. "Just give it to them and then we can go. God knows what Ajeet's been telling Victory-Rose." To Leah-Leanne-Leona, she said, adult to adult, "Honestly, he spends far too much time on those conspiracy theory websites. You should do something about those. Get them banned."

"I'll give you the card," Everett said. He sprang the tiny memory chip out of its housing with his fingernail. "The photographs are on it." He set it in the middle of the desk. No one moved to take it. "You do believe me, don't you?"

"I'll take care of it, Everett," Moustache Milligan said. He slid the chip into a ziplock plastic bag.

"There are a few things we'd ask you to do," Leah-Leanne-Leona said. "Precautions. Just in case. If you really want to help us, keep this to yourselves, okay? Don't go telling people—and no tweeting it or putting it up on Facebook. If anyone does get in touch, whether it's Mr. Singh . . ."

"Dr. Singh," Everett interrupted.

"If you say so, Everett. If it's Dr. Singh himself, or if it's anyone else, get in touch with us. No matter what they tell you. If he has been kidnapped for a ransom, they always warn you not to get in touch with the police. Don't do that. Let us know immediately."

"Ransom? Oh dear God. What did they pick us for?" Laura said. "We're not rich; we haven't two pennies to rub together. We can't afford a ransom."

"'If,'" Everett said. "You said 'if' he has been kidnapped for a ransom. What other kinds are there?"

"Do you want me to list them?" Moustache Milligan said. "I'll list them for you. I tell you this, it won't make you feel better. There's what we call tiger kidnappings. It's usually a relative of a bank employee gets taken hostage while the manager opens up the vault and removes the cash. Then there are kidnappings for hostage swaps. There are kidnappings for specialist knowledge—doctors get lifted to patch up some hood who's been shot up in a gang fight.

Then there's express kidnappings. They lift you and every day march you down to the cash-point to take out the daily limit until the account's empty. It's a flourishing business, son, kidnapping. And then there are the people who just disappear. Gone. Missing persons. It's mostly those, missing persons." Moustache Milligan lifted his ballpoint and looked directly at Everett. "Now son, if you want to give me a statement, you and your mum can go home and let us find your dad."

Everett leaned back his chair and breathed the paint fumes deep inside him.

"Okay, I came down into London after school to meet my dad . . ."

3

All the way up the A10, through Dalston and along Stoke Newington High Street, Laura didn't speak. Not a word. She tapped her fingers on the steering wheel and mumbled mangled bits of lyrics from the smooth-listening MOR radio station until Everett wanted to punch his fist at the radio, punch any button, hit any station with a bit of noise and beat and life. Anything rather than listen to his mum getting the lines wrong.

See that girl, hear her scream, kicking the dancing queen. It's not that! Everett seethed inside. *Clown Control to Mao Tse Tung* . . . Major Tom! Everett wanted to shout. Major Tom Major Tom Major Tom. Get it right. The song was forty years old, but Everett knew it better than his mum. There was a word for misheard lyrics. Everett had come across it online: a mondegreen. He'd liked the word. He remembered it.

By the time they got to Evercreech Road to pick up Victory-Rose, Everett understood. This was anger, of a kind he had seen once—only once—before. He'd seen it the day he came back from football practice and found all the lights on in every room and every door open and the radio blaring through the entire house and his mum in the kitchen, mopping the floor, mopping and mopping and mopping. *Something kind of ooh ooh, jumping up my tutu*, she'd been singing along to Girls Aloud.

"Mum what are you doing?"

"This floor is disgusting. It smells. That's disgusting. Kitchen floors shouldn't smell. There's ground-in disgusting things between the tiles. And I'm not having those things over my nice clean floor."

She had pointed at Everett's football boots. He slipped them off. Stocking feet on cold concrete step.

"Are you all right?"

"Fine fine."

"Are you sure?"

"Yes I'm sure. Absolutely sure."

"You cleaned that bit of floor three times."

"No I didn't."

"Yes you did."

"Well, what if I did? It needs cleaning. It's disgusting. This whole place is disgusting. I can't keep anything nice; why can't I keep anything nice?"

"Mum, are you okay?"

"Yes I'm okay. Okay? Here's me saying: I. Am. O. K. Why do you keep asking me? Of course I'm okay, I'm always okay. I have to be okay. Someone has to and that's always me. Oh shut up shut shut up; shut up your stupid blabbering . . ." Laura had screamed at the radio, slapped at the tuning buttons, then ripped the radio plug from the wall. Everett felt embarrassed, ashamed, scared. This was not a thing he should see. It was like the walls of his safe and predictable world had turned to glass and through them he could glimpse huge, monstrous, threatening shapes.

"I'm sorry, Everett," his mum said. "Everett, me and your Dad. He's taking . . . he's not coming . . . Well, we think it might be better if we spent some time apart. I don't know how long. Maybe quite a long time. Maybe . . . permanently . . ."

That was how Everett Singh found out that family life as he had always known it had ended, standing in his sock soles on the cold concrete back step, his school blazer over his goalkeeper kit. Boots in hand. Mum holding a squeegee mop. The radio blaring Girls Aloud. It had ended long before, he had realised. It had been ending for a long time. His parents had been lying to him for years.

He had seen the Angry nine months, two weeks, three days ago. He had hoped never to see it again, but here it was in the car with him. Granny Singh had taught Victory-Rose a Punjabi song, which she sang loudly and badly as Laura strapped her into the backseat. Laura put on Singalong with Beebles.

"Shall we sing our song, Vee-Arr? Our favourite song? Shall we? Shall we?" They sang, loudly and badly, all the up through South Tottenham and Stamford Hill.

I'm not the one to punish, Everett thought. There's no one to punish. But you need someone to ground your anger, like a lightning rod, so I'll do. I always do. Everett understood the mondegreen thing now. If his mum could sing her own words, her own interpretation, she had control, even if only of a pop song.

He went back over the details of his police statement in his memory. "At approximately 17:45 on December 15, I was waiting outside the Institute of Contemporary Arts on the Mall," Moustache Milligan had read from the report sheet. "I was waiting for my father Dr. Tejendra Singh to meet me at six o'clock for a public lecture on trends in nanotechnology. I saw my father proceeding up the Mall from Horseguards on his bicycle. He was coming from his office at Imperial College and was clearly, distinctively, and appropriately dressed. I noticed that he was being followed by a black car with darkened windows, of German make, possibly an Audi. I noticed that the car was driving abnormally slowly and that my father seemed oblivious of it. About a hundred metres from me the car abruptly pulled out, overtook my father, and pulled in front of him, causing him to swerve and stop. Three men exited the vehicle—"

"They got out of the car," Everett had said.

"Three men exited the vehicle," Moustache Milligan had continued. "Two of the men seized my father and forced him into the backseat. The third man put the bicycle into the boot. The car then drove off up the Mall in the direction of Constitution Hill. I took a series of photographs on my mobile phone, but I did not call out or attempt to alert any other passersby."

"Is that correct?" Leah-Leanne-Leona had said.

"Suppose." It sounded thin and full of holes. There were no witnesses, no corroboration, only Everett's own word and a shaky mobile phone photograph that, if you looked at it cold and hard, could be anything.

"Is that correct, Everett?"

"Yes."

"Sign here. Press hard—you're making a couple of copies."

In his room, in his space, away from the noise. Everett opened up Dr. Quantum. Tejendra had given him the tablet computer for his last birthday. It was a good present, the best present. Too much computer for his age—he'd still been a kid then. Laura had immediately forbidden him ever to take it to school, even to show it off. Everett concurred, for once. He had good senses and was fast—faster than anyone would think a Known Geek to be; it was what made him the goalkeeper for Team Red.

Into the mail. Open subject: *mall kidnap*. A swipe with the finger here, a tap there, and it was into his pictures folder. Everett spread his fingers like a bird opening its wings. The photograph opened up to fill the screen. Everett zoomed in on the tiny scrap of fluorescent yellow in the backseat. Tejendra: that was Tejendra; he could almost read the black Assos logo on the weatherproof jacket.

Rules for twenty-first century living: Never give the police your only photograph.

The doorbell rang. Everett, exploring the photograph pixel by pixel, half-heard it. Someone was always ringing the bell, trying to sell something, despite the sign that said, politely, *We don't buy door to door.* Then he heard the voice, and shoes on the wooden floor in the hall. Dragging feet; a low Northern Ireland accent. Paul McCabe. Everett went to the bedroom door, opened it a crack. Paul McCabe stood in the hall, hunched over in his raincoat. No one had worn coats like that for forty years. It made him look like a cheap private detective. He always seemed round-shouldered, skulking, guilty of something. Even in his office at Imperial College he never looked at home, as if he had wandered in one morning in the 1980s and was waiting for the day when someone official would discover he was a fraud and throw him out. His voice, talking to Laura, was soft and hesitating. He always seemed to be apologising in advance. Paul McCabe must have heard the bedroom door open, because he turned and looked straight at Everett.

"Everett. Yes yes yes, are you well? Good good. Terrible affair, terrible. Sincerest good wishes. The police called; everyone at the department is terribly upset, terribly. Colette is distraught, quite distraught."

No way back now. Everett had grown up a physics brat, running free between lecture halls and labs, whiteboards covered in symbols and high-powered research equipment with exciting yellow warning stickers: Lasers! Radiation! Nanohazard! The faculty staff was his alternative family, but he had always found Paul McCabe, Tejendra's Head of Department, too jolly, too much the embarrassing uncle. Paul McCabe pursed his mouth, as if tasting unpalatable words.

"Actually, Everett, it's you I've come to see."

Paul McCabe looked uncomfortable in the living room, seated in the middle of the sofa, hands draped over his knees. He hadn't taken off his coat. In the kitchen Laura made tea, a thing she normally never did after nine o'clock. The caffeine kept her awake. Only table lamps were lit, and the flickering lights on the Christmas tree cast an insane shine over the scientist.

"The police called me about your father, Everett. Incredible, simply incredible. On the Mall. In broad daylight—well, you know what I mean. But it's incredible, incredible, in modern London, that it's not been caught on some CCTV camera somewhere. We are the most surveyed nation on earth."

"I got a photograph of the car. I got the registration number."

Paul McCabe sat up.

"Did you? Really?" You look like a meerkat, Everett thought. "That's good work, they should be able to do something with that."

"So what did the police ask you about?"

Laura pulled out a side table and set a mug of tea on it. Paul McCabe waved away a KitKat.

"Thank you, thank you, but chocolate gives me terrible migraine. Terrible. The police? Oh, just the usual procedural stuff. What where when, had your dad been suffering from unusual stress, had we noticed any . . . uncharacteristic behaviour recently."

"Had you?"

Paul McCabe spread his hands apologetically.

"Everett, you know me. I'm the last person finds out what's going on in my own department. Though, if you don't mind, perhaps I could turn your question back on you?"

"What do you mean?"

"Had you noticed your dad behaving . . . uncharacteristically, recently?"

Everett pictured Tejendra in his mind, flicking through moments, memories, Saturday afternoons, Sunday mornings like snapshots. The moments on the Skype calls when Everett found himself talking to dead air, Tejendra distracted, somewhere else. The time on the stand at White Hart Lane when he completely missed a sweet Danny Rose goal because he'd been frowning at a message on his iPhone. The time he'd pedalled straight past Everett outside the Tate Modern when they went to the opening night of the Rothko exhibition. Moments, memories, little snapshots when Tejendra seemed in another world entirely. A common thread held all those moments of strange together.

"You know the double-slit thing?"

"What? The experiment?"

"The classic experiment. That's what Dad said. The classic experiment that shows that reality is quantum. It starts just asking what light is made of, is it a particle or is it wave, and it's so simple, just light and shadows. But when you get really close in, really up tight and detailed, it's not one or the other. It's both and. Both and neither. He really wanted me to get it, to see how it worked. He'd explain it to me again and again. It's not the particle going through two slits at the same time; it goes through one slit in this universe, and through the other in another universe."

"When was this, Everett?" Paul McCabe held his mug in two hands, watching Everett over the top of it like a clever bird. He took a sip of tea.

"Back just after school started again. I mean, we always talked about physics and stuff, but just all of a sudden he really needed me to understand it. Maybe it was going into year ten. And you know something? I did understand it. I saw how it worked, I knew what it meant. I understood the Many Worlds Theory."

"Now you know what Richard Feynman said, Everett."

"'I think I can safely say that no one understands quantum mechanics.'" Everett held Paul McCabe's gaze. The scientist looked away. Nothing was ever direct with Paul McCabe. Everett had been to the department enough times to see how he worked with his staff: a suggestion here, a hint there, a glance. "But what if I do?"

"You'd be the greatest physicist of your generation," Paul McCabe said. "Or any generation, I think." He set the tea mug down on the table without so much as rippling the surface. He slapped his hands decisively on his thighs. "Well, I'd best be going. Just to say, this is a dreadful time, dreadful, and everyone at the department wishes you all the best, the very best. It's not knowing, that's the worst bit. The worst. I'm sure it'll all work out all right, Everett." He stood up, straightened the coat he had not taken off. "Thank you, Laura. If there's anything any of us can do to help . . ."

Paul McCabe turned at the front door. Behind him the rain slashed in silver horizontals. The evening's evil weather had deepened.

"Oh yes, Everett one last thing. Your dad, did he give you anything recently?"

"Like what?"

"Like a memory stick, or a data DVD, or even a file transfer?"

"I don't think so."

"Are you sure?"

"I'm sure." Everett felt Laura behind him. The cold wind from the street got under the Christmas cards, lifted them, sent them fluttering to the ground.

"Well, as long as you're sure." Paul McCabe turned up the collar of his coat. "Oof. Dirty old night. Everett, if you do get something from your father, would you be so good as to let me know? It may not make any sense to you, but it might to us. It could help. You will let me know, won't you? Thanks. Good night, Laura."

He pulled the door hard against the wind.

"Well, what was that about?" Laura asked. "I always thought he was a strange little man."

That's what that was about, Everett thought. Those last two questions. The rest was just polite games.

The visitor had left almost all his tea.

4

How Everett had missed the ping from the drop box: he had been trying to identify Paul McCabe's soft voice at the front door. He hadn't used it much recently anyway: file swapping at school had gone quiet since Aaron Leigh got a threatening letter from Viacom's lawyers. But there was the button bouncing up and down on the tool bar at the bottom of the screen. A file was waiting. A touch took Everett to his drop box on a server in Iceland.

"Everett!" Laura had this way of putting an emphasis on the end of his name and going up in tone when she wanted him to know she was exasperated. Ever*ette*. "Lights out. School day tomorrow."

"Okay, Mum." It was nothing to knock off the light and dive under the duvet to read by screen glow. It reminded Everett of when he was a small kid, face lit by screen-shine, the duvet propped up like a tent by his clunky old netbook turned up on its side like a proper book, the display switched to vertical, watching the Dr. Who rerun on iPlayer. It had always been best on winter storm nights like this, with sleet slashing across the windows and the wind rattling the gutters. Down under the duvet had been another world then. Everett-world.

There was a single folder in the drop box. *Infundibulum.* No sender information in the check box. Date: eight pm this evening, as Everett was sitting across a table from Leah-Leanne-Leona and Moustache Milligan in Belgravia police station. Size: thirty gigabytes. He opened the folder carefully, ready to back out should anything computer-eating spring out. Inside was a data folder, an executable, and a note in Notepad. It didn't look like a scam. Malware liked to disguise itself as a game or an update. Malware disguising itself as anti-malware was as clever as it got. This just sat there, a big obvious executable. Everett flicked up a clever piece of software he'd traded from Abbas in school. It tracked IP addresses. From that he could identify the sender. Abbas's software came up blank. The address had been made anonymous. Something like iPredator, Everett thought, a Swedish site that encrypted IP addresses and kept them safe from prying eyes. This was starting to get exciting.

Nothing else for it. Everett clicked the download button. There was no save or run option. The executable installed as it downloaded. The screen went crazy with dozens of green timer bars, filling in the blink of an eye, unpacking and unfolding into new icons and menus. Data was downloading from the drop box as fast as the wireless link and the house broadband could handle it.

"Whoa, whoa," Everett said, trying to click close-boxes. It was fast, too fast even for him. This was a full metal assault on Dr. Quantum.

"Everett? Are you still on that computer?"

Say nothing. Admit nothing. Everett tried to catch the hurtling installation panes. For every one he hunted down, trapped against the edge of the screen, and closed, a new one opened. The screen went dead.

"No," Everett whispered, filled with dread that he had truly killed his computer.

Dr. Quantum blinked, then rebooted. There was a new icon on the desktop, front and centre. A single white tulip. *Infundibulum.* Everett breathed out, a long, slow sigh.

"What are you?" Everett breathed. He tapped the icon twice. The tulip blossom unfolded into digital petals. The screen filled with moving translucent veils of light, folding around each other, merging like slow waves breaking, passing through one another, spilling off sprays of ghostly silver pixels. Everything was movement and change. As soon as Everett began to grasp a pattern the banners of light morphed into something unpredictable and new. Everett thought of dragonfly wings, eerie jellyfish, translucent flower petals, the clouds of interstellar gas you saw in photos from the Hubble Space Telescope, ghosts of ghosts. He thought of the shimmering, flickering curtains of the aurora borealis high above the Arctic night. Then he saw the scale, a hair-thin cross at the centre of the screen. It drew three dimensions: left to right, down to up, front to back. A small palette of tools hovered at the edge of the window. Everett picked the magnifying glass and zoomed in on the horizontal axis. At each level of magnification, the images were the same: veils of light, like wings, or angels, or the glowing tendrils of vast space gods. In and in: the same. It looked no different. Big patterns were made of smaller patterns were made of tiny patterns. It was veils of light all the way down.

He'd seen this before. It was when he was a kid. He'd been on the home computer when he'd opened a programme because he'd liked the look of a word: *Mathyka*. It sounded like a book of spells or a gateway to a magic world. It had opened up a gateway, not into a mystical realm but into forever. Everett now knew that the black beetle-like object at the centre of the screen surrounded by halos and streamers of brilliant colours like lightning bolts was called a Mandelbrot set. He could programme one—it was easy. He'd seen that the bolts of colour that cracked off from the points of the black beetle-thing contained little black specks in them. When he zoomed in on one of those specks, it was another little black beetle, complete with coloured halos and lightnings, complete with specks, which when he zoomed in, were black beetle shapes, with haloes and lightning bolts and specks that became beetles with . . . In and in and in and in. He had a scream-dream that night. He was falling through the dark eye at the centre of the Mandelbrot set, falling through a lightning storm of colours and black eyes that opened into whole new Mandelbrot sets, on and on and on.

"How far does it go?" he'd asked his dad.

"All the way. It never ends."

This wasn't a Mandelbrot set, though he could see now that it was built from that same Mathyka software that Tejendra used to model his theories of how the universe worked. This was . . .

"Infundibular," Everett whispered, in the screen-light, under his duvet, with a mid-December storm gusting and howling around the eaves. He remembered where he'd heard that word before.

Tejendra had been a late convert to Dr. Who. He became a fan after he had a place of his own, where he could watch without Laura shaking her head at the geekiness of it all. It was all right for kids, but for grown men . . . After a Saturday game, or a wander up the Lea Valley, Everett and his dad would sit down and watch the show while their latest culinary creation evolved on the hob. "Infundibular," Tejendra had said. "That thing, that police box. Bigger on the inside than the outside. It's easy in maths, having things that are much bigger on the inside than the outside. Now, if they were really clever, they'd make it properly infundibular, which is, the farther you go in, the bigger it gets. There'd be a smaller box inside that box, but that box would be bigger on the inside than the one containing it, and inside that one, a smaller box that was even bigger inside and so on, all the way down, so that by the time you got to the centre, it would be smaller than an electron but inside it would be bigger than the entire visible universe."

Infundibulum. The farther in you go, the bigger it gets. There was no doubt in Everett's mind about who had left the anonymous folder in his drop box. Neither was there any doubt that this was what Paul McCabe had been asking about with his parting question. He had tried to make it sound so offhand, but it was the only reason he had come to the house. Sudden fear knotted at the base of Everett's stomach. Paul McCabe knew about this Infundibulum, and it was important to him. Did he know what it was? To Everett it was eerie mathematical patterns, sent by his father to him and him alone. To Paul McCabe it was important enough to drive an hour and a half around the M25 to slide it in as a casual aside. Did he not have access to it? Had Tejendra not wanted him to have it? Had Tejendra not trusted his own department head with it? Was Everett the only one Tejendra could trust with it?

Everett clicked down the silent, swirling hypnotic ghost-patterns. He went back to the drop box. The file had been uploaded at eight. Tejendra had been driven away in the black Audi at six. Everett was sure that whoever kidnapped him would not have handed him a laptop and said, *Sorry, we forgot, go on, please upload that file of abstruse mathematics*.

He remembered the attached note. Four words: *For you only, Everett.* No name, no signature, no greeting or sign off. *For you only, Everett*.

Thoughts, theories, suspicions swept Everett up like a strong current. He knew this state of mind too well, when he seemed to think without thinking, ideas and connections and possibilities scampering away from him like ferrets escaping from a sack. It was usually when he read a line in a book or on a blog, or the real world surprised him, in the stop-start-stop rhythm of traffic jams up Stoke Newington High Street, or the patterns the starlings made as they flocked and swooped over Hackney Marshes. His thoughts exploded outwards like a firework. He understood something about the way the world worked.

Tejendra must have set the file to automatically upload. But he couldn't have known that this was the day he would be kidnapped. He must have set a dead-man's switch. If he didn't enter a code, most likely at a set time every day, the Infundibulum folder would be uploaded. The folder would go to Everett. Not to Laura, or his friend Vinny who had the next season ticket seat at White Hart Lane, or any of his colleagues or students at the university, not even to Colette. Not to Paul McCabe. To Everett. His dad must have suspected that something like what had happened could happen. He must have suspected that he was in danger. Danger of kidnapping, Everett wondered, or something worse? He wished the thoughts would stop galloping through his head. He wished they would stop whispering things he didn't want to hear, showing him things he didn't want to imagine. When had his dad planned this? How long had he lived with the fear of the men following him, the black car? Had it been before he and Laura split up? Parents kept secrets inside secrets, Everett realised.

"Non-nuke," Everett muttered under his breath. "He doesn't build atom bombs, so he's not important. As if."

The bedroom felt huge and dark and under siege. The glowtube decorations turned his jacket, hung on the back of the door, into a killer attack bot from hell. For the first time since he was a small kid, Everett felt afraid in the dark. Eyes in every corner. Monsters under the bed. There could be a black car outside, remotely scanning the room for every keystroke and tap he made on Dr. Quantum's interface. Sleep would never come this night. Everett waited until the line of light from under his mum's bedroom door went out, then slipped out from under the duvet and went silently down the landing. He knew the location of every creaking board and noisy stair. He clutched Dr. Quantum to his chest. He couldn't leave it. He'd never be able to leave it. Even as he opened the fridge to rummage for cheese slices and yoghurt drink, he kept one eye on the tablet on the kitchen table. He hugged it to him as he called up a Modern Warfare BlackOps duel on Xbox Live. He couldn't concentrate. His reactions were Dad-slow. His ass got kicked again and again, but he kept playing and playing, dying and dying.

In the morning Laura found Everett asleep on the sofa with the Xbox humming and the Christmas tree lights blazing, Dr. Quantum pressed hard against the side of his face.

5

The police came round for breakfast. Victory-Rose was milk-moustached and chocolate-bearded with Coco Pops. Chris Evans was rattling on the radio. Everett was fuzzy and muzzy from bad sleep, but he knew it was police at the front door even before they rang the bell, briskly, twice. Their streetlight silhouettes behind the glass were too close together, one tall, one small, one man, one woman. Police and Mormon missionaries stood like that. Everett scraped the last of the Flora out of the tub and spread it on his toast. Low-fat spread melted strangely, separating into globules of fat and water.

"Freezing out there," D. S. Milligan said. "High pressure must have come in in the night. I'd give yourself a good half-hour extra on the school run. Might even get a white Christmas. Is that coffee? Any chance?"

Everett poured him a Tottenham Hotspur mugful. Leah-Leanne-Leona sat down opposite Everett.

"Have a seat, why don't you," Everett said. "Have you found him?" Victory-Rose frowned at these big people in their dark coats bringing cold into her home. She might burst into tears at any moment. Laura sat down, positioning herself behind the cereal packets to hide her vest top and shameful saggy trackies.

"Sorry, Everett," Leah-Leanne-Leona said. Everett sized her half-smile, her screwed-up pig eyes, the little kick of her foot. You really really hate me, Everett thought.

"We have had a look at the photographs on that memory card you gave us," Moustache Milligan said. Laura turned the radio down. "Is there some of that toast going? You couldn't stick on a couple of slices?"

Laura got up to drop two slices of whole grain into the toaster.

"You wouldn't have white, would you?" Moustache Milligan asked.

"This is a hi-fibre household," Laura said firmly.

"I'll need it back," Everett said.

"What?" Moustache Milligan said through coffee.

"The memory card."

Leah-Leanne-Leona slid a transparent vinyl CD sleeve across the table.

"We've got everything we need off it. We had a good look at your photographs on our image enhancement software. Would you like to see the prints?"

She set her briefcase on the breakfast table, making room between the cafetière and the milk carton. She took out a big glossy high-resolution print of the number plate.

"We ran a trace on the number. It belongs to a Mr. Paul Stefanidis from Hounslow. He supplies Cypriot goods to restaurants and corner stores."

"So?"

"It's hardly likely your dad was kidnapped by an Eastern Mediterranean grocer."

"They can clone plates. Ringers, all kinds of things like that."

"Everett, this is Mr. Stefanidis's car. He drives an Audi. He was driving up the Mall at the time you said—you did photograph his car. He was on his way to a dinner of the London-Cyprus Business Forum."

"What are you saying? I made this up?"

The toast sprang up. Everyone started at the sudden noise. Laura scooped two slices onto a plate and set them down in front of D. S. Milligan.

"Ah lovely. Any butter? I know it's not supposed to be good for you, but that spread stuff just tastes chemically to me."

"We're a polyunsaturate household," Laura said. Milligan noisily scraped half-fat spread from the freshly opened tub across his toast.

Leah-Leanne-Leona produced another glossy photograph, set it on the table, and turned it around to face Everett. It was his parting shot of the back window, the three bodies framed in it. Three backs of heads, all dark haired. Three upper torsos, all clothed in dark fabric.

"This isn't right," Everett said. "Dad was in his bike gear. He was wearing his hi-viz rain jacket. It was bright yellow."

"Well, Everett, we work a lot with photographs from members of the public. A lot of them are taken on the fly, on mobile phones, in all kinds of light and weather conditions. They don't have time to focus or zoom or even frame properly or anything like that. You'd be amazed at what people think they've photographed, that, when we run our expert eyes over them, really aren't there at all."

"You changed it."

"What's the resolution on your camera, Everett?"

"Four megapixels. And a 4x digital zoom."

"And you were zoomed in."

"Of course I was zoomed in."

"And it was raining."

"Yes. So?"

Leah-Leanne-Leona pointed to a teardrop shaped flaw on the right edge of the photograph. The bottom of the droplet was an arc of gold.

"That's a raindrop on the lens."

"It was raining. I said that." He knew where this was going. There was no way out. They had him, at the kitchen table, in front of his mum and his kid sister. They would take it apart pixel by pixel.

"What colour are the street lights, Everett?"

"Yellow. Sodium-vapour lamps."

"So it's possible that another raindrop on the lens, over that figure in the middle seat, might have caught the streetlight and made it look yellow."

"You changed it."

"Here's the original." The policewoman slid it into position beside the enhanced shot. It was a blow-up, big enough to show the pixel grain. There it was, the size of his thumb and as unmissable: a drop, a tear, a drip of rain right over Tejendra in the back of the car, distorting the image, filling it with diffracted yellow street light. That didn't happen. That was not what I saw, Everett thought. You changed that too.

"I didn't make this up. Why would I make this up? Why would I photograph a complete random stranger's car?"

"Begging your pardon, Mrs. Braiden, but family problems can make us do strange things," Milligan said. There were toast crumbs in his moustache.

"*Mizz* Braiden," Laura said stiffly. She was furious, she was humiliated; the police had called her son a liar and a fantasist at her own kitchen table and seen her in her baggy trackies and vest top and her own daughter with her mouth ringed brown with Coco Pops. "And we are not a problem family."

"Well, I'm glad that's cleared up." Leah-Leanne-Leona scooped the photographs back into her briefcase. "But we really want you to know, Everett, that your dad is still classified as a missing person and we will continue to investigate this case." She stood up. Moustache Milligan hastily abandoned his second slice of toast.

"Thanks for the toast and coffee," he said. "Best meal of the day, breakfast."

Laura saw them out. It was light now, and Everett saw them drive off in a Skoda. Cops in reasonably priced cars. While Laura was at the door Everett took the memory chip up to his room and pushed it into Dr. Quantum.

"Everett." Her voice from the hall was tight and angry.

"In a minute."

"Not in a minute. Now."

"I'm doing something." He opened the image on the chip the

police had returned to him, then the image he had sent to himself while waiting in the police station.

"I don't care what you say you're doing. I want to talk to you."

"I'm doing something!" He moved the images next to each other, adjusted the sizes to match perfectly.

"We need to talk, Everett. This is making Vee-Arr very unhappy." When Everett's mum was very very angry she dropped her voice and talked Oprah speak. *Classic passive-aggressive*, they said on Divorcedads.com. "Everett, I had two police in my kitchen asking me for toast and butter and calling us a problem family. Now will someone please tell me what is going on?" Everett expanded photographs with thumbs and forefingers, tapped up the magnification. Tappety tap tap. Creakety-creak-creak. The noisy board on stair number four. She was coming upstairs now.

"Everett . . ."

There. *There*. He met his mother on the landing. He held Dr. Quantum up in front of him.

"I'm not a liar."

"Everett . . ."

"I photographed what I photographed. There. Look. I sent myself a copy before I gave the chip to the police. This is the original. There's no raindrop there. That Dad's back; that's Dad's head. They put the raindrop in."

"What are you saying, Everett? I don't know what you're saying."

"The police lied, Mum. They lied about the photograph. They probably lied about Mr. Cyprus Grocer Man. They sat down there at the table and lied and tried to tell you it was me was the liar."

Laura put her hands up to her mouth. She sat down on the top step and leaned against the banister.

"Oh, God. I cannot cope with this."

Everett settled on the carpet. He too leant against the banister. He felt like the bottom of his heart had opened and everything it had held, all the certainty and trust and joy and solidity, had spilled out into a gulf of doubt. Even toast and spread and breakfast radio was tainted.

"Let me see that." Everett passed Dr. Quantum to his mum. She traced the details of the photographs with her fingertips. "Why?"

"I don't know." It was a lame answer. It was not an answer. *Why* was not the question. The question was *what*. What happens next? Everett had chased that question to terrible conclusions. Leah-Leanne-Leona and Moustache Milligan might not know who had taken Tejendra—they might even believe what they had been told to sell to the Singhs over the breakfast table—but the people who had ordered that a raindrop be added to Everett's photograph knew. People who could boss the police around knew. People who knew that, when Tejendra came back, he would blow their lie sky-high. People who therefore knew that Tejendra could not expose them that way. People who knew that Tejendra could not come back. At each understanding Everett felt himself lifted higher, seeing farther. If only he could stop seeing the connections sometimes. If only he could stop thinking. He could never stop thinking, seeing those connections. It was what made him Everett Singh. The people who could order the police to tell lies, the people who had disappeared Tejendra, they didn't know that. Their mistake.

"I'll find him."

"Everett, love, no."

"I'll find him."

"Everett, you can't do that."

"I'll find him, right!"

Victory-Rose had got down off her chair and wandered to the foot of the stairs. Mummy and Evtt, as she called her big brother, were up on the landing together. At the sound of Evtt's raised voice she began to cry.

"Rosie darling, I'm coming." Laura's whisper to Everett was low, but every word was clear. "You are not to do this. Do you understand me? You are not to do this. This is not a game. He's gone and I don't know where he's gone and I don't know why he's gone and I don't know what's going to happen and I don't know anything except that I am very very afraid and I am so scared that if you get involved, if you ask too many questions, if you tell the wrong people they're lying, you'll go too."

"You believe me?"

"I don't know what I believe, but I am so very very scared, darling."

Victory-Rose was crying hard now, and as Laura went to her Everett saw her shoulders tense and shake and he realised that she too was crying: crying for him.

6

Everett saw where the ball would go even as Yolandi made her run up the left side of the pitch and sweetly tapped it to Ryun in hectares of space in the centre. Efron tried to move to cut Ryun off, but the pitch was like a bog after three days of constant December rain and Efron moved like a walrus. He had the size for a central defender but none of the skill. Ryun was around him and into shooting space while Efron was still working out what to do with his feet. The ball kicked up a little trail of water. Everett was already in the air as Ryun struck. Top left corner. Fist meet football. Everett punched it out to Anuska, who had dropped back deep. She trapped it and ran the length of the pitch with Gold Team defenders splashing through the grassy mud in her wake. She was always fast. The ball flipped around the Gold Team box in a series of crosses and shots and corners and half-hearted clearances while Everett banged his gloved hands together and bounced up and down on his goal line trying to keep warm. The final whistle blew. Team Red and Team Gold trooped off as a new flaw of freezing rain blew in.

"I hate you, Everett Singh," Ryun said in the changing room after the whistle had been blown and the teams had trudged off through the slanting rain. Fresh from the shower, he screwed water out of his ears with a corner of towel.

"You cannot beat me," Everett said, trying not to look at him scrubbed and shower fresh. "My kung fu is too strong. There's a way you look around to clock everyone else, then lean back from the ball just before you hit it. You do it every time. Every. Single. Time. And that's how I get you."

"What if I didn't?"

"You'll do something else and I'll see it. I know you, Ryun."

Ryun Spinetti was Team Gold's best striker, but in the two years since Everett came on to Team Red he had never been able to get a ball past him. He was also Everett's oldest, closest, and best friend. Football enemies, nerd friends. Team Gold. Team Red. Team Sky Blue. Team Lilac. What kind of name for a team was Team Lilac? Everett suspected that the sportswear manufacturer that made the shirts had had a load of lilac fabric they couldn't get rid of. Stupid names for phony teams in a made-up competition with no real sense of the things that made competing meaningful. Things like place or history or tradition or shared loyalty. Things that got you roaring on a Saturday at White Hart Lane.

The boys' changing room hissed with the sound of Lynx body sprays. Everett refused to shower in the presence of others. Home was only fifteen minutes away down the poo-smeared walkway known as the Dogs' Delight and through the tree-shaded peaceful gloom of Abney Park Cemetery. He customarily pulled on a blazer and, in this weather, his Puffa jacket over his goalkeeper's strip and clumped home in studded boots for a wet-room shower and death metal on the waterproof mp3 player. Luxury. Privacy. Just Everett and cascading hot water. He could spend a long time, shut away from the rest of the world by the heat and the sound of the rushing water. Laura asked what he was doing in there all that time. The answer was nothing. Everything. Thinking. Not thinking. Letting the ideas come.

"See you." Everett was always the first out of the changing room.

"Hey! Everett!" Abbas called as Everett headed out the door. "So, more Thursday afternoons with the Gob." The Gob—Mrs. Packham—was the school counsellor. Everett had spent three months of last period Thursday afternoons in her office after his parents split. It got him out of Religious Education.

"I'll just have to think up some new lies to tell her."

It was always too much to hope that Tejendra's disappearance could be kept secret from Bourne Green Community Academy. Facebook to tweet to text; it was round everyone even as Everett was sloping up the Dogs' Delight that morning. Year Ten knew better than to prod him and poke him, make jokes about his dad having run off with another woman or another man. Everett would never be one of the hip or the jock or the slacker tribes, but everyone had seen the dark anger that could explode out of him when provoked and as quickly subside. They didn't welcome him, but they respected him. You did not bully Everett Singh.

The text chimed as he turned out of the Dogs' Delight on to the curving cemetery path. NAT HIST MUS. SOON AS. He broke into a run. Rain stained the faces of the Victorian grave memorials.

Call it pattern recognition. Call it goalkeeper's instinct. Call it weird quantum stuff. Call it just something about the Renault Mégane—the way it came a little too slowly up Rectory Road; the way the woman driving and the man beside her were a little too well dressed, sat a little too upright; the way they both looked a moment too long as they drove slowly past Everett at the Number 73 bus stop. Call it a sense for suspicious cars. The Renault turned into Gibson Gardens. Everett kept watching. His breath caught as he saw its nose come out from behind the white van parked on the double yellow lines on the corner. It had turned on the side street. It pulled out on to Northwold Road. No mistake. It was looking for him. They weren't afraid to act in plain sight. The Renault was in a stream of slow-moving traffic. It stopped at the pedestrian lights while a kennel-maid tried to guide ten tiny dogs on ten different leads across Northwold Road to the Common. Everett watched the Renault out of the corner of his eye. The man in the passenger seat was a skinhead with sharp cheekbones. His suit looked uncomfortable on him. The woman driver had a young face but old, dark eyes. Blonde curls fell to her shoulder. She looked like a rock star. She wore gloves, which she tapped on the top of the steering wheel as she waited for the girl in the Wittle Wascals Dog Hotel windcheater to untangle the darting dogs. The lights changed. The Renault moved smoothly off. Where was the bus? It was always late, the Number

73, at this time of the afternoon. The driver just sat at the terminus doing sudoku. Everett could see it across the small triangle of open ground that was Stoke Newington Common.

"About bloomin' time," said the Caribbean woman in the shelter with a dozen orange Sainsbury bags slumped around her ankles. Across the Common the driver folded his paper. The bus pulled out into the traffic. It sailed around the corner of Stoke Newington Common on to Northwold Road. But here came the Renault. Rock-Star-Blonde woman saw him, but a VW people-mover ahead of her saw a parking space, stopped dead, and signalled. The constant traffic streaming up Rectory Road in the opposite direction trapped the Renault. The Number 73 swung in to the stop. Everett leaped aboard, pushing ahead of Too Many Shopping Bags Lady.

"'Scuse me, 'scuse me," he muttered as he plunged towards the backseat. The stationary bus held up the traffic and opened a gap ahead of it. The Renault pulled into the gap and overtook the VW. Everett ducked low on the seat. He glimpsed Rock-Star-Blonde check out the bus. Then they were past and the bus pulled out from the stop. He scrambled round in the seat to look out the rain-smeared rear window. The Renault had stopped dead in the middle of the road and was making a three-point turn. Traffic hooted; white van drivers leaned out of their windows to shout and wave their fists.

The Renault clung to the Number 73 all the way down Albion Road and long Essex Road. Stop start, start stop. Doors open doors closed. Beepings and bells and warning and robot announcements. Passengers on passengers off. Jerking down through northeast London: and there it was, the Renault, sometimes four cars back, sometimes two, sometimes right on the bus's taillights. Several times Everett saw the Renault pull out and go past. Within a minute he would feel a prickle, a presence like the tip of a blade on the back of his neck and knew that Rock-Star-Blonde was back behind him again. They could follow the bus route street by street, stop by stop, on the downloaded route map. They were watching to see at which stop he got off.

The bus ground down Upper Street and into Pentonville Road. Everett felt a surge of relief when the Number 73 swung out of the traffic into a bus lane. Then he glanced behind and saw the Renault follow. Only taxis and police were allowed to do that. And cyclists. So these were police, or the people who ordered the police. The Renault sat on the bus's taillights. He had to get away. He had to shake them before the Natural History Museum. Everett slipped out his mobile, flicked the flash off and shot off fifteen photographs of car, passenger, the ice-cold driver. The bus ground across the chaotic junction at King's Cross. People, traffic, confusion, and ready access to other modes of transport. A good place to lose his tail. Everett jumped up and hit the bell. The bus swung in to the stop opposite the stations; St. Pancras, towering and Gothic, seeming to tip over on top of him, King's Cross low and aloof, standing back from the street ruckus. Everett leaped from the bus and ran, headlong and crazy, into the grind of afternoon traffic. Cars and vans bounced to a halt. Horns blared. Fists shook. Mouths yelled silently behind windscreens. A moped swept around him, the rider throwing back a stream of swearing. Everett made it to the central traffic island. He glanced back. Skinhead-in-a-Suit was out of the car and in pursuit. A little G-Wiz city car stopped level with his toes and parped its silly little horn. Skinhead-in-a-Suit turned, glared at the woman behind the wheel, grabbed the fender, and lifted the front of the little car off the ground. Machinery creaked and cracked when he dropped it, but the diversion was enough for the lights to change and Everett make it to King's Cross plaza. He plunged down the Underground, elbowing commuters out of his way.

Everett had the Oyster subway card out of his wallet before he realised the danger. They could find out where he'd been through his Oyster card. Gloucester Road, the station for both the Natural History Museum and Imperial College, was enough of a clue to who he was meeting, and why. But the ticket machines were slow, and there was the inevitable group of tourists peering at the instructions and randomly pressing buttons. Everett glanced behind him. Skinhead-in-a-Suit stood on the stairs, surveying the crowded ticket hall. Everett slipped his backpack from his shoulder and pressed closer to the tourists. His Puffa jacket was anonymous in the ticket hall, but his yellow football shorts and the even more yellow thermal compression gear he wore underneath were instantly identifiable. He moved the backpack to conceal his legs. The machine fired tickets at the delighted tourists. Everett stepped up and pressed buttons. The machine was so slow, so slow. Single. Yes. Select method of payment. Cash. Did he require a receipt? No thank you. Come on come on come *on.* Ticket and change rattled into the steel trough.

The ticket barrier was ahead of him. Don't run. It will make you stand out. Be part of the crowd. The machine scanned his ticket; the gate clanged open. Everett glanced behind him. For a moment, just a moment, his eyes caught Skinhead-in-a-Suit's, but for that moment, it was as if they were the only two people in King's Cross tube station. Skinhead-in-a-Suit bounded down the stairs and pushed through the crowd. A Transport For London worker in a peaked cap and an orange hi-viz vest moved to cut him off. Skinhead-in-a-Suit straight-armed the man away and vaulted over the barrier. Everett ran. Before him was the main escalator, as steep and deadly as a ski-jump. Everett took a deep breath and ploughed down the moving steps. "Excuse me, excuse me," he shouted. Standers pressed in to the handrail; the less-quick walkers on the fast side of the escalator moved out of the way of the kid running like a madman down the moving staircase. The steps were steep, the steps were treacherous, the steps were endless. You hit a rhythm and you kept it. Keep moving keep moving don't look back if you look back you'll miss the timing and you'll fall and bounce off these sharp step edges all the way to the bottom. Everett's backpack bounced heavily against his shoulder. Behind him he heard a growing commotion. Keep moving. The escalator threw Everett on to the Circle line concourse. Now he could look back. Skinhead-in-a-Suit came down the escalator like a rugby player, casually sweeping anyone who might obstruct him out of his way.

A gust of warm air. The shriek and clatter of a tube train arriving. The Circle line was not the most direct route, but Skinhead-in-a-Suit would catch him in the warren of tunnel and staircases that led to the Picadilly line. Everett dashed through the doors as they were closing. Instants later Skinhead-in-a-Suit arrived. He banged his fists on the doors. They won't open for that, Everett thought. Whoever you are, they won't open for you. The man sought out Everett clinging to the pole in the open area by the doors. He put his hands flat on the window and stared straight at him. As the train moved off, Everett raised his hand: *Bye. Lost you.*

Everett made it into the Natural History Museum ten minutes before closing. The Museum Experience Colleagues harrumphed at his football studs on their tiled floor. Colette Harte was waiting for him underneath the dinosaur skeleton. Her hair was purple this week.

"You all right, Everett?"

He showed her the slide show he had taken from the back of the bus: the Renault, Skinhead-in-a-Suit, Rock-Star-Blonde.

"Do you know these people?"

"She's way overdone the eighties eye makeup," Colette said. "And he looks like an extra in Grand Theft Auto. Sorry, Everett. No. Never seen them before."

The first time Everett Singh had met Colette Harte, she'd terrified him. Thin as a stick, tall as a tree, with metal in her eyebrows and dyed pink hair, sculpted up with gel like an anime heroine. "Is that a skull-and-crossbones tattoo on your back?" he'd asked. She had leant towards him, seeming to come down from a huge height made huger by platform boots, and whispered in his ear, "I'm the Pirate Queen of East Cheam." And winked. He had been six then, at a faculty barbecue Tejendra had thrown in the back garden on a summer Sunday. The wink made them friends. The wink said it would always be all right. Colette Harte had been a new graduate student. Eight summer barbecues on, she was a research fellow, working with Tejendra. Her face metal and platform boots only came out for nights at those clubs that sounded so strange and dangerous to Everett, and her hair changed colour every month rather than every week, but the skull-and-crossbones still nestled in the small of her back and she was now and forever the Pirate Queen of the Quantum Physics Department. Everett had texted her that morning as he pushed through the rain across Abney Park Cemetery. *P McC came—thought I had sumfing. Help?*

"They tried to follow me down here," Everett said. "I think they were waiting for me outside school, but they didn't know I was going straight from the changing rooms."

"I like your use of 'tried,' there," Colette Harte said. Announcements rang out through the great Central Hall: the museum, café, and shop were closing in five minutes. Five minutes. "So, do you?"

"What?"

"Have something?"

Everett unzipped his backpack, pulled out Dr. Quantum, and booted it up. He expanded the *Infundibulum* icon. Colette bent close. Everett heard her swear under her breath.

"Close it down, Everett."

"It's what they were looking for, isn't it? It's what Paul McCabe meant." He powered down Dr. Quantum and slid it back into his backpack.

"Yes." He'd never heard Colette's voice like this, never heard fear in it. "Not here, Everett. Let's go."

Mingling with the slow drift of exiting visitors, they left the museum. Once she was in the open Colette lit a cigarette. Departing visitors put up umbrellas and pulled up their collars and hunched over against the rain.

"Are you hungry? Let's get something to eat. You fancy sushi? I know a good place up west."

"Ya! Mama is right over there." It was a good place. He'd been there with his dad and Colette enough times to learn the rules of sushi. Rule 1: no conveyor belts. They looked cool, but you never knew how long those little transparent plastic bubbles had been going around the track. Rule 2: fish in the wasabi/soy. Never the rice.

"A tad too close to my work colleagues, Everett."

By the time they flagged down a taxi they were both soaked through. The restaurant was off the Tottenham Court Road and small and warm and family-run, with intimate booths where you could talk. The manager made Everett leave his football boots at the door. He sat cross-legged on the tatami mat, slowly drying out his many layers.

"Okay, let's have a look at it."

Everett opened up the Infundibulum application and passed Dr. Quantum to Colette. The booth was quiet and dimly lit, and the light of the moving veils of light illuminated her face.

"So, do I have something?"

"You have more than something." Colette set the tablet down on the low table. "You have everything."

The sushi arrived. It was neat, the rice was glossy, the fish bright and firm. Good sushi. Everett mixed soy and wasabi with his chopsticks. The Maneki Neko cat in its niche on the wall waved its left paw. Right to attract money, left to attract customers.

"Your dad, me, Paul—we're all part of a long-term, big-budget project looking for experimental evidence of the existence of parallel universes," Colette said.

"I know all about that." Everett swiped a piece of sea bass through the soy-wasabi.

"You don't know all about it, Everett."

Everett bristled. Everyone, everyone, *everyone* felt they had the right to tell him their opinion of him. What about his opinions?

"Dad taught me the theory. I can do the quantum field equations better than our physics teacher. I don't think he even knows what a quantum field equation is."

"I know you can, Everett. You can probably do them better than me, but you didn't listen to what I said. I said, *experimental evidence.*"

"Proof."

"Physical proof. Yes. You have it on your pad there."

Everett was the Shaolin master of chopsticks. Everett could eat raw seaweed with them, even slippery noodles. Everett never fumbled. He fumbled now. The sticks crossed; the little cylinder of rice fell to the plate.

"What you have is a directory of the multiverse. I didn't know your dad had given it a name. Infundibulum. Those are locations of the known parallel universes. Not all of them. You couldn't fit all of the ones we've discovered so far on to your computer."

"How many have you discovered?"

"Ten to the eighty."

Everett knew mathematical notation. His friends who were good with hardware had expanded Dr. Quantum's onboard memory to a terabyte. That was ten to the twelve bytes of information. As a number, taken out of the realm of computers and information, that was a one with twelve zeroes behind it. A thousand billion. A number you could still think. Ten to the eighty, a one with eighty zeroes, that was a number beyond imagining. You would run out of millions of billions of trillions. Everett's belly felt hollow; his head reeled. He was falling through the endless unfolding of the Mandelbrot set again. Big, exciting, terrifying numbers.

"My dad found all this?"

"Your dad's been working on this for a lot longer than you think."

Everett remembered summer. It seemed so far away from the dark and cold of the year's end. Another world. School holidays and university holidays matched pretty well. The access agreement meant he had whole weeks at his dad's new apartment over in Kentish Town. Evenings they'd walk up over Hampstead Heath to Parliament Hill, and there among the kite fliers and the joggers they would look at London and it seemed to Everett as if Tejendra were seeing a different city, an alien city fallen from another universe. Walking back through the twilit streets his dad had talked, words bubbling out of him, tumbling over each other. He had talked about other worlds, as close to you as the breath in your lungs but farther than the farthest star. Worlds so like this one that a Tejendra Singh and an Everett Singh were walking down through Highgate only a shade different, so that it was Russell Brand in that house, not Ricky Gervais; some so different that life, the Earth, stars, even matter had never formed. He had talked about them so powerfully and convincingly that Everett had turned around, certain he had heard those other Everetts whisper his name.

"I knew," Everett said. "I *knew*."

"He told me more than once that he thought you were more gifted than him," Colette said. "He had to work at it; you could see it. There it is, Everett. He gave it to you. The multiverse, on your iPad. The problem is, we don't know what to do with it. That's just what we call the wave function graphs. It's like trying to explore London and all you've got is a phone directory with just names and addresses of people and their phone numbers. There are Singhs of 43 Roding Road and Singhs at Ormonde Place and Singhs at Queen Elizabeth Way, but you can't tell from the phone book where they are in London—east, west, north of the river, south of the river—to get there. You've got their home address, but you don't know what it's like—whether it's a footballer's mansion or a crackhouse. You get my drift, Everett?"

"We're Braidens now, not Singhs," Everett said. "My mum says."

"No you're not."

"I'm not. Never was, never will be."

"I should buy you a beer, Everett."

"I like Kirin better than Sapporo."

"I was joking, Everett. Eat your sushi."

He ate the nigiri. The rice was properly vinegared, the grains round, and the texture just right—not too sticky, not falling apart. Colette pushed her pickled ginger around her plate. She laid her chopsticks down crossed.

"Everett, did your dad ever mention something called a 'Heisenberg Gate'?"

"It's a theoretical point where parallel universes touch and open on to each other. Like a wormhole between worlds."

"What if it's not theoretical?"

The waiter brought a tiny cast iron kettle and poured tea, hot and clear and fragrant. The restaurant, the décor, the booth, the scalding tea were finally driving heat into Everett's chilled bones. Colette slid a memory stick across the table.

"God forgive me, if they found out about this, they'd throw the key away. Take this, Everett. Watch it all. Then call me."

Everett slid the memory stick into an inside pocket, next to his heart. He zipped the pocket shut, but he felt as if everyone could see the memory stick, glowing through the fabric, betraying him. He drank down the rest of his tea while Colette paid the bill. It didn't taste quite right anymore. The golden Maneki Neko cat waved its paw up and down, up and down while Everett laced on his football boots. His studs went clack-clatter out into the threatening night.

7

The front door of 43 Roding Road stood wide.

"Mum?" She might have stepped out a moment; something down at the shop, or nipping next door to the McCulloughs to borrow a stapler or a knife sharpener or to drop in a parcel. But since Dad had gone, Laura had been extra careful about locking the door, even for a step down the road. And Tuesdays was always KidSwim down at the leisure centre with Victory-Rose. They were never back before eight. Tuesdays Everett let himself in and rattled something up from the kitchen; that was the rule. Leaflets from pizza companies and plastic window companies had been blown around the hall, and the runner of carpet was soaked by rain. The door had been open for hours.

Not Mum, then. A core of ice ran from the pit of Everett's belly to his heart, but he edged into the hall. The living room door was open. There could still be someone in the house. He peeped around the edge of the door frame. The room had been shredded. Every drawer had been pulled from the chest and tipped out, every DVD taken from the rack, opened, the disks skimmed across the floor. Magazines lay like broken-backed birds. Sofa and chairs were overturned, facedown to the floor, cushions scattered, covers unzipped. The Christmas tree lay on its side. The lights flickered and pulsed like insanity. Feet had ground the fragile glass decorations into the carpet. Every single present had been ripped out of its wrapping and torn open. Everett tapped up his smartphone and called the police. Then he called Laura. For a long moment he thought she wouldn't answer.

"Everett, love, there's cold chilli chicken in the tub in the fridge . . ."

"Mum. If you're on the way back, I think you should leave Victory-Rose off with Bebe Ajeet."

"Everett, what is it? What's wrong?"

"Someone's been in the house."

She arrived as the police were going through the crime site. They were local police, in uniforms, but they still drove a Skoda. She stood in the living room door with her hands to her mouth in horror as the policewoman tried to ask questions. The policewoman followed Laura up the stairs to her bedroom. His mum gave a small moan that was like nothing Everett had ever heard from a human throat.

"Oh my God oh no, oh God. It'll never feel clean again. I can't sleep in there, I can't, I just can't. It's dirty. They've been through it. We'll have to move."

Everett looked at the wreckage of his room and understood. Filthy. Everything felt filthy. Clothes boots bedclothes books boxes of cables and old toys and cars and football magazines and posters ripped off the wall. Everything. They had been into everything, and run their fingers through it and left their smear and stink all over it. He felt sick.

"It's all going out, all of it, I can't have any of it near me," Laura said. "Why us? What have we got?"

Not "us," not what have *we* got, Everett thought. Me. What have I got? He hugged his backpack to his chest, Dr. Quantum hidden inside, the Infundibulum hidden within that. It was imagination, but the pen drive Colette had given him felt warm.

The policeman joined them on the landing.

"They've given this place a right seeing to. They were definitely looking for something. Usually it's just in and out, a couple of kids, grab the first thing that's lying around and scarper before anyone notices. No, this was a piece of work, all right. The lock on the front door was picked, and I don't know what they did to the alarm but it's flashing numbers and letters. They took their time."

The policewoman had her arm around Laura's shoulders.

"Is there someone you can stay with tonight, love?"

"My mother-in-law, she's looking after my daughter."

"Mum, I'll stay with Ryun."

"Everett . . ."

"He's got a spare bed; Bebe Ajeet doesn't have enough room for us all. Ryun's mum will be cool about it."

"Are you sure?"

He had only made the decision a moment ago, but he was sure, sure as sunrise, because he was also sure who would call tonight at Grandmother Ajeet's door, with his shy, shuffling way, and his softly threatening accent and his sincere sympathies and his offer of *Is there anything we can do to help? Oh, and another thing, has anything come through from your dad, like a package or an email, or something? Are you sure?*

"It'll be cool. I'll get Ryun's mum to call. I'll call you anyway. Go on. I'll be okay."

The police waited for Laura to call a locksmith to secure the house and salvage a bagful of overnight for her and Victory-Rose from the strewn mess of the bedrooms, then dropped him round to Ryun's. As he suspected, Skodas were rubbish cop cars.

8

Ryun's mum's kitchen was everything Everett's mum's wasn't: clean, ordered, bright, warm, with a dad in it. Everett had known Ryun Spinetti since primary school, and down all those years his memory of Mr. Spinetti was of him constantly laughing. He found huge, gut-shaking laughs in everything. Everett had seen him crying with laughter at the Spinetti cats, one in a cardboard box he had placed in the centre of the kitchen floor, the other prowling around it, dabbing paws at each other. Fun with Tejendra always seemed deliberate, thought out, never free-flowing and spontaneous. Even John Spinetti couldn't find it in him to laugh at Everett's ransacked home.

"You stay as long as you need. Open house here."

"If your mum needs any help, Everett . . ." Ryun's mum shouted from the distances of the vast kitchen. "Anything at all. Horrible, just horrible. God save us it never happens to us." She crossed herself and kissed her knuckles.

"Ryun, have you got that high-def monitor set up?" Everett asked.

In Year Five Everett Singh and Ryun Spinetti had recognised each other by a line from *Transformers* and realised they were not alone in the world. The geek of the earth are a tribe, and they are mighty. They had built a friendship in front of a screen.

"It's all set up."

"There's something I want to take a look at."

They took tea and Mrs. Spinetti's legendary M&M cookies up to Ryun's room. Since moving to Bourne Green school Everett and Ryun had found their interests drifting from the virtual to the physical: specifically into football. But the desk was still cluttered with old screens and USB ports and media readers, pushed aside by the new monitor, the size of a tabletop. Ryun closed down Facebook and a World of Warcraft screen. Everett unzipped the memory stick and pushed it into an empty USB slot.

"What is this?" Ryun asked.

"I don't know."

Everett opened the folders. Video files, in a format unfamiliar to Ryun's computer. Everett went online, found a player that could handle them and installed it.

"Hey, that could be full of disgusting Russian viruses. . . ."

Everett opened the first video clip. The time-code in the corner said that it had been shot on January 16th, 11:12 a.m.

"That's your dad."

And Colette, and Paul McCabe, and some from the faculty Everett recognised, and some he did not recognise at all. This was a place he had never seen in the university: a long, windowless, low-ceilinged room. Bare metal pillars held up the roof. Fluorescent tubes were arrayed in precise lines across the ceiling; every third one was lit, casting a wan, grey, sick light. It looked like an underground car park, or a bunker. Was it even in the university at all? Desks laden with laptops and flatscreen monitors were arranged in a wide circle. Halogen desk lamps cast pools of illumination that caught the hands on the keyboards, the faces looking at the screens. In the outer shadows were bulky, boxy objects, person-tall. Everett wished he could move the camera, pan, and focus on those dark masses. Cables, gaffer-taped to the floor, ran through careful gaps in the circle of desks to the object toward which all the screens and faces were turned. At the centre of the circle stood a metal slab. Everett guessed it to be three metres tall, maybe one and a half wide. The camera gave little sense of depth, but he guessed its front to back dimension was the length of his forearm. Every square centimetre of the slab's surface was covered in circuitry cables, wiring and pipes. Yellow *Caution: laser* triangles were stuck next to cryohazard warnings. Superhot to supercold. In the centre of the slab was a hole. It was not a very big hole. Everett thought he could have thrown a tennis ball through it, nothing bigger. The edges of the hole smoked with vapour from supercooled liquid gasses.

"That must be a ring of superconducting ceramic," Everett said.

Ryun understood these things. "Cool," he said.

"Very."

Parabolic radio dishes stood around the slab. One of the technicians Everett did not recognise moved among them, focusing them on the hole in the slab. The cables from the dishes led to what looked like a hi-fi radio receiver. An amplifier powered a bank of floor-standing speakers.

Tejendra spoke. His voice sounded tinny and artificial on the video. He said, "Okay this is radio frequency communication experiment eight. Can I have a twenty-second count on the gate? On my mark. Three, two, one. Count." Screens sprang to life around the circle of desks. Digits counted down from 00:20. 00:19. The experimenters stared intently at their screens.

"Power is at one hundred percent," Colette said. Paul McCabe pulled on a call-centre telephone headset. 00:08. He tapped the microphone. 00:05. The numbers flicked down. 00:00. And the empty circle at the heart of the slab of technology became a disc of white light.

"Oh, wow," Ryun breathed. The white disc was bright enough to outshine any other light source in the room. It threw long shadows among the pillars. The faces of the watchers were bleached out.

"The Heisenberg Gate is open," said Colette. "We are in inter-universal contact with E2. Professor McCabe?"

Paul McCabe cleared his throat. When he spoke, his voice was thin and shaking.

"Hello, this is Imperial College London, Department of Physics." The speakers hissed static. "E2 E2, this is Imperial College London, Department of Physics." Paul McCabe's voice was stronger, more certain. Static. Everett could feel the tension in the room as if he were there, then. A third time Paul McCabe spoke. "E2, E2, this is Imperial College London."

The speakers crackled; then a voice spoke. A man's voice, heavily accented, speaking words Everett did not understand but were at times on the edge of familiar. Was that Spanish, Portuguese? But those sounds were definitely not European; they were more like the Punjabi in which Bebe Ajeet would chatter away with her son, his dad. Or Arabic? He heard no more because the room erupted. Whooping, cheering, applause. High-fives and air-punches. Colette crushed Tejendra in a huge bear hug; Tejendra shook hands enthusiastically with Paul McCabe. The two men clapped each other on the back. Champagne corks popped. Glasses were raised against the light shining from the hole in the universe. The clip ended.

"What was that, what did we just see, who was talking?" Ryun asked.

Everett had already opened clip two. Setup: the same. The room, the laptops and screens, the radio dishes, the speakers, the pierced slab smoking with the vapours of liquid nitrogen. Date: one week after the first clip. The same people. Except . . .

"Is that David Cameron?"

"And that other guy's the minister for Employment and Learning," Everett said. He couldn't remember his name. They changed so often, and they all looked the same.

"We've arranged a radio link with E2," Paul McCabe said. His voice was oily with deference to the politicians. "Tejendra, could we have a countdown please?"

Tejendra silently punched up twenty seconds on the screens. Everett could see the resentment in the way his dad followed orders. When his dad was tense or angry or upset he went deadly quiet and moved slowly, as if he were in deep waters and any noise, any movement, might draw sharks. Everett understood his anger. This had gone from science to politics. It had been taken out of his hands. 00:00. Again the light from another universe flooded the room.

"Hello E2, hello E2. This is Professor Paul McCabe from Imperial College London calling."

At once a voice came back; the same voice Everett had heard in the first clip, but speaking English with a strange, half-familiar accent.

"Hello Paul, hello Imperial; this is Ibrim Hoj Kerrim of the Chamber of a Thousand Worlds."

"Ibrim, it's great to hear from you. I'm honoured today to have our prime minister, Mr. Cameron, with me."

"The gift honours the giver. With me is Saide Husaen Eltebir, pre-eminence of the Pavilion of Felicities of Al Burak."

"What's he talking about?" Ryun asked.

"I think he's their prime minister," Everett whispered.

"Who's they?" Ryun whispered.

Everett watched the prime minister put on a headset.

"Hello?" he said uncertainly. "Hello? Mr. Eltebir?"

"If I may make so bold," said the strange, singsong voice beyond the disc of light, "His Pre-eminence has not received the language implants. With your permission, I will translate."

A new voice spoke, deeper toned, in that same language Everett had heard on the first clip. Ibrim Hoj Kerrim translated simultaneously.

"His Pre-eminence greets and salutes his esteemed trans-universal counterpart and extends the welcome of the many peoples of the Plenitude of Known Worlds."

Prime Minister Cameron looked flustered for a moment, then started, "Thank you for your gracious words, Pre-eminence—"

The clip ended abruptly.

"Is this some kind of movie or something?" Ryun asked. "Was that really the prime minister or a lookie-likie?"

"It was the real prime minister. This isn't a movie. This is real."

"Real what?" Ryun asked, but Everett had already clicked open clip three. They gasped simultaneously.

They were high over a city. Sun dazzled from domes, domes high and low, domes of white alabaster, domes covered in red terracotta, domes patterned with colourful ceramic tiles, domes of silver, domes sheathed in pure gold; dome after dome after dome, arcades of tiny domes arranged in lines and squares, domes a hundred metres across and a hundred metres tall topped with shining golden crescent moons, cascades of domes like waterfalls, domes shallow as saucers, bulbous onion domes. From between the domes rose towers; pencil-slim minarets and kilometre-high skyscrapers more like sculptures than buildings. They seemed crocheted from titanium and glass, too thin and delicate to support their own weight, but they stood in clusters and clumps like trees in a forest. The camera shifted. It must be on some kind of aerial drone, Everett thought. Now he looked down on wide avenues and boulevards shady with trees. The camera dived down between rows of tall apartment blocks, each level overhanging the one beneath. Deep arcades lined each side of the streets, shelter from a sun that was brighter than any that had ever shone on Stoke Newington. The camera only caught fleeting glimpses of the citizens of this other city, walking in the shade of the cool arcades. Everett saw men in elegantly cut, Indian-style round-collared suits, women in brightly coloured, dazzlingly patterned full dresses with puffy upper sleeves. Headgear was the norm: round caps and coloured fezzes and a wild range of turbans for the men, thin veils of white lace for the women, piled high on headpieces clipped into the hair so that they looked almost like halos. All in a glimpse before the camera drone swooped back up past the wrought-iron balconies and out from under the overhanging, shade-casting roofs. The apartment blocks enclosed private courtyards and gardens. Everett saw ponds, fountains, lush green spray-wet ferns and ornamental trees, the glitter of water-wet tiles. Then the camera wheeled across the sky. Clouds and cityscape. Everett thought he saw an aeroplane coming in to land; then there was a silver flash of water and the camera came to rest on a massive port complex on the bank of the river opposite the city. On the water hydrofoils and small fast ferries darted between tankers and bulk carriers the size of city blocks. Tugs manoeuvred the big ships into dock. The camera drifted over canals and wharves, cranes and container yards. It made a turn over a petrochemical works, tanks and pipes and fuelling piers. Everett tried to read the words painted tens of metres tall on the sides of the tanks, but they were in an alphabet unfamiliar to him. The curves and loops reminded him of Arabic. As the camera wheeled away he looked again at the oil plant. This was not an oil refinery. This was a loading terminal. The big tankers at the fuelling jetties were filling their tanks with crude. This was oil country. Then as the camera wheeled high above the bustling river, Everett saw the pattern. The slow turn in from the south, the long east-west reach, the sharp loop to the south that turned abruptly north around the narrow peninsula of green. He recognised this river-scape.

"It's the Thames," Everett breathed. "It's the River Thames. This is London, or something like London, but in a parallel universe."

Now the camera drifted toward the long tongue of the Isle of Dogs. In this London it was a green parkland, glittering with formal pools and fountains. Canals and water channels traced silver geometric lines between the precise parades of trees and clipped hedges. Domed pavilions and open-sided halls shaded by seashell roofs stood in open courts among the trees and hedging. At the centre of these pavilioned gardens, rising from the centre of an artificial lake, was a sprawling palace of courts and arcades rising up, dome upon dome, to a huge central dome sheeted in gold. From it rose a single enormous flag, plain white, bearing two red crescents back to back.

An edit, a jerky jump-cut to the dingy, pillared room. The two watchers gasped simultaneously. The slab with the hole into other universes at its centre was gone. In its place was a thick metal ring, draped in cables and warning signs, three metres in diameter. Everett sensed more and new machinery in the recesses of the room. Screen-glare suddenly hurt his eyes. The hole at the centre of the ring was a disc of white light. Out of the light came a spindly insect silhouette, hovering against the painful glare. The glow from the border between the universes went out. It was a moment or two before the camera adjusted to the ambient light; then Everett and Ryun saw a white plastic aerial reconnaissance drone holding position on its four ducted fans before unfolding landing gear and settling to the ground in front of the big ring.

"They sent it through," Ryun said. "There. Whatever there is."

"Freeze that," Everett ordered. The camera had been laid down, left on, aimlessly filming one of the computer screens. Ryun was quick with the mouse. "Look at the window." Everett tapped the screen. "Look at what's in it." At first glance it was a conventional Google Earth satellite shot; mainland Europe, the great peninsula of Scandinavia, the jut of France, the isolated square of Portugal and Spain. "That's Ireland, but where's Britain?"

There was Denmark and the Netherlands; there in the Atlantic was Ireland. Empty water lay between. A thousand miles to the south lay Britain, a hundred kilometres off the coasts of Portugal and Morocco, moored in the mouth of the Mediterranean.

"That's England?" Ryun said. Yes, and we've seen its capital, Everett thought. And from those shots—obviously from the drone that he had seen return through from this parallel Earth, but so carefully placed before that scene, and this oh-so-casual setting down of the camera, that accidentally happened to be left running accidentally pointing at this screen, he could guess at its general history. The Romans had come to this island at the edge of the known world. They had conquered; they had brought their language and culture; they had left. Then had come the Moors, the armies of Islam, who had stayed and built a strong and powerful country and an enduring civilization. There never was an England here. Al Burak, the radio voice had said. Was that the name of this other Britain? Everett could guess another thing from the unsubtle editing, the just-so placing of the camera: who had taken this, and why.

"What's the time code?"

"Oh five twelve; 14:32."

Eleven days ago. Ten days before Tejendra was kidnapped on the Mall. He had intended Everett to see this, the same as he had intended Everett to have the Infundibulum. He had been preparing his legacy. He had known he was in danger.

The final clip. Everett clicked it open. A camera veered and came to rest looking down at a well-polished brown lace-up shoe. The lace was undone. Hands came into the shot and tied a bow. Brown, elegant hands, with a white scar nicked across the second joint of the little finger of the right hand. The clip ended.

"What?" Ryun said. "Show me that again." Everett clicked the clip. "A dude tying his shoe."

Except it's not a dude, Everett thought. I know that scar. An electric carving knife put it there three Diwali festivals ago, though the man who owns it tells people it was a laser because it sounds cooler. That scar, those long brown hands, those well-kept shoes belong to my dad. But why make this the last clip? Why include it at all? A dude tying his shoelace.

The suddenly opening door, the plane of light that cut across the screen-lit room, made both Everett and Ryun start.

"That's two guilty consciences if ever I saw them," Ryun's mum said. "Whatever are you looking at? Ryun, if you've found a way around those safety locks again, that's it, no more internets. Have you finished with those plates and mugs? I'll throw them in the dishwasher overnight—I've found mugs in here with an inch of mould in the bottom, Ryun Spinetti."

They handed her the crockery in silence. When the door closed again, they breathed.

"This is real," Ryun said.

"This is the most real thing there is," Everett said.

9

Everett called from the old telephone box at the bottom of Ryun's street. He no longer trusted his own phone. The world was full of listeners. There were watchers behind every door and wall and in every car. The telephone screen had been smeared with something red and sticky, and the box smelled of urine and something he couldn't identify

"Colette, I watched it." He didn't mention Ryun. Simpler not to. Already, the lies were spreading. "We need to meet."

The Piazza at Covent Garden was grey, rain-swept, and gusty with an umbrella-wrecking wind, but it was open and even on a foul morning there were people about. The rain had driven the street performers from the Piazza, but London shoppers were tougher. They huddled under umbrellas, pulled up hoods, turned up collars, dashed through the rain, hands busy with umbrella handles and paper carrier bags in Christmas colours. Christmas. I've seen a London where it doesn't rain like this, where there are no tattered decorations and last-minute dashes to the shops, Everett thought, looking across the Piazza to two women safe and dry in Costa coffee sipping cappuccinos. Are you in that other world too? Do you go out to drink coffee, are you friends, what kind of lives do you lead? He blew on the froth of his own cappuccino at the table under the glass roof of the Market Hall.

"We've opened Heisenberg Gates to nine other parallel universes," Colette Harte said, taking a spoonful of the foam from the top of her coffee. "Our term for them is 'planes.' The first one we made contact with is the plane we call E2. That's the one you saw in the clips, Islamic Britain at the end of the Med. It's the one most of the other planes contact first—it's about seventy-five to a hundred years ahead of us technologically. Gate technology is a mature science there. The problem is, they only had one other plane they could gate into; a plane we call E3, another early adopter of Heisenberg Gate technology.

"E2 and E3 were contacted back in 1995 by another plane that independently developed gate technology, E4. E2 and E3 are very different earths from ours; E4's almost identical to our plane. They have a theory on E2 that E4 and us—E10—are part of a cluster of similar parallel universes that split off recently. You could gate into E4 and not even know you were on a parallel earth. This would look the same—they might even be having the same weather. You're there, I'm there. But there are some differences: Al Gore is in his second term as US President, there wasn't a 9/11, the prime minister is Michael Portillo. Oh, and something happened to the moon, something they haven't told us about."

"So; my dad?" Everett said.

Colette grimaced.

"Let's start with the three *P*'s. Planes you know about. There are two more *P*'s to get your head around: Plenitude and Panoply. Plenitude—*the* Plenitude, the Plenitude of Known Worlds—is an alliance of planes in contact with each other. There are nine known worlds; ours is number 10. Things are moving fast, Everett, and I'm not central to it anymore—the politicians have taken over—but there are diplomats and negotiators coming through from the Plenitude. You heard Ibrim Hoj Kerrim from E2 on the audio recordings—he's part of the team. There's a woman from E3 and her counterpart from E4, who's a man. Like I said, I don't know what's going on anymore; it's politicians talking. We've appointed a government minister, there's an EU representative and a US envoy. The Russians are there, the Chinese, India. Think of the Plenitude as a United Nations for parallel universes."

"Ten worlds," Everett said. "That's not even a fraction of a fraction of a fraction of it all. Not even a hair's-breadth."

"The rest—all the other parallel universes—is the Panoply. The multiverse; the whole shebang. There's room out there. Other planes, other worlds. Other Plenitudes. Maybe bigger. Maybe less friendly. Maybe a lot less friendly. I've heard a rumour that there's a group inside the Plenitude that wants it to be a little less of a UN and a little more of a defence pact."

"We're E10; E2, E3 and E4 have had the Heisenberg Gate for a long time," Everett said. "What about E1?"

"That is the question. No one's saying—or maybe just not to me."

"Is my dad still on this world?" Everett asked. Colette was taken aback by his abruptness.

"I don't know, Everett. I think he may not be."

Everett knew what question he had to ask next.

"Did he go through the gate because he wanted to, or did someone take him?"

Colette took a deep breath. She laid her hands flat on the table.

"Okay. Before he disappeared, he said he'd found something."

"In the Infundibulum."

"The way it's worked so far is that all the Known Worlds in the Plenitude found each other because they developed Heisenberg Gates. It's like radio stations tuning into each other. There was a definite destination at the other end. But the thing about the gates is they can open a portal into any plane of the Panoply. Any one of billions of parallel universes. The problem is, you don't know where you're opening that gate. You could step out five miles underground, fifty thousand feet up in the air, or halfway through a wall; you could arrive right in front of a hungry saber-tooth or a pissed off T-Rex, or whatever they become with a few hundred million years of extra evolution, or a world that's been blasted to radioactive glass. You don't know. It's like GPS coordinates, when what you need is a map to see where you're going."

"He found the map."

"He found something. He told me."

"When?"

"Three days before he disappeared."

Everett remembered that Friday. He'd called. They'd planned where to meet before the game, and what they might cook on their cuisine night. Oh, and there was a good lecture on Monday at the ICA. Nanotechnology and how it was going to change everything. And all that time, as they sat next to Vinny in their season ticket seats, as Everett made his special chilli with chocolate, Tejendra had opened gates to parallel universes, talked to scientists and prime ministers from other Earths, found the key to ten to the power of eighty worlds.

"Did he tell anyone else?"

"Yes."

"Paul McCabe," Everett said.

"Yes."

Everett shivered. The cold was settling into his bones again; a deep cold, seeping in from the spaces between the universes. A cold world where no one could be trusted. Those shoppers dashing through the cold, driving rain; those street entertainers bravely setting up their show on the Piazza; they could be spies, they could be enemies, they could be doubles slipped in from another world. In just three days Everett's world had been shaken to its core, expanded to a billion worlds, smashed to atoms of fear and mistrust. He feared he would never feel warm again.

"They took him because they thought he had the Infundibulum."

"Who controls the Infundibulum controls the Plenitude and the Panoply. It could be not ten worlds, it could be ten thousand worlds. Ten million worlds. It could be an empire."

"But he doesn't have the Infundibulum."

"No."

"I do."

"Yes. And I wish your dad had never given it to you. Everett, you'll never be safe. You, your mum, your sister, your grandparents, your uncles and aunts and your cousins whether they're in Britain or India; your friends. Me. They will do anything to get it. They will never go away. You're in possession of the most important artefact in the multiverse."

The street performers had set up their act. Defying the weather, they rocked back and forth on the wet cobbles on unicycles, juggling blazing torches between them.

10

The timer on the oven in Ryun's kitchen read 03:45. Everett's mum had never been able to set any device with a clock in it. Every time Everett put them right for her she would do something and knock it wrong, sometimes within the hour. Mrs. Spinetti kept strict time: hob, oven, digital radio, microwave, all perfectly synchronised. The hum of the refrigerator pump seemed loud enough to rouse the entire house. Everett had tripped and banged and creaked his way out of the bedroom and down the stairs, but the Spinettis, being loud and noise-loving, heard nothing and slept soundly. Everett helped himself to juice from the fridge and by the light of a dozen digital clocks opened up Dr. Quantum.

Everett brought his finger down on the Infundibulum icon. A flick would send it to the trash. Deleted. Erased from all the universes. He didn't doubt that this was the original, the one, the only. He had a theory now. His dad had seen something in the glowing clouds of data. He had turned it into a key that would open the gate to any world in the Panoply, safely, precisely. He had been kidnapped for what he knew. He'd feared that. So he'd made sure they took his insight, but hid the thing that insight applied to. How did he think they would fall for that? Colette was right. Everett would never be safe—none of his family and his friends would ever be safe—while the Infundibulum existed. Get rid of it. Everett's finger hovered over the touchscreen.

He should delete it. He ought to delete it. He must delete it.

Everett tapped the icon twice. Dr. Quantum filled with the glowing aura-veils of the multiverse. Tejendra could have deleted it himself. That would have been safe. But he sent it to Everett knowing it would put his family in danger. Tejendra was first and always a Punjabi dad. Family was everything. There must be something more in the dataset. Something hiding in the clouds of light that were the worlds of the Panoply.

Everett felt the planes flock around him like winter starlings. Ghostworlds; other kitchens in other Londons. Only in this one did Everett Singh hold the key to all those other worlds. He reached out his hand, opened up the Infundibulum and grabbed a handful of universes. Everett turned the clouds of digits to the left, to the right, set them spinning, wove glowing ribbons of code together and parted them; he opened up a rift in reality and threw himself into an endless crevasse of light. Universes above him, universes beneath him, universes before and behind him and to each side. *What did you see in there, Dad?*

Endless, endless numbers, universes. You could spin through it for centuries and never notice the thing that tied one code to another.

Tied.

A pair of hands. A pair of polished brown shoes. Tejendra had always taken good care of his shoes. A pair of straggling laces. Hands tying them in a bow. Tying. *Why show me this?* Everett had wondered in Ryun's bedroom. Vistas of parallel Earths, alien cityscapes, alternative geographies, then a man tying his shoelaces. Because it's a message.

A knot. An object looped through itself in three dimensions. That was topology: the mathematics of shapes and surfaces and how seemingly different objects could be transformed into each other. Three dimensions was the least number you could make a knot in. One dimension was a straight line. There was no space to loop a line round and pull it back through itself. Forward and back, that was one dimension. A circle, that was two dimensional. Curve the line round and connect one end to the other. But you still could not tie a knot, because there was no way you could make the line cross over itself. Forward and back, left and right, but no up or down. Three dimensions—up, down, forward, back, left and right—were the least number you needed to be able to tie a knot. But you could tie them in a lot more. You always needed that higher space, that extra dimension, to reach in from.

Everett had always been able to think in more dimensions than three. It had always baffled his dad. Everett could never explain it. It took years, decades to learn to think outside the box of three dimensions. *I just see it*, Everett said. Like he could see patterns in the world, make connections between things that didn't seem connected, visualise how Yolandi would cross the ball just there and Ryun would go for the bottom right corner when Team Gold took on Team Red. One dimension two dimension three dimension four. Five dimension six dimension seven dimension more.

Everett touched the screen. He grabbed a piece of Infundibulum, turned it this way, that way, looked at it from every angle. He tugged; it stretched into a long filament of code. He expanded the view. He had noticed that the codes formed into clusters beginning with the same strings of digits, but there he could see no pattern between one cluster and the others that surrounded it. He copied the first nine digits and entered them into a search pattern. Clusters lit up across the wavering veils of the Infundibulum. He took the filament and joined it to the nearest cluster. A loop. Form from the chaos. He did a speed save. He scanned the Infundibulum for his next patch of matching code. There. A match. But there were also some matching points on the loop he had just formed. Through. A knot.

The first knots were painstaking, eye-aching work. Time and again he had to blink the swirling clouds of numbers out of his head, look at the dim, cool digital clock lights in the dark kitchen. Four thirty-eight. As the number of knots grew, he knew better what to look for. He could see the patterns. Knitting reality together. A knitting pattern. Everett laughed aloud. It was taking shape beneath his hands. It all connected. It was easy. So easy. His fingers raced across the screen, flicking up new sections of the Infundibulum, finding the link points, reaching through higher dimensions to bring them together. In, under, through, back.

Everett sat back and stared at the screen. The Infundibulum. The multiverse. But it wasn't complete. There was a final transformation. Knots within a knot. He zoomed out to the maximum, dropped handles on the locations that matched code—it was instinct to him now—and applied the mathematical transformations that tied them into a sealed knot. Knots made of knots made of knots. The farther in you went, the more complex the knots became. Bigger on the inside than the outside. An Infundibulum.

Everett got up from the seat. Crates rattled as the last milk van in Hackney whined up Roding Road. Oh six oh seven. The house would be up and moving soon. He took more juice from the fridge and looked at what he had done. He had taken the data-points and woven them into a map; a map not in two flat dimensions, or even rolled up into a three-dimensional cylinder, but a seven-dimension map, folded into and through itself. The map. The most valuable thing in all the universes. He had made it. And there was no one in this house, no one in this street, no one in his family, no one among his friends, not even über-geek Ryun, who could understand what he had done.

Everett stroked the screen and set the Infundibulum tumbling like a ball of string. This way, that way, any way I want. I can find any point in any universe. It's not just random pieces of code. It means something.

"What do you want me to do with it, Dad?" he asked aloud.

Even as he asked himself the question Everett knew the answer. Colette had said she didn't think Tejendra was on this world anymore. But which world? How did the Heisenberg Gates find each other? By resonance, by matching those patches of code, like radio stations. Bring the map to the gate.

"Come and get me, that's what you're saying to me," Everett

whispered. The central heating clicked on. The pipes creaked. Everett had not noticed how cold he had become. The cold between the worlds.

Everett fired up Skype. The number called several times before it was answered.

"Everett. This is early for you."

"Professor McCabe. You remember you said to call you if my dad sent me anything? Well, he has. I think you should see it."

11

Rock-Star-Blonde woman didn't look any less elegant for having been woken in the dark before dawn. Or any less deadly. Supervillains like her probably never slept anyway. She'd swapped the Renault for an S-Class Merc. Tasteful. No need to blend in with the background now. And Skinhead-in-a-Suit didn't look any less like a thug. His chauffeur cap added an unsuspected hint of stupid. Everett watched him slide up into the disabled parking bay outside the coffee shop. He opened the rear door. He had the boots and britches, the high-collared jacket, the string-back driving gloves. The lot. Rock-Star-Blonde set one black high heel onto the curb, then the other. She was tall. She moved like a golden silk scarf falling through water. Her skirt was calf-length and tight, her jacket nipped at the waist, flared at shoulder and hips. She wore a little round pillbox hat at a stylish angle, with a scrap of veil. She looked killer.

But I have something you need, Everett thought.

The slacker students, the coffee-shop coolios, the hip kids, the guy with the Mac writing his Oscar-winning screenplay all looked up and could not look away as the woman entered and stalked up to Everett's table.

"Everett." Her lips were glossy red.

"I'm him." Everett stood up. Tejendra's family had been very strong on good manners, but he would have felt compelled to stand anyway. The woman commanded by her presence. The tightest smile played across the woman's lips.

"I am Charlotte Villiers. I am plenipotentiary of the world designated E3. We have a matter to discuss. Shall we?" She nodded very slightly towards the car and the waiting chauffeur. Everett was very glad he had sneaked away from the general post-morning-assembly milling around and changed clothes in the toilets before slipping out and away from school. You could not credibly play this wearing a school uniform. Charlotte Villiers flared her nostrils at the glowtubes attached to his waterproof. Everett scooped up his backpack and left a few pounds of coins on the table. He'd always wanted to do that, like they did in Tarantino movies—just throw some money down and walk.

"Sit with me, Everett," Charlotte Villiers said. The central locking clicked. The car moved off into the traffic. And all Everett's bravery faltered. Plans made in the dark before dawn look cheap and rickety in the morning light. Get the Infundibulum to the gate. The rest he would make up as he went along. He had always prided himself that he could see the ball coming. What if this time he couldn't? What if there were people as good as him? Better than him? His stomach lurched in fear. But they weren't better than him. They weren't even as good as him. He'd woven together the Infundibulum. None of them had, in ten Earths full of people, not the Moorish Britain of E2, not the identical-twin E4 where something had happened to the moon, not the E1 they didn't talk about, not the E3 of the elegant Charlotte Villiers. Only Everett Singh—and his father Tejendra Singh.

Charlotte Villiers—she was one of those people who could only be known by both her names—looked out of the rain-streaked window. Her scarlet lip was curled in disdain at the street people in their heavy winter coats and hoodies and bum-freezer jackets. This is my home, these are my people, Everett thought. You don't look at them like a tourist.

The car headed north through rain and heavy traffic, following blue signs for the M25.

"We're not going to the university?"

"That's correct," Charlotte Villiers said. She opened her small handbag and surveyed her face in a compact mirror. Everett glimpsed dark metal, an ivory handle, an engraved barrel. A gun.

Satisfied with her appearance, Charlotte Villiers put away the compact and clicked the little bag loudly shut. You only did that little act so I could see what you have in there, Everett thought.

Out on the orbital motorway Skinhead-in-a-Suit—Skinhead-in-a-Chauffeur-Cap now, Everett supposed—could open up the S-Class. Charlotte Villiers smiled at the surge of acceleration. Everett had seen this model track-tested on *Top Gear*. He knew the nought-to-sixty, the HP, and the top speed. *You watching that boys' rubbish again?* Laura would shout. *Homework!* The memory caught in his throat. She'd be waiting for him. She'd have something cooked for him. She'd call him. She'd call Ryun. She'd call the police. Sorry, Mum, I have to do it.

The Merc was well over the speed limit, blazing along the outside lane; Skinhead-in-a-Chauffeur-Cap sending hatchbacks and Ford Mondeos scuttling out of his way with flashes of the headlights. Plenipotentiary. That was like an ambassador, but more. Über-ambassador. In the days before phone and internet, when messages took months to get from one side of the planet to another, a plenipotentiary *was* the State. An agreement made with her was binding on her government. Inter-plane diplomacy must be strong.

Over the Dartford river crossing. South.

"Where have you got my dad?"

"You father is working at a secure research facility."

"A Plenitude Research Facility?"

"In some areas your technology surpasses ours; in others, we surpass yours. We've been familiar with what you call the Heisenberg Gate for decades. It's only natural we would bring the talent to the technology."

So he's on your world, Everett thought. He asked, "Working or being held?"

Charlotte Villiers sighed softly.

"Mr. Singh, all this cloak-and-dagger paranoia. This is not how the grown-up world works. This is a sensitive business. There are security concerns. It's no different from your father working in one of your nuclear weapons facilities."

The Mercedes peeled off into a big clover-leaf junction; M25 to M20. Signs directed to Channel ports and tunnel. Skinhead-in-a-Chauffeur-Cap hurled the Mercedes past long lines of coast-bound trucks. They had left the rain behind at Maidstone; clouds raced them on a westerly wind. Winter sun shone on a dripping landscape. Already the roads were drying. The car slipped between relentless traffic into a lane heading for the Eurotunnel shuttle terminal.

"I don't have my passport with me," Everett said.

"You won't need a passport," Charlotte Villiers said.

Half a kilometre from the check-in booths the car turned left onto a service road that led out of the valley where the tracks and shuttle trains came out of the tunnel, up onto the chalk downs. The road climbed up the ridge, dipped down into a shallow bourne and skirted a field of half-drowned winter wheat. Water stood in the furrows. In the centre of the field was a fenced-off enclosure, a hundred metres on a side. No building, no radio mast, no structure of any kind. The fence was the most remarkable thing about it. Skinhead-in-a-Chauffeur-Cap turned onto a side road that cut through the waterlogged field to the enclosure. The road was pitted and crumbled at the edge from under-use. Patches of grass and tough winter weeds pushed through the eroding blacktop. A gate opened at the car's approach. CCTV cameras swivelled and tracked. Now Everett saw that the road dived steeply into a cut in the ground formed by a concrete-walled bunker, invisible from car-level. At the end of the sloping concrete approach were two heavy black steel doors. The doors parted. The car drove down into darkness. A creak of tracks and gears made Everett look around. The doors closed on an ever-narrowing rectangle of light until they shut it out altogether. They were in a tunnel. The headlights picked out dead light fittings, ducts, sagging cabling, ventilation fans, steel doors with faded numbers stencilled on them. Ahead was a patch of white light. It seemed to take the Mercedes a long time to reach it. Distances and speeds, time and space were distorted in this tunnel. Ms. Villiers sat up, straightened her posture and her gloves, checked her face again in the small compact mirror. Two strokes with the lip gloss and she was all killer once more.

Everett could see Paul McCabe waiting in the white light. He looked rumpled and unironed, as if he'd been wearing these clothes when Everett's call woke him. Beside him was a short man with olive skin and an elaborately styled beard and moustache, as elegant and groomed as McCabe was unkempt, wearing a round-collared suit of ivory and grey brocade. Beside him was Colette Harte.

The car stopped. A woman in black military fatigues and a SWAT team cap stepped out of the darkness to open the door. Everett blinked, dazzled by the light pouring from the four batteries of floodlights on tripods. But he did notice the assault rifle slung across her back.

"Everett! Excellent, excellent!" Paul McCabe pumped Everett's hand. "Your trip was good, yes? We sent the good car for you, you know. VIP treatment and all that, yes yes. I'm only here five minutes myself. Bit of an early call, you know?"

Charlotte Villiers stepped out of the car. Everett thought he saw Paul McCabe bow to her—the smallest, briefest dip of the head, but a mark of subservience.

The man in the elegant suit touched his right hand to his heart.

"Mr. Singh, an honour. I am Ibrim Hoj Kerrim, plenipotentiary of E2."

It took all Everett's control not to say, *I know, I recognise your not quite-Spanish, not quite-Moroccan accent, I've heard your voice on the radio. I've flown over the rooftops of your London.*

"It's a pleasure to meet you, Mr. Kerrim."

The plenipotentiary smiled. It was the kind of smile that transforms faces. He had bright eyes and very good teeth. I would like to be able to trust you, Everett thought. I need people to trust.

"I understand you possess a jewel of great price," Ibrim Kerrim said.

"The map of the Panoply," Everett said. A murmur rang around the ring of people. "Yes. I worked it out."

"A remarkable feat," Ibrim Kerrim said. "You are a precocious talent." Everett noticed a little jewelled hook behind the E2 plenipotentiary's left ear, like an enamelled hearing aid. He'd said something in one of the clips about language implants. Was this little ear-gem feeding him English?

"Well, my dad—," Everett started

"An extraordinary man, extraordinary," Paul McCabe said quickly. "Should have had a Fields Medal. Maths must be in the DNA." For a moment Everett thought he might ruffle his hair. Everett would have had to hit him, armed soldiers or no armed soldiers.

"I'd like to see evidence of this device," Charlotte Villiers said. You know it's in my bag, Everett thought. This was the dangerous time. Show her the Infundibulum and she might take it off him. He was surrounded by people with guns. He'd glimpsed what Charlotte Villiers kept in her smart little purse.

"It's better if I show you it working," Everett said. "You do have the Heisenberg Gate here?"

Paul McCabe and Charlotte Villiers exchanged glances. Ibrim Kerrim said quickly, "I would like to see that. Professor McCabe?"

"As you wish, Plenipotentiary."

A Person-in-Black opened a hatch in the tunnel wall. Beyond it was a smaller, less finished tunnel hacked into raw chalk. Lighting cables swagged along the roof, neon to neon. Heavier-duty power ducting ran along the foot of the wall. The air smelled of damp and dust and electricity. Two Persons-in-Black took the lead, then Everett with Paul McCabe, immediately behind them Colette Harte. Next came the two plenipotentiaries, last of all two more Persons-in-Black. The floor of the tunnel was gritty under Everett's feet. It sloped down to a distant hatch. Everett froze at a growing rumble that shook drops of condensation from the light-fittings, chips of chalk from the ceiling.

"We're almost exactly parallel to the Eurotunnel," Paul McCabe said. "You'd be amazed how close we are to the tracks. Amazed. The vibration is irritating: we've had to mount the entire gate chamber on springs to damp it down. But I think the privacy's worth it—and so handy to transport links."

"What is this?"

"Long before you were even thought of, Everett. In 1974 there was a serious plan to build a Channel Tunnel. They even did a test drilling. The economics didn't work, the political climate changed, the plan wasn't feasible—whatever, they just stopped digging. Years later they incorporated it into the main tunnel. The service shaft, however; that they shut up and left and forgot about. But it's perfect for us—until such a time as we can go public. Which reminds me."

Paul McCabe dropped back to whisper with the plenipotentiaries. Colette Harte fell in beside Everett.

What are you doing? she mouthed to him.

I have an idea, he mouthed back and then said, to divert attention, "This is like *Doctor Who*."

One of the guards laughed.

The hatch at the end of the tunnel was iris-locked. Woman-in-Black bent to the reader. The laser scanned her eyeball. The door opened.

"I think you'll find, Everett, this is more what you mean," Paul McCabe said. Lights flicked on as he stepped through the hatch. "Welcome to Earthgate Ten."

The chamber was a dome hacked out of raw rock, ten metres in diameter, its apex lost above the ring of floodlights that poured white glare on the object that stood in the centre of the steel mesh floor: a slab of circuitry and wirings the height of a house. At the centre of the slab, an empty circle, three metres across. A ramp led up to the empty circle. No ramp led down on the other side. Heavy power cables swagged away from the pierced slab to shadowy, glossy units ranged around the chamber walls. The air hummed with power. Cables coiled, glistening in the sharp light, beneath the mesh floor. The slab was surrounded by the familiar ring of desk, computers, monitors, laptops.

As Everett stepped onto the grille he felt it give slightly. The springs Paul McCabe had mentioned. He heard the dull rumble of a train, out there in its own hole in the rock; the lights shook, but the black slab stood firm. Black slab: Heisenberg Gate. Everett climbed the ramp and touched the gate. It was cool and still. Not a tremor, not a hum of power.

"I need access to your system," Everett said.

Charlotte Villiers opened her lips to protest, but Paul McCabe quickly passed a tiny digital display to Everett.

"Be quick; the code changes every thirty seconds."

Everett slid Dr. Quantum out of his backpack and booted it up. He found the wireless network immediately. The key code didn't even have time to change. And *in*. Bad security. The key opened everything; the wireless and the control panel to the Heisenberg Gate, everything. Paul McCabe and his plenipotentiaries must feel pretty secure from hacking with all that rock and the armed Persons-in-Black.

"How do I operate the Heisenberg Gate?"

"Ah, now, Everett, I really do think . . ."

"I see no harm in letting the young gentleman access the gate controls," Ibrim Kerrim said. Paul McCabe at once dipped his head and scuttled away from Everett and his computer. Colette showed Everett the interface.

"It's really pretty simple," she said, calling up a window with input forms on it. "Just three numbers. When, how long, and where. The timer's basically a safety lock on gate-to-gate jumps, so you can't jump into a gate that's already open to somewhere else. We don't know what would happen in that scenario."

"I'm not doing gate-to-gate jumps," Everett said. He squeezed the Heisenberg Gate control panel into the bottom corner of Dr. Quantum and opened up the Infundibulum.

"Oh my God," Colette whispered. Ms. Villiers brushed her aside in her haste to get a look at the map of all the universes, known and unknown. Screen-glow lit her face death blue. Her lips moved as she frowned at the multidimensional knotwork.

"Seven-dimensional third-order topological knots," she murmured. "The farther in you go, the bigger it gets."

Everett whipped Dr. Quantum away from her sharp eyes and turned to face the Heisenberg Gate. He set the timer to fifteen seconds, the duration to five seconds. Then he zoomed into the Infundibulum, grabbed a piece of code from deep inside the tangled mathematics and slotted it into the destination bar. The lights dimmed. The chamber hummed to a sudden surge of power. The Heisenberg Gate sparkled like a Christmas tree with LEDs. Yellow warning lights rotated and flashed. Paul McCabe bent to a computer monitor.

"Good God," he said. "Good God."

Ibrim Kerrim came to stand beside Everett. A new option appeared on Dr. Quantum, a big green button with the word JUMP written on it.

"E2," Everett said. "Your world. Your city, five miles from your gate."

He jabbed down on the JUMP button. The empty circle at the centre of the slab turned to light. Hands were thrown up to protect eyes. Charlotte Villiers took a pair of round-eye dark glasses from her bag and put them on.

The Heisenberg Gate opened. The wind from another world buffeted everyone, whirled a fragment of newspaper down the metal ramp. Everett's gate had opened on a shady arcade, shops on one side, a row of columns, and, beyond them, tall cars and long trams. A woman in a full-skirted, puff-sleeved dress had stopped, startled, staring. She dropped her parasol. Her hand went to her mouth in shock. Everett raised his hand in greeting.

The Heisenberg Gate closed. The generators powered down. The lighting returned to normal. Ibrim Kerrim stooped to retrieve the piece of newspaper.

"This is this morning's *Daily Intimator*," Kerrim said. "This is what I read over my morning coffee."

Everett rotated the Infundibulum and pulled up a new map. He dragged codes into the jump window. A red bar across the bottom of the screen filled: the Heisenberg Gate capacitors recharging. The JUMP button came to life.

"E8," Everett said. "In three, two, one."

Light again flooded the jump chamber. The Heisenberg Gate opened. Everett glimpsed the dome of St. Paul's, the ugly architecture of Paternoster Row like a mouth of bad teeth; then water surged out of the gate. Funnelled down the ramp, it swept Everett from his feet and drove Kerrim and Charlotte Villiers and Paul McCabe back against the desks. Everett fought to keep Dr. Quantum out of the deluge. Then the Heisenberg Gate slammed shut.

"That particular London flooded in a storm surge in 1972," Paul McCabe said. "They moved the capital to Birmingham."

Everett picked himself up. The water had drained through the mesh floor; drips and drops fell from the metal grille-work.

"We're all right," Colette said, glancing from monitor to monitor. "We haven't lost anything important. All major systems are operational. We are good to jump."

"Well, that's nice for you, but what about these shoes?" Charlotte Villiers hissed.

Everett spun up another set of coordinates. The Heisenberg Gate readied itself for an inter-universe jump.

"E1," he said.

"No," Ibrim Kerrim said. His voice filled the room. Everett's finger hesitated over the JUMP button. "No, young sir. That world is quarantined. Access is absolutely and permanently denied."

Everett challenged him with his glare. Kerrim's eyes held his.

Everett dashed his hand across Dr. Quantum's touchscreen. "Round and round and round she goes . . ." He pulled a random piece of code onto the control panel. "Where she ends up no one knows." He brought the heel of his hand down on the button. The Heisenberg Gate opened. The crew in the control room looked out across a red-sand dune-scape under an indigo sky. The moon stood huge and terrifyingly close on the horizon, the size of Everett's upheld hand. A handful of sand trickled out of the gate onto the ramp. The desolation was not absolute. In the distance, something disturbed the crest of a dune silhouetted against the monster moon. A ripple in the sand zigzagged across the dune faces at incredible speed. The soldiers stepped forward, assault rifles at the ready. The sand swelled; the thing beneath was coming to the surface. A dark object broke the sand. The gate closed.

"Where was that?" Ibrim Kerrim.

"I can't tell you," Everett said. "But it's the same point in that world as the one I dialled up in your own world. There's no London there. I can do this for any Earth in the multiverse." One final twist of the Infundibulum. He pulled out the code. "E3. Your world, Ms. Villiers." The light dimmed, the air hummed, and the Heisenberg Gate opened inside a long, high-vaulted hall with a steel-ribbed panoramic window at one end. Beyond the window were clouds; the people in the hall were tiny dark insects against the vast skyscape. An enormous dark object was moving across the skyscape, huge as an approaching planet.

"And you are a very clever young man, Mr. Singh," Charlotte Villiers said. The ice in her voice made everyone turn. The gun Everett had glimpsed in her bag was in her hand now. In her hand, pointing at him. "We've seen quite enough party tricks. I'll take the Infundibulum now."

"What is the meaning of this, Plenipotentiary?" Ibrim Kerrim thundered. In the moment's hesitation, Colette moved. She lunged from her seat and slapped the gun away from its aim on Everett.

"Go Everett, go now!"

Everett Singh thrust the Infundibulum under his arm, nodded all the good-bye he would ever give to Colette, and dived through the circle at the centre of the black slab.

The Heisenberg Gate closed.

12

It didn't hurt a bit. That surprised Everett. He'd imagined that there would be some physical sensation to leaving one universe and arriving in another. Some wave of agonising transformation moving down his body, a wrench of every part of his being, the sensation of being broken apart down to the atoms, down to the superstrings, spread out to every part of every multiverse and then brought back together again. Even a mild dizziness and a pressing need to hurl. Nothing. Like walking from one room into another. Didn't hurt a bit. What hurt and hurt a lot was hitting the deck on the other side.

Everett hit E3 and hit it hard. People scattered as the kid from nowhere—where did he come from, did anyone see him?—went skidding across the tiled floor. He got groggily to his feet. There was something stabbing in the left side of his chest. Something felt loose in there. A rib. Not a rib. The Heisenberg Gate had closed while he was getting to his feet. He had only a few moments before E10 reopened it and sent someone through to find him. Get away, hide yourself. Which way? Where to go? Everett turned around and walked through the point in space where the gate had opened. Reverse psychology: if you go through in a certain direction, they'll naturally assume you'll keep going in that direction. Double-back on yourself.

His ankle hurt. But at least the people weren't staring. As much. He was, he had to admit, conspicuously dressed. Men in big-shouldered suits with wide laps and turned-up trousers. Shirts, no ties: instead, enamelled brooches of different geometric shapes at the collar. Some wore greatcoats, tailored at the waist. Women too favoured long coats, trimmed with fur, wasp-waisted jackets, tight pencil-skirts that went to mid-calf. Girls' fashion was long, hooded cardigans over leggings. Boys ran to military-style jackets and knee-length shorts over long socks. Hats. This was a hat universe. Sharp trilbies with decorative bands for the men; the women dainty little pillboxes and fascinators perched at perilous angles, swathed in lace and net. Girls wore hoods, boys bandanas, which Everett thought made them look badass. Tweed and twill, cord and knitwear. Proper shoes, very shiny. Denim had never been invented in this universe. Everett in his jeans, his glowtube decorated North Face weatherproof, his thick-soled but very comfortable trainers, and his backpack, looked like an astronaut, Not an astronaut, a traveller from much farther away than that. A *quantum*naut.

He was in another *universe*.

The hall curved around a central spine of ticket desks and chutes where porters dropped baggage. People milled around Everett, too busy on their businesses to spare more than a glance at the bizarro kid. A shout, a kid pointing and staring could change all that. Head up. Keep walking. Look like you belong here. The outer wall carried advertisements for hotels and banks and resorts. Blown-glass video tubes the size of cars hung from the ceiling at regular intervals; marked *arrivals* and *departures.* Some kind of a port. An airport? The people pushing past had anxious airport faces and carried clutch bags, tightly clutched, and leather briefcases and satchels. The outer wall opened into a panoramic window. Everett stopped, dizzy with wonder. The pain in his chest was forgotten. A metal and glass tube twenty metres long led from the centre of the curved window. At the end of the spoke an airship nosed in to the dock. This was the vast object he had glimpsed through the Heisenberg Gate from underneath Folkestone. Even from Everett's head-on perspective it dominated the skyline. The upper part of the nose cone carried a stylised coat-of-arms, lions and unicorns and shields. The lower part bore the words *British Overseas Air Services*, and a name, *Sir Bedivere.* Beneath the two sets of lettering was a band of windows. Everett held his breath in excitement. Behind the glass, uniformed figures in peaked caps moved, checking equipment. A shadow passed over him. Everett looked up. A cylinder of girders and conduits and pipes and elevator shafts rose a hundred metres above him and blossomed into four spokes, each set forty-five degrees out of phase with the docks on Everett's level. An airship had just cast off. An airbridge retracted, pipes were reeled in, dripping water that fell in smearing drops on the glass roof below. The airship was a sleek, streamlined flattened torpedo, much more sophisticated and elegant than the lumbering sausages Everett had seen on Discovery programmes. It must have been two hundred metres long, but it manoeuvred lightly and nimbly on its fan engines in their sleek pods. As it backed away from the dock it turned so that Everett could see the rows of windows that ran its entire length. People stood at the windows, looking down, waving. *Deutsche Kaiserlich Luftservis* was written in massive letters along the airship's lower flank. Then the engine pods swivelled, the rudder moved, and the airship drifted out of Everett's sight.

Enchanted, Everett moved through the crowds to the outward-curving window. He looked down. Vertigo made him sway on his feet. He was high, very high. As far beneath him as he was beneath the uppermost dock was another set of four docking-spokes, and that was the same height again above the ground. Airships were nosed in to each dock like piglets at the teat. Everett calculated: the entire tower was six hundred metres high. Even at this intermediate level, he was higher than any building in London. His London. He felt dizzy again. Maybe there was an aftereffect to the Heisenberg jump. Maybe it wasn't anything physical. Maybe it was philosophical; that moment when something tells you that you are farther from home than anyone in human history.

Everett looked down on this new London. He saw angels and brick. He saw the spires and domes, the saints and lions and Greek gods and cornices of Christopher Wren and Nicholas Hawksmoor churches, all Portland stone and angel figures with their wings wrapped around them looking down into the teeming streets; and he saw the brutal sheer brick cliff-faces of Battersea Power Station and Bankside and even the daunting face of University College London, a building that always made Everett imagine Batman sweeping down from its heights. Baroque Gotham, that was the architecture of E3 London. Electricity cables swooped between the domes and the blank-faced brick monoliths. Rooftops carried ugly power pylons; the city lay beneath a spiderweb of power lines. Elevated railways veered between the ancient buildings. Here were the arched glass roofs of great railway stations. There were more parks than he remembered, though they were crisscrossed by elevated railway lines. From the landmarks he recognised Everett reckoned he was around Sadler's Wells. He could see fifty kilometres. Everett gasped. At the limit of his vision was a wall that stretched as far in each direction as he could see. A burning wall—smoke and vapour went up all along its length. Everett pressed his hands against the glass and leaned forwards. No—not a wall. Chimneys. Kilometre after kilometre of chimneys and cooling towers belching smoke and steam into the atmosphere. He didn't doubt that they circled the whole of London.

Noise: voices raised against the general background of passengers heading for flights. A disturbance in the crowd, back where he had come from around the curve in the corridor. Only one thing could do that. He had stayed gaping like a fool too long. Run. He stopped himself. Don't run. Walk sedately. There were the elevators. Elevators up, elevators down. Three car loads of passengers arrived through the shaft and still the down elevator remained up on the top level. Come on come on.

Ting. The diamond-shaped lights on the call panel went green. The doors opened. Everett apologised his way into the press of people. As the doors closed he saw Charlotte Villiers, her hat like the prow of a warship, moving through the crowd. A wedge of men in dark blue uniforms and headgear like white fireman helmets cleared the way for her. Police always look like police, whatever the universe.

She turned her gaze on the lift as the doors closed. The lift started downwards with a speed that made Everett feel like the bottom had dropped out of his stomach. The Heisenberg jump had been less sick-making. Ting. Second tier: domestic flights. Ting. Ground level and transport. Everyone was heading for the exits and meeters and the greeters and the men in suits with travellers' names written on cards. And here was the trap, because beyond the meeters and greeters and the name holders and the world beyond the glass were more of the men in dark blue and white helmets. They had pieces of paper in their hands. They carefully checked the face of everyone leaving against the piece of paper. The crowd would propel him right under their eyes.

Everett peeled out from the crowd. Porters scooted around him on electric trolleys piled high with luggage. He slipped into the washroom. In a cubicle he bolted the door and tried to think of a plan. It was a good place to think. He'd always had good ideas in places like this. Something about being alone, private, free from disturbance. He sorted through the travel kit in his backpack. It had been a hasty pack that morning, after he'd had the idea of using the Heisenberg Gate to go in search of his dad. While the Spinettis had banged around trying to get ready for school and work, he quietly pilfered things a guy might need in another universe. Screwdrivers. Plugs and adapters. Insulating tape. Pencils, paper. Knife fork spoon. Ryun's dad's multitool and mains tester. Gas lighter. Matches. Headache tablets. Torch and spare batteries. Guilt stabbed him again as he brought up the wedding and engagement rings from the bottom of the side pocket. If he had had time, he would have gone home and taken his mum's. She was always promising to throw them away or have a getting-rid-of ritual or just send them to one of those "We-Buy-Gold" people who advertised on afternoon television. Mrs. Spinetti always took her rings off when she worked in the kitchen and left them on the porcelain ring-tree beside the sink. Opportunity. One two. Gone. He hadn't felt guilty at the time.

There was too much else pounding in his heart and his brain. Now he looked at them in his hand and felt sick with regret. He imagined Mrs. Spinetti looking for them on the ring-holder and not being able to find them and tearing house and family apart to find them and when she couldn't find them being fretful and tearful and filled with a terrible sense of loss. Everett felt worse about those rings than being alone in a strange and perilous new universe.

"I need them," he whispered under the sound of a cistern flushing in another cubicle. "I really need them."

Football strip. He'd forgotten he was wearing it the night he came home and found the house ransacked. Charlotte Villiers had done that, he was certain, with her thug boyfriend. Probably those two cops too—Leah-Leanne-Leona and Moustache Milligan. Football shorts over compression tights and school blazer might have looked geeky in his home London. In this London he would blend right in. The shoes were an issue, but there was nothing he could do about them. He wished he'd stolen a bandana.

Changing clothes quickly and quietly in an airport toilet cubicle was more of a challenge than Everett had imagined. Not that he had ever imagined trying to slide off jeans and pull on sports gear with one knee jammed against the paper dispenser and one foot trapped under the U-bend while trying not to send the contents of his backpack sliding across the polished floor into the neighboring cubicles.

Everett shot the bolt, looked at himself in the mirror as he washed his hands. Passable. He wouldn't fool the police on the door—"the Missionaries," he called them, from an old photo Tejendra had shown him, of his great-grandfather Narinder from the colonial days, pulling white men in white solar topees around in a rickshaw. Everett didn't intend to fool the Missionaries—not that way.

He held the matchbox in the palm of his hand as he walked through the arrivals hall. He was looking at waste bins. It took three before he found one stuffed with old newspaper. It was the work of a moment to light the match, stick the unlit end under the cover like a little wooden fuse, and drop the box into the trash. He heard the whole box of matches go up with a satisfying woosh as he walked casually away. There was an outcry. Someone hit an alarm. People panicked and fled from the blazing bin. The Missionaries on the door looked over. Everett knew so obvious a ruse wouldn't fool them either. But the consternation distracted enough people in the arrivals halls to give him the moment he needed. He quickly lifted cases off a laden luggage cart while the porter's back was turned, made a space, slipped into it and pulled the bags in around him. He pulled the final case over his head and wrapped his arms around his knees. After what seemed like an age oppressed by the smell of expensive leather, Everett felt the trolley jolt and move. He knew he was out of the terminal when he felt the regular click of paving slabs under his butt. Click click click and stop. Daylight, as the porter lifted the topmost cases. He stared dumbfounded at Everett. Then Everett pushed away the bags, leapt from the trolley, and without heed for cars buses taxis, whatever they drove in this London, ran as fast as he could away from the terminal entrance, ran until all he could see of it was the metal tower of the airport rising above the rooftops like a massively elongated Eiffel tower, and the airships nosed in around it.

13

"Go three streets down onto Kingsway, turn left, then second left on to Evelyn Street," the driver at the taxi rank said. There were six drivers, leaning against the tea stall, mugs of tea in their fists. Their taxis were alien, streamlined things, teardrop curves, tyres concealed by fairings, big grilles on the front. Two of them were plugged into a charge point beside the tea stand. "Big flight of steps out front. Can't miss it. Want me to take you there?"

"No money," Everett said. "Anyway, you said it was just a couple of streets."

"Go on, you cheeky . . . ," the taxi driver said, half joking.

If you can't ask a policeman, then a taxi driver will know; that must be a truth in every London. As soon as he had put a safe distance between himself and the airport Missionaries, Everett slowed to a walk to try to make sense of this London in which he found himself. The streets were like canyons, narrow and lightless in the shadows of the great buildings. The racket of an overhead train made him look up. Signal lights changed from red to green through the gantries and tracks. There were stations up there. Above them were swags and runs of power cables. Higher than anything but the airships, angels and classical gods and mythological creatures looked down from their places in the sun. The streets buzzed with traffic. Everett recognised the functions: buses, trucks, taxis, private cars. Trams glided down the middle of the streets, shedding sparks from the overhead wires. But the buses ran on electricity as well, drawing it down from an overhead web of wires through long, flexible antennae that brushed the cables. Some of the trucks and cars had similar pantograph arrangements. Many of the parked cars were plugged into red pillars marked with an embossed coat-of-arms, the way that post-boxes were at home. Everett estimated there was a red charge-pillar every twenty yards. Cars, trucks, buses shared that futuristic-but-old-fashioned look, like the way people in the 1930s imagined the twenty-first century would look. One thing was familiar: there were almost as many bicycles on this Tavistock Place as the Tavistock Place he had come from. But it was quiet. So quiet. Gone was the permanent internal-combustion growl of Everett's London, the shriek of brakes and the gasp of airbrakes. Here things hummed and purred and rumbled on rubber-tyred wheels.

The air smelled. Steamy, smoky, chemical. It caught at the back of Everett's throat. It tasted oily, dirty, greasy on his lips and tongue. He imagined it coating his lungs, breath by breath. Everett had tasted and smelled this once before in Delhi, on a foggy January day, when Tejendra took him to visit his Punjabi relations—hydrocarbon smog. This had a different tang from the exhaust fumes of five million Marutis and autorickshaws. There was a hellish, acrid, sulphurous tang. Coal smoke.

At the corner stood an object Everett recognised. A telephone box. Not the red metal and glass slab that even in Everett's years had started disappearing from the streets; this was an ornate bubble capped with a jaunty little spire, the ironwork wrought like leaves, the lettering organic and decorative. Inside was a metal keyboard, the brass buttons polished by years of fingers, a handset, and a screen the size of a matchbox. Everett found a square magnifying lens on an angle-poise arm and pulled it down over the screen. Words appeared, white on green. *Royal British Telecommunications. Please choose a service. Call/Interweb.* There was no mouse or trackpad. There was a small brass ball at the bottom of the keyboard.

"Cool OS," Everett said to himself. He manoeuvred the cursor over the word *Interweb*. He assumed it was the equivalent of online. *Go do*. Everett liked that. So much more full of intent than *Enter*. He hit the key. As he did he noticed the top line of the keyboard. Not QWERTY. It read: PYF. "Oh wow. Dvorak layout as standard."

New text appeared, white on green: *Please insert one shilling or Royal British Telecommunications payment card.* Too much to hope it would have been free.

"All right then. Library." Which was how he came to be asking the taxi drivers drinking tea at the stall. Three streets down onto Kingsway. Turn left. Second left. Great Russell Street. Big flight of steps. The library was built like a Greek temple. Everett tried to recall what stood in this spot in his London, but the street patterns were different and he wasn't sure of his location. He thought it might be just shops. Nothing as magnificent as the Sir John Sloane Library. The pillars that held up the great triangular porch were stone women in marble robes. There was a name for figures holding up a roof, Everett remembered. Caryatids. Each caryatid held an open book, titles carved into the stone covers. Science. Law. Drama. Medicine. Theology. Rhetoric. Everett jogged up the steps between the gazing caryatids. The interior of the library was as massive and intimidating as its exterior. It seemed kilometres to the uniformed commissioner behind his high desk in the centre of the marble lobby. His hat was very elaborate.

"The reference section, please."

"The Newett Wing," the commissionaire said. "Straight through periodicals. No eating or drinking. We close at five sharp."

The Newett Wing was a vast room beneath a glass barrel-vaulted roof. Sunlight poured down on the readers bent over their private reading desks. Shelf stacks ran down each side of the room. Faces looked up, frowning, as Everett passed. A kid in a reference library. Everett had seen the strange people who spent their days in libraries researching genealogies and histories, journeys into the past that must never end because the meaning of their lives would end with them. It was no different in this universe. Libraries give you power, Tejendra had said.

"Excuse me."

The woman at the desk looked up, eyes wide. She couldn't have looked more shocked had Everett fired a gun beside her head.

"I'm looking for the telephone directory?"

She raised a bony finger and pointed. Everett turned to follow the direction she indicated and saw all the library-pale researcher faces looking up at him. Then—only then—he realised. He hadn't seen a single non-white face since arriving in this world.

On his way to the stack Everett's attention was diverted by the neat, uniform spines of an encyclopaedia. *Encyclopaedia Britannia.* In these pages he could check out all the theories and hunches and strangenesses about this world. It wouldn't take a moment. Look up the number later. Curiosity now. Volume 22. Oaxaca to Origami. He set the heavy volume on the reading desk and opened it. *Oil. See: vegetable oils, subsection rape seed oils, palm oils, olive oils, animal oils: see whale oil, blubber, the South Atlantic whalery.* Nothing on mineral oil. Everett flipped pages back and forth. No. No crude oil. No petrochemicals. No oil. Everett's head reeled. A technological civilization without oil. Everett had seen the electric cars and the trains and the charge points and the web of cables weaving London together, and even the wonderful, improbable airships—he'd tasted the coal smoke on the air and felt it catch the back of his throat—and had imagined a post-oil world. It had all run dry. It was more than that. They had never had oil. An entire high-tech civilization had been built without liquid fuel. The coal age never ended.

"Steampunk. Cool," Everett said, loud enough to earn a glare from an earnest young woman in serious glasses. No, not anything like steampunk. Not now. Post-steampunk. Electropunk. Electricity coursed along the nerves of this London, through every city of this world, as the veins of Everett's home city were clogged with petroleum. Coal of course—he could still feel its fumes scratching the back of his throat—but surely nuclear as well. Hydro, wind-power, anything that could generate electricity.

Everett ran his finger along the spines of encyclopaedias. Earl Marchfold—Emmenthal. *Electricity*. He greedily scanned down the references. *Electricity generation. In 1789 Henry Cavendish explored the relationship between electrical charge and magnetism and in 1790 constructed the Magnetic Rotating Generative Mill, a prototype hand-cranked generator. Cavendish's celebrated insight—that the same device run in reverse would function as a motor—came to him in his infamous dream of the angel of lightning that turned the axis of the Newtonian universe. The first commercial plant was at Bowden's Mill in Manchester in 1799, where a single water wheel–powered generator operated sixteen electric power looms. . . .*

Everett reeled back as if the page had slapped him. His imagination was spinning, tumbling histories and possibilities over and over. Electric motors invented before steam engines. This Henry Cavendish had done nothing as momentous in Everett's universe. In this universe, he had invented an electrically powered Georgian era. Everett speed-read down the article. *Sir Michael Faraday's development of the electrical traction motor in 1819 . . . Alternating-current transmission lines . . . first all electrical direct-current railway from London to Oxford in 1830. . . .*

They had never had an age of steam. The age of electricity began in the eighteenth century. Coal formed the steam that generated the electricity, but not trains or cars or quaint steam-powered buses. No liquid fuel. Everything electrically powered. An idea was coming to Everett, towering and expansive like a tsunami the width of the horizon. Back to the racks. Volumes *South Pole–Tennessee* and *Original Sin–Port Harcourt. Space exploration.* Everett ran his thumb down the brief entry. This Earth had never sent men to the moon or rovers to Mars or robots to the moons of Jupiter and Saturn or probes wandering out of the solar system on million-year-long glides to other stars. They had never made it out of Earth orbit.

"No, you went exploring somewhere else, didn't you?"

Everett opened the second volume. *Parallel Universes. The physical existence of a multiverse was derived from Edwin Bell Collins's Principles of Multivalence in 1889.* Everett flipped pages. *The Einstein Gate was theorized in 1912 by German quantum physicist Albert Einstein . . .* In this universe Einstein was a quantum theorist. An American beat him to what sounded like a version of special relativity by twenty-six years. The Einstein of Everett's universe would have hated that. *Spooky* was how he described quantum theory. He skipped on. *Contact was made with the Plane E2 in 1978. . . .*

Everett closed the book. His heart was racing. They had opened the Heisenberg Gate on to the multiverse thirty-three years before his world. And everyone knew it. It was in the encyclopaedia on the shelf in the library. One more thing. One last nugget of information about this world before he put the encyclopaedias away and went on to the stack that held the telephone directory, the primary reason he had come to the library. It was even in the same volume. He ran his finger down the thumb-notches.

Plenitude of Known Worlds.

The Plenitude of Known Worlds is an inter-universal supervisory organization overseeing the development, construction, licensing and use of the inter-plane transit device known as the Einstein Gate. It also facilitates cooperation between member planes in areas of inter-universal law, security, trade, development, political and diplomatic representation, exploration and expansion. . . .

Planes E2, E3, E4 and E5 are the founder members of the Plenitude. Current membership stands at nine worlds.

"You're out of date," Everett whispered. "It's ten now."

Each member world holds a rotating Primacy and for the duration of that Primacy the Central Praesidium is based in the Plenitude Headquarters of the Primarch's home world. Earth—E3 by its Official Panoply Identifier Number—headquarters are in the Tyrone Tower, Cleveland Street, Bloomsbury, London.

Everett jabbed his finger down onto the picture of the Tyrone Tower—a spire of buttresses and mullioned windows and turrets and mythological creatures that out-Gothed even the baroque skyscraper Everett had seen from the sky port. "That's where you've got him," he hissed. "I know it, I know it. Can't be anywhere else."

"Young sir?"

Everett looked up, startled and guilty that his anger had been overhead. The woman from the main desk leant over him. Reading lights uplit her face, casting sinister shadows.

"Just to let you know, we close in ten minutes. Minutes, ten."

Everett hadn't noticed the reading light on his desk come on. He had been too engrossed in books to be aware of the sky darkening behind the glass vault of the roof, the long Reference Room empty as the readers and researchers and eccentrics drifted away one by one. *All the important stuff ends up in books,* Tejendra had once said. *Take that out of the Internet and all you have left is opinion.*

But: ten minutes! The London Telephone and Business Directory ran to seven volumes. *Pawnshops, gold buyers, and precious metals valuers*. It might be too late; he didn't know when closing time was in this London. Most of them were just a name, an address, and a telephone number. Some were highlighted in a display box and had a line or two of description. Payday loans. Low rates. Gold and jewellery bought. Keenest prices. Here was one with a half page display. *Money too tight to mention? Can't stretch to payday? Instant redemption. No early payment fees. Nevin Financial Services. Late nights. . . .*

"Thursday!" Everett clenched his fist in triumph. He jotted down the address. He went down the stacks until he came to Maps and Cartography, found the *Henson-Jenson All-Streets Compendium* for London, located the address, and took out Dr. Quantum. It looked as alien as a starship in the softly lit, wood-and-leather library. He didn't like using precious battery life before he had worked out the local electricity supply. He took a photograph. The camera click seemed as loud as a book falling from a stop shelf. Earnest Woman looked up, frowned, did a double-take at Dr. Quantum. She was the only other reader in the long quiet room. One last piece of information from *Encyclopaedia Britannia*: *Great Britain's electricity supply is at 110 volts, sixty hertz*. Result. No different from the US in his home world. There were two-pin sockets on the reading desks, and Everett had already worked out that it was only ten minutes' work with his multitool to re-engineer his socket adaptor.

"Thank you!" Everett called breezily to the librarian as he left. Outside the streets were dark and cold. A yellow smog was distilling out of the night air. Passersby turned up collars and pulled scarves tight. Everett shivered. He would have loved one of those greatcoats. Maybe when he had money. No, you're going to need every penny. The exercise will keep you warm. And better get going now; it was no short distance.

14

Nevin Financial Services was Nevin the Pawnbroker. The window on Lambic Lane was a false front, made up to look grander and less seedy than it was. Nevin Financial Services' main office was down a greasy alley, lit only by three neon circles—green, blue, and red—that crackled and dripped fat blue sparks to the cobblestone. The symbol of the pawnbroker was the same in any universe. The window here was filmed with years of grime. Rows and racks and shelves holding hundreds of pledged articles made cleaning the inside of the glass impossible. Everett had heard of pawnbrokers—there was even one in Stokie, off Stamford Hill, but neither he nor anyone he knew had ever seen it. He had to go to a parallel universe to visit one. He knew how they worked—you put up an item of value as security, and if you didn't pay back the loan and a small fee, the pawnbroker kept the item to sell. Here were the items no one had ever redeemed. Devices that looked like radios, or those really old Sonys that played cassette tapes, with their earphones wrapped around them. Things like typewriters with little television tubes where the carriage should be, and magnifiers on swivel arms. Medals set on cardboard. Jewellery: rings, necklaces, carved ivory brooches, and sculpted black jet. Dolls. Ornate lamps. Items that looked antique even to Everett's limited understanding of this world. Collections of stamps. Old records. A small enamelled box with a painting of an airship on it, bordered with Union Jacks and the words, in gold: *Excelsior Brand: mint comfits.* Everett started at the sight of two eyes looking back at him from between the forfeited items. Nevin the pawnbroker.

The door jingled as Everett entered.

Nevin the pawnbroker took his ancient profession seriously and was dressed in a sharp suit in the wide-lapelled style of this world. He wore a carnation in the buttonhole, a little wilted at this late hour. Everett thought he was the second-most-person-to-look-like-a-complete-crook, after Thug-in-a-Chauffeur-Cap. The office was walled floor to ceiling with gas cases filled with forfeited objects, great and small. Electric motorbikes to comic books. A stuffed bear to a tiny embroidered heart. Everett could feel the weight of misery dragging at his heart. Nevin screwed a jeweller's magnifier into his right eye socket and examined Everett's goods.

"Sell or pledge?"

Everett's original thought had been to sell the rings for hard cash. To pledge them was to declare that sometime he would redeem, then put them in a padded envelope and drop them through Mrs. Spinetti's letter box. Everett didn't like to think of himself as a thief, however noble his motivations.

"I'd like to pledge them."

"Forty guineas for the wedding band, tenner for the engagement ring."

"Ten pounds? Those are diamonds, those are."

"They're marquesites, they are."

Anything less than diamonds in her engagement ring and Angela Spinetti would have called the entire wedding off. Everett took the ring, touched the jewel to the glass countertop and lightly left a two-centimetre scratch.

"Diamonds."

"All right, smart arse. Thirty for the sparkler."

"Guineas."

Nevin looked Everett up and down, seemed on the verge of asking a question, then shook his head and took out a docket book.

"I'm too bloody soft, that's my problem. Standard terms, thirty three percent APR, no redemption fee, over six weeks. Right with you, son? Sign here and here."

He signed with a beautiful metal fountain pen. Of course,

Everett thought. Not so easy to make plastics from coal. He'd never used a nib pen before. It scratched and squeaked on the paper. His signature looked like a spider car crash. Nevin tore along the dotted line and gave Everett the docket. He took out a large, complicated leather wallet, polished smooth from decades of passage from hip pocket to hand. Nevin turned it this way, that way, opened up different pockets and pouches. He marshalled the notes and coins on the glass counter like troops. Sparks from the dodgy neon lit the room nightmare blue. As Everett reached for the money, Nevin flicked out a finger, snake-quick, and dragged one coin back.

"Going to have to get the scratch professionally removed, ain't I?"

Everett glanced over his shoulder from the shop door. Nevin was setting the two rings in a glass case, his receipt folded through them.

I'll be back for you, however many universes I have to cross.

Money in his pocket. It didn't feel exactly clean, but he could look at it without thinking of Mrs. Spinetti fretting over her lost rings. One hundred pence made a pound, like home, but like US currency, the coins all had names. Guessing from American coinage, Everett estimated a shilling was ten pence, a half-crown twenty-five pence, a crown fifty pence. A tanner was five pence, and there was a rare little coin called a florin that seemed to be the equivalent of the twenty pence piece. Money in his pocket. It wouldn't last long. And while Everett was in the pawnshop the streets had emptied. A sudden flaw of wind edged with sleet sent papers tumbling down the street. It blew harsh December through Everett's sportswear. It was December everywhere in the multiverse. Suddenly he felt terrifyingly alone. A stranger in an alien world. Nothing was the same here. Nothing. He couldn't go back. He couldn't suddenly declare game over, switch off and go back to tea and chocolate HobNobs. He couldn't whip out his phone and call home and the car would be there in half an hour. He was farther from home than anyone of his world had ever been. He was the most alone person in the multiverse. No—and the realisation sent a thrill of hope and at the same time, of fear at what he must do. He was not alone. Out there, in there, in the Tyrone Tower, was his father. But home was so far, and there was so much to do, and he was tired. So tired. Tired in every cell; tired in every atom. The only way home was to follow his plan through. And there were so many holes in it, so many flaws, so much reliance on lucky breaks. It was hopeless. It was the only plan that had a chance of working. But it had no chance of ever working if he froze to death trying to sleep in a doorway, or got picked up by the police for vagrancy wandering the streets. But one night in any of the hotels he had seen, their windows bright and their lobbies loud with gorgeously dressed people gathering for Christmas dinners and jamborees and balls, would wipe out all his hard-won money. These were the bits he hadn't thought out. The fact was that he needed to sleep—and right now needed to eat.

A train clanged and roared overhead like a battle. Did they run all night? Could he just buy a ticket to the next stop and ride round and round, lulled to sleep by the clack of the rails and the jostle of the points? Everett had ridden night trains at home. He didn't expect them to be any less scary in this London. He looked up at the figures softly silhouetted behind the misted-up windows. People going home. Home to Barnet and Earlsfield, Harrow and Wealdstone, Hackney and Stoke Newington. The idea seized him so sudden and hard it was painful. Go there. It's the territory you know. The street names may be different, but the geography they're laid along is the same. There may be a 43 Roding Road. There may be a summer-house out the back of Number 27, that would make a winter bedroom for an inter-universal traveller. There may be a Dogs' Delight and allotments at the end of it, allotments with garden sheds and chair and sofas and all the things allotmenteers brought to make their gardens like outdoor living rooms. If there are none of those there may even be a Victorian cemetery with an old chapel in the middle. Everett didn't mind the dead. They slept deep and sound and never snored. Another train passed over on the down-line. Everett walked purposely toward the red neon circle-and-V symbol of the London Overground through a shower of soft blue sparks. The wind of another London sent newspapers flying around him like birds.

15

The girl got on at St. Paul's. Everett would not have noticed her except that she came up the carriage and sat down opposite him. She didn't need to do that. The carriage was almost empty. Everett had been checking the map on Dr. Quantum. He slipped the pad as secretively as he could into his backpack. Warnings beeped, the doors closed, the train accelerated in a shriek of wheels along the high line that looped around the floodlit mass of the great domed cathedral. Everett was suddenly paralysed with homesickness. St. Paul's—identical in every detail to the one he knew—seemed like a piece of his own world dropped into this one.

"What you gawping at?"

Everett's face reddened. The girl thought he had been staring at her.

"Just St. Paul's."

"Ain't you seen it before?"

"Well, yes, of course. But it was the cathedral really. Not you."

"So is I not worth a gawp?"

She was, Everett had to admit. The girl was extraordinary. Extraordinary her clothes: leggings tucked into pixie boots, a military-style jacket pulled over a T-shirt slashed to navel-height. Extraordinary her hair: a big afro of pure white. Extraordinary her face: Everett had never seen skin so pale, eyes so arctic blue. She looked like she was carved from ice.

"I'm sorry if you thought I was staring."

"Doesn't matter to me."

The girl turned away from him, flipped up the collar of her jacket, and slid down into her seat. She pulled a deck of cards from a satchel she wore at her side and leafed through them, lips moving silently. It was warm in the carriage, and the rolling rhythm of the tracks lulled Everett into the half-hypnosis of the night train. He jolted himself out of sleep to see the girl snatch her gaze away from him again. She carefully laid out cards from her deck on the none-too-clean upholstery. Extraordinary too the cards. They were illustrated like tarot cards, but the symbols and characters were strange to Everett. Gothy Emma, the Queen Bee of the Bourne Green emo girls, carried around a tarot deck and pretended to read love fortunes and call down curses on people who badmouthed her on Facebook. Those had hanged men and popes and fools with dogs at their heels. This was a different bestiary. Here was a brass man, and a man in a leotard on a unicycle juggling worlds. Here was a god with four faces and a woman with a sword in each hand and crowned with the sun. A serpent tied in a figure eight—or an infinity symbol—its tail in its mouth. An ancient man on crutches outside a door that led into blackness. A single hand reaching out of a stormy sea. The girl muttered to herself as she laid each card in a careful pattern. House On Legs in the centre of the cross; Chariot Drawn by Swans laid at right angles across it.

"You're doing it again."

Everett started. "What?"

"The gawp thing."

"I'm sorry; it's, well, I've never seen cards like those before."

"Course you ain't. No one has. These here cards is bespoke to me. Personalised, in person. Completely unique. The one and only Everness Tarot."

"What are you doing?"

"Look at 'im. Not just gawping, but nosy with it. Since you ask, looking. Little up the ways, little down the ways, little out to the sides."

"Like telling fortunes?"

The girl's eyes widened in affront. Everett had never seen such pale eyes. They were slivers of ice.

"It is not like telling fortunes. Not like that at all. It's like I said, it's looking. Seeing things how they is, how they really is deep down, under everything and everything." She smiled. It transformed her. It turned her into another person. "Do you want me to show you?" She gathered up the cards and skipped across the carriage to sit beside Everett. She shuffled the fat deck. She had all the tricks and riffles. Bebe Ajeet had been able to do that. She was a demon at gin rummy. The girl held out the deck in the palm of her hand. "Tap it three times."

"No magic words?" Everett said.

"This isn't magic." She raised the deck to the level of her eyes. "Now cut it."

Everett cut the deck in three, put the top in the middle, the middle on the bottom and the bottom on the top.

"Take the top three cards and lay them out in a row."

Everett turned them up, one at a time. A man with a spear, wreathed in flame. Two flying figures blasting a field of wheat. A skyscraper with an eye at its summit. The girl waggled her head from side to the side in a way that was so like that Punjabi gesture for almost-yes that Everett almost laughed. Almost. The girl's icy seriousness was terrifying.

"Behind you, beneath you, before you," the girl said. "Now, the next three."

A man pulling a cart with a donkey in it. A struggling man entombed in rock. Two sisters with their tongues linked by a chain. As he turned over the last card the girl's eyes widened. A tiny gasp went out of her. She bent forward, peering at the cards. Spooked, Everett leaned forward too, and as he did he felt the tiniest tug on the backpack strap he had wound around his leg. He lunged forward just in time to stop Dr. Quantum from vanishing inside the girl's military jacket. She hugged the computer to her.

"I'll scream rape."

Everett snatched up the cards, opened the ventilation window and held them out in to the slipstream. The girl shrieked.

"No!"

"Give it back," Everett ordered.

"But I want it. It's bona. Give it to me."

"Put it down."

The girl only hugged it tighter.

"But I likes it. I'd be good to it. Where's the on switch?" She turned Dr. Quantum over and over in her hands. "Oh, this is fantabulosa bona. No magnifier, look how thin it is. This isn't from our world."

Everett felt a spike of ice run through his stomach. His eyeballs, his brain, his heart throbbed. His belly muscles spasmed. He wobbled, woozy in the lurching train carriage.

"That gawp thing. You're doing it again. Sit your little self down, omi, before you go arse over tit."

Numb with shock, Everett sat down. The girl gingerly set Dr. Quantum down on the seat.

"Cards. Now."

Everett placed the deck of cards beside the machine. The girl's hand struck like a snake, snatched the Tarot back into the inside pocket of her jacket. Everett put Dr. Quantum back into his backpack and closed the zip. He saw how the girl never took her eyes off it.

"Nah, I mean it's obvious it ain't from this world," she said. "We've nothing like that. It's plastic, ainit? Real genuine plastic. Got to love that. Where you get it from, eh? Did you nick it? Oh . . . oh . . . I get it. It ain't just the comptator. It's you, ain't it? You're cross-planes as well. What world? Ain't E2, they're proper zhooshy they are. And you, cove . . . Well. I don't think so. So where you from? Hey, are you one of those nano-assassins from E1?"

"A what from E1?"

"That's what they say. That they look exactly like us but inside they're this mass of nanotechnology. You can only tell if you look them right in the eye, right in the dark bit, and it's like fly's eyes. Of course, if you close enough to do that, they've already eaten your brain."

"Is this true?"

"What true, omi?"

"About E1?"

"Nah. Just a story. No one knows. Are you from E1, cove?"

"Look into my eyes."

The girl leaned forward. She smelled of patchouli, like Gothy Emma, and something muskier, earthier Everett could not identify. It seemed too mature a scent for her. Everett guessed her age at thirteen. He wasn't very good at guessing girls' ages. She held Everett's eyes for a moment, then looked away.

"Naah . . . Just zhooshing you. Where are you from? Honest?"

"E10."

"E10? Where's that, what's that. Never heard of that. E10?"

"We made first contact with the Plenitude in February this year. We've exchanged plenipotentiaries."

"Naah, never heard anything about that. Then again, like, it's all going on up in that big tower, and what's any of it got to do with the price of cheese."

"Quite a lot if you wanted to steal my computer."

The girl cringed back, embarrassed, but she let her hand lightly stroke Everett's backpack.

"Oh, but it is bona . . . Does everyone have toys like this where you come from?"

"It's new tech, but it's nothing special. Everyone has portable computing." Everett pulled out his phone and turned it on. "I won't be able to get a signal here, but this is a mobile phone, a telephone. Except it's got all these apps, and I've got my music on it, and pictures, and what I think you call Interweb . . . and a decent camera." Everett clicked a photograph of the wide-eyed girl and showed it to her. She covered her face with her hands, embarrassed again, then took the phone to look at herself. "You can zoom in and out with your fingers," Everett said, showing her the gestures that navigated the screen.

"Bona*roo*," the girl said. "You E10ers are good. Almost as good as them E4 coves, but they got that thing with the moon. Okay, well so I knows something about E10 now. Your tech is bona, but your togs are well vile. So where you going?"

Everett didn't answer. He didn't trust her yet.

"Oh, don't come that with me, omi. Them planesrunners, them scientists and businessmen and Plenitude coves, when they're here, they rides round in limos with bodyguards and jumpguns and everything. Here's you on the Trafalgar Line dressed like a dill with a million dinari of E10 tech on you. Do you know where you're going, omi?"

Still Everett didn't answer. The train hurtled into an archway in the face of a monstrous apartment block. The rattle of tracks and engines rose to a roar: they were in a tunnel. The carriage was flashlit by arcing electricity. Everett glimpsed windows beyond the windows, brief glimpses of other lives. The girl wiggled closer to him.

"Omi omi omi, I been counting the stops. 'Less you get off at the next one, you're going the same place I am. Last stop. Terminus. All change. You ain't been there. You're going to need a guide."

"Why should I trust you? You haven't even told me your name."

The girl sat up, stiff and affronted.

"Well, I can say the same of you, planesrunner."

"Everett. Everett Singh."

"That's like an Airish name."

"It's Punjabi."

"God, you really don't know nothing, do you, Everett Singh? You see me . . . Nah. Let's put it this way; there's coves up there'll lift all your dally tech, and they'll even take your naff togs if they think they can get a shilling for them, and they cut your kidneys out as their way of saying a personalised thank-you. Everett Singh, Everett Singh, what you doing here?"

The train creaked to a halt at a blindingly lit station built inside the apartment unit. Cast iron balconies rose tier upon tier on either side of the tracks, the apartments sheer as cliff faces. Power cables and washing lines crisscrossed the canyon of brickwork. High above, another railway line crossed at right angles, higher even than that was a glass vault, ribbed with iron. Pigeons swooped down from the heights, wings whirring, skimmed the platform. Doors opened. Passengers got off. No one got on. Everett and the girl were the only people in the carriage. Warnings shrieked; the doors closed.

"Next stop Hackney Great Port, Everett Singh. . . ."

"I need somewhere to stay," Everett blurted out as the train pulled out of the station.

"Course you do, omi. Why didn't you say so? You see, I may have tried to lift your toy, but at least I was honest about it, you know? Me you can trust, Everett Singh."

Everett would have questioned her logic, but a place for the night was a place for the night. Then the train banged out of the brick-and-iron cavern—which Everett now realised was many buildings, grown together over decades, even centuries, a city within a city. The breath caught in his chest. Here was a greater wonder. Airships. Dozens of them; perhaps a hundred, moored in nose to nose around docking towers. So many airships they shut out the smoggy night sky. The train-line ran between the ceiling of airships and the ground. Down there were low, long warehouses; low-loaders and sleek electric trucks. Railway cars shunted along shining silver rails; between them darted forklift trucks, containers balanced in their prongs. The bellies of the airships were open; hull sections lowered on winch cables. Some offloaded cargo; others took on containers and pallets of freight. Everett watched an airship winch up its loading pallet and close its cargo bay. And from an open cargo bay, blinding with working lights, he saw a face as dark as his own look down. Everywhere was noise and activity and industry under steaming arc-lights.

"Sweet home Hackney Great Port," the girl said. "Come on, planesrunner, we gets off here."

The train slowed to a stop beneath a steel-and-glass vault and emptied its passengers onto the platform. End of the line indeed.

The elevated track stood above a marshalling yard. Freight trains and shunters clanged and groaned in cascades of sparks and flashes. The air smelled of grease and lightning. Everett would have watched for hours, but the girl pulled him on down the clattery steps. They were last through the turnstiles. Out in the street the wind whipped sleet around Everett's shoulders and legs.

"Don't stare," the girl said. "Makes you look like an amateur."

But Everett couldn't help but stare, down at street level. Industry was king here, and people minded their manners. More than once the girl pulled Everett out of the way of a forklift, container raised high above them, or stopped him from stepping into the path of a shunting engine. They hopped over silver rails, scurried through labyrinths of stacked containers from which the wind, blowing over their angles, drew a melancholy wolf-howl. They hurried down sleet-lashed streets between the bright neon signs and windows of pubs and coffeeshops and Chinese noodle bars and Jamaican curry houses. From the open doorways came light and gusts of warmth and voices and music. The music made Everett think of '80s retro synthpop; the kind of thing dads asked for at wedding discos, but with a chunkier beat. Lots of singing. From one pub, a waft of beer, cigarette smoke, and "Hark! The Herald Angels Sing." Outside, the smell of old urine. Christmas lights sagged in the window and around the door, flickering fitfully. Mare Street; he was on Mare Street. And above, hauled in around their docking arms, the airships hung over him like the leaves of immense trees.

He would never have survived here alone.

The girl led him in under the hulls of the airships. Sleety rain fell in cascades from their skins. Two men stepped out of the waterfall. Water ran from ankle-length waxed coats and shapeless broad-brimmed hats. They were big, square, darkly silhouetted against the glow from the airship's interior, and the girl did not look at all pleased to see them.

"Where's your guv?" The man's voice was deep and guttural.

"You know, she comes, she goes," the girl said. "Me, I'd be the last to find out."

"Who's your cove?" The second man had a strong Dutch accent.

Everett sneaked his bag behind his legs.

"I'm trying to sneak him in so I can charver the arse off him," the girl said.

The Dutchman creased over with laughter. Guttural Man was less amused.

"Well, see, here's a message, polone. Tell this to your captain: the Iddler's giving her to Christmas Eve to hear her proposals, no more. You got that? Christmas Eve."

The Dutchman was still laughing as they walked past Everett and the girl into Hackney Great Port.

"The Iddler?"

"Iddle diddle davy, pig's bum and gravy," the girl said nonchalantly, but Everett was not fooled. The two hoods had shaken her. But she wasn't going to tell him who or what the Iddler was.

"And Captain?"

"You know, Everett Singh, the reason I'd never ever even snog you let alone let you close enough for a charver is 'cause you's always asking questions. Question question question. Captain. Yes. My Captain." She ducked through the curtain of falling water. "You coming or do you want to stay out here all night?"

The airship's belly lay open, platforms and hoists and lifts lowered to the ground. Everett squinted up through the light. A name was stencilled on the underside of the nose. *Everness.*

The girl had called her cards the Everness Tarot.

The girl stood on the aft cargo platform. She pulled up her sleeve and tapped a watch-like device around her left wrist. Motors whirred overhead. Two cables descended from inside the airship. Loops were attached to the cables; the girl slipped wrist through one, foot through another and turned the dial on her watch-that-wasn't-a-watch. The cable hauled her up into the light.

"Hope your grip's good, Everett Singh!"

Everett slipped both arms through the straps of his backpack and grabbed for the cable as the loops rose past him. For a moment he dangled by the wrist; then his foot found the second loop.

"You still haven't told me your name!" he shouted up at the girl, vanishing into the light.

"Sen!" she shouted back, grinning down between the soles of her boots. "Sen, and I's a pilot!"

16

Everett felt the softness move under him and turned over and smiled and thought, that'll be the wind, moving the airship at its mooring. He sat up, electrically awake. Every nerve and hair awake. I am on an airship!

He remembered now. He had ridden the cable up into the open belly of the airship. He had gaped up in amazement. *Gawp*, that had been her word. So much bigger and yawning and stupid with amazement than *gaped*. Everything in the airship was in the key of *vast*. Vast the cargo holds. Vaster still the skeleton of arches and vaults, pierced through and through again with holes, that clasped the airship's skin to its ribs. Most vast of all, the roof of lift cells that ran the length of the airship's spine—a double row of gas-filled spheres each the size of an apartment block, lashed together with netting and webs of cables and flexing, pulsing pipes. The interior space of the airship was the size of a cathedral, with a cathedral's sense of height and space and lightness. No, that was not the image at all. It was more gooey and physical than that. A lung. He was inside a giant lung.

The girl—Sen, her name was Sen—had reached out and grabbed him by the waistband of his football shorts and hauled him in to the decking. He had disentangled his hand and foot just in time. In his state of amazement he could easily have been hauled high up among the gas cells.

"You bed down in here, omi." Sen had shown Everett a nook where three cargo containers met. "I sometimes beds down here myself. I mean, I'm supposed to be on watch, but sometimes you just fancy a kip. See?" Webbing and gas-cell skin had been piled into a rat's nest. Sen offered two handfuls to Everett. "Snug as a bug."

The fabric was soft as liquid, so flexible Everett thought it might run through his fingers, breath-soft. When he tugged at it, it snapped rigid, then relaxed again into softness.

"What is this stuff?"

"Them's carbon nanotubes," Sen said. "Everything in *Everness* is carbon tubes. Strong as steel, light as a wish."

"We don't have anything close to this," Everett said.

"Something you don't have, Everett Singh?" Sen skipped away. "I'll come get you in the morning. You'll be all right in here—no one knows this is here—but don't go wandering about. Wait for me."

She waggled her fingers in farewell and vanished. Everett gingerly lay down on the pile of webbing. It was deep; it was yielding. It was soft. He pulled it around him like a coat. Weariness fell on him like a landslide. Sleep pulled him down, but he fought himself awake to wrap Dr. Quantum up in airship silk like a fly in a web and lie down on top of it. He didn't trust Sen not to come slipping and sneaking in the night to the little hidey-hole. For the bona. Everett looked up at the vast spheres of the gas cells. An airship. He was on an airship. An airship in another world. A parallel universe. This morning he had woken in one Earth. Tonight he slept in another. A moment of panic jolted him, then he tumbled headlong into huge sleep.

And now he was awake and he was still on the airship on a parallel Earth. Morning light turned the open hatch into a swimming pool of light. The air in the hold was so cold he could see his breath. Everett looked up again at the lift cells. He marvelled at the way they were packed so efficiently into the space—a classic problem in mathematics, that—how the ribs and spars of the ship's skeleton respected them, the high catwalks and the scramble nets, the drop-lines dangling from the upper skin, the winches that ran along overhead rails. A sudden hissing vent of a pressure-release valve made Everett jump. Condensation dripped from the support spars. The cold was outrageous. But the engineering was thrilling. Everett clutched the backpack containing Dr. Quantum to him and followed his curiosity. The deck beneath his feet was metal mesh; below were ballast tanks and what looked like battery banks for the ducted fan engines. This must be a strange world to grow up in, Everett thought. A strange world within a strange world. Nothing was solid; nothing was substantial; nothing was anchored to the ground. A floating world, shifting at every whim of the wind. Here was a staircase that led up to the main catwalk that ran like a spine between the rows of gas cells. The steps looked frail and fragile as ice. They easily bore Everett's weight. He jumped up and down. Not even a creak. Strong as diamond. Up on the catwalk he looked back and forth along the central axis of the airship. One way bridge, the other way stern. Could he remember from the previous night how the ship was oriented? He went up to the nearest gas cell. It bulged tautly against the netting that connected it to the ship's skeleton. The skin looked as stretched and distended as a party balloon. Everett prodded it with a forefinger. The skin yielded. He pushed his finger into the cell all the way to the last knuckle. The skin deformed smoothly around him. This was how the people of this world had engineered out the frailties and fragilities that had doomed the old hydrogen-fuelled zeppelins of Everett's world. Carbon nanotubes, soft under gentle pressure, rigid under shock. Experiment time. Everett balled a fist and drew back to punch the skin as hard as he could.

"That's right, you put your big ham fist right through it," a voice said in the broadest Glasgow accent Everett had ever heard. "Ye thieving Iddler hellion ye." Everett turned, glimpsed a figure. Orange jumpsuit. Cavalry-style jacket. Face: brown as his own. Object in the hand, pointed at him. Everett heard a soft coughing noise and something hit him solidly in the face, something huge and dark and heavy and yet soft as a sock filled with mince. He went down on to the catwalk. Down and straight out.

The woman looked down on him. She wore a man's—a man in this world's—ankle-length greatcoat smartly tailored at the waist, lapels embroidered in twining floral patterns of gold thread. A white shirt, high collared, tan riding breeches tucked into boots with lots of buckles and straps. At first Everett thought she was bald, then saw that the woman's hair was cropped within millimetres of her skull. Her left ear was hooped with piercings from top to bottom. Rings on every finger and both thumbs. Silver bangles around both wrists. Her skin was the deepest black, her eyes the largest Everett had ever seen, but they did not seem soft and trusting. They were wide to everything in the world; they missed nothing; they saw and judged all. They looked at Everett with contempt and wonder.

"What have we here?"

Everett tried to sit up. He slumped to the deck. Everything hurt, hurt down to the bones. His head felt like his brain had been slam-dunked into his skull. From a mighty height. Struggling on to his elbows, Everett could just focus on Orange Jumpsuit, perched at the top of a flight of stairs, knees pulled up to his chest.

"You shot me! In the face!"

"And I'd do it again." The accent was pure Glasgow; the face was pure Punjab. The object resting on his knees looked like a weapon in any city, any culture.

"So the Iddler's sending kids to do his dirt, is he?"

Everett rolled painfully over to find the source of this new, American-accented voice. A white man, blue-eyed, axe-faced, with an Uncle Sam goatee that made him look older than he was. Pinstripe pants, a brocade waistcoat over a shirt closed at the neck with a cravat. His long coat had a half-cape. On his head he wore a wide-brimmed hat with a feather stuck jauntily into the band.

"What? Who?"

"What's your name, son?" said the woman. The two men seemed to defer to her.

"Everett," Everett groaned. "Everett Singh. And who the hell are you?"

The woman's wide eyes widened farther at the boldness.

"I am, *the hell*, Anastasia Sixsmyth, and I am, *the hell*, master and commander of this airship, which you have been trying to sabotage."

"No, wait wait wait wait, I haven't, I'm not trying to sabotage—"

"Is that so? Then what's this?" The master and commander held up Dr. Quantum. "Some kind of new explosive, I'd hazard. Just made to slip in under the charge capacitors and no one would ever notice." She held up the smartphone. "And don't tell me this isn't a remote control." She ran her thumb across the screen. "Ooh. Bona. Tell me this, how come the Iddler trusted all this shiny tech to an idiot like you?" She waved away any possible answer Everett could have given. "No, don't bother. You won't be around long enough for it to interest me. Mr. Sharkey, Mr. Mchynlyth, our uninvited guest is leaving now."

The Punjabi-Scot unfolded from his perch and grabbed Everett's right shoulder. The tall American took the left. They hauled Everett to his feet.

"Goodbye, Mr. Singh," Captain Anastasia said. "Oh, and as you won't be needing these, it would be a shame to let them go to waste." She held up the smartphone and Dr. Quantum, then tucked them away inside the tails of her greatcoat.

"No, you mustn't!" Everett's toes kicked at the decking as the two men dragged him across the metal mesh. He struggled, but they were big, they were strong. He was damaged. He was alone. They dragged him to the open hatch and held him out over the edge. Everett looked down ten metres at the hard metal surface of the cargo deck. "You can't do this!"

"I think you'll find I can do whatever I like on my own ship," Captain Sixsmyth said. "Or did you miss that 'master and commander' bit? Gentlemen . . ."

The American and the Punjabi-Scot easily lifted Everett off the ground.

"And ah one . . . ah two . . . ," the Punjabi-Scot Mchynlyth chanted.

A single fleck of white fluttered down out of the vast high vaults of the airship, turning and tumbling, flashing as it caught the morning light spilling up through the open hold. The American Sharkey reached up and dexterously snatched it out of the air. A card. A white card with a pattern on it. An Everness Tarot card.

"Sen?"

Motors whined. Sen descended like an ice angel out of the lofty recess of *Everness* on a drop-line.

"Let him go. He's bona."

"Oh so?" Captain Anastasia held up Dr. Quantum. "So you know what this does, then?"

"It's some kind of comptator, is what," Sen said defiantly. She swung gently at the end of her line, the toes of her boots five centimetres from the decking. Captain Anastasia turned the rectangle of plastic over and over in her hands, looking for a way to operate it.

"Excuse me, ma'am, I could show you . . . ," Everett offered. Captain Anastasia nodded to the American and the Punjabi-Scot, who set Everett down but stayed close, one on each shoulder. She held the computer out to Everett as delicately and distastefully as if it were smeared in excrement. He found the tricky little on switch. When the welcome screen booted, he pressed his thumb to the biometric panel. Captain Anastasia leaned close over the screen, frowning at the desktop. This is where it stands or falls, Everett thought. These people can help me or they can throw me out. I have to get them to help me. But there's nothing I can do, except tell the truth and nothing but the truth.

"Now this is a mighty slick comptator," Captain Anastasia said.

"That," Sen declared, "is because that's not from anywhere on our world. That's cross-planes tech, that is." She sounded very pleased with herself, but at the word "cross-planes" the American Sharkey, Mchynlyth the Punjabi-Scot, and Captain Anastasia all took a step back.

"I haven't got a disease, you know," Everett said.

"No, you ain't. But what you got is special status," Captain

Anastasia said. "And what we got is trouble. Sen! What for you bringing this planesrunner back here? And you, Mr. Singh, what for you wandering round on your ownsome into Hackney Great Port without the usual truckload of sharpies and Security Service buffoons and the Dear knows what else behind you?"

"Sharpies?"

"'Knowing this, that the law is not made for a righteous man, but for the lawless and disobedient, for the ungodly and for sinners, for unholy and profane, for murderers of fathers and murderers of mothers, for manslayers,'" Sharkey the American said.

"Mr. Sharkey, far be it from me to disrespect a man's religion, but this is perhaps not the most apposite time for the Word of the Dear. Sharpies, Mr. Singh. Police. There is no situation in life that cannot be made worse by the presence of police. And that leaves me in a delicate situation, because sure as eggs is eggs, them sharpies and special security agents will come looking for you, and, well, we keep our own customs here in Airish Town. Sharpies, the exciseman, the tipstaff; we live well enough without them. But at the same time I can't simply dump a valuable piece of cargo off my ship. Sen, fix your guest a bite of breakfast." She turned to leave, her coat tails flapping.

"Captain Sixsmyth!" Everett said.

She stopped but did not turn.

"You've still got my computer."

"So I have."

Captain Anastasia strode on, her boot-heels clicking from the decking,

"Thanks, Ma!" Sen shouted.

Ma? was the word on Everett's lips, but Captain Anastasia raised a dismissing hand.

"Don't thank me, I haven't decided what to do yet. But I shall require words with you, Mr. Singh, in my quarters. And Sen, get some hot water and soap around him. Teenage boys are rank; it's all those hormones."

17

"Master and commander of *Everness*, and my mother," Sen said. The galley was tucked into a cubby on the upper starboard side of the airship, so small Everett feared being spattered by hot fat from Sen's frying pan. The table folded down, the chairs folded up, and the air was blue with smoke, but the view from the curved window was magnificent. The night's rain was clearing, swept from the sky by a brisk wind that sent lines of clouds marching out of the west. It was the kind of day Everett loved, bright, cold, low winter sun striking glints and highlights from the hunched backs of the airships. As he watched, a ship lifted from its moorings, engine pods swivelling, turning as it rose to catch the westerly wind. And there was another, approaching low and slow over the Hackney Marshes, huge as a cathedral, cloud shadows moving over its skin. Where are you from, where are you going? Everett thought. What do you carry that is half as wonderful as you are?

The scrape of fork against pan brought him back down. Sen slid the plate of eggs across the narrow table. They were grey. Transparent liquid leaked from the rubbery scrambled mess.

"Do you do all the cooking?" Everett asked.

"Special occasions. Usually it's Mchynlyth. He's rubbish."

Everett winced.

"I've an idea. How about I cook you breakfast?"

"Omis can't cook," Sen declared. "It's against nature."

"Not on my world, it's not."

"Well, if you think you can."

"You'll thank me."

The galley was so small they had to shuffle past each other

around the table. Again Everett caught Sen's musky, alien perfume. Why did she have to smell like that? Earthy, animal. It was wrong.

"Lesson one." Everett rescued the frying pan from the dishwasher. "Never wash your frying pan. It destroys the natural nonstick oil layer. Salt, and kitchen roll." He scrubbed away on the tiny work surface with paper hand towels. "So, your mother."

"Adopted."

"Adoptive."

"What?"

"You're the adopted one. She's the adopter. Adoptive."

"Ey! You cook, planesrunner. I talk. You can't even speak bona palari."

Everett looked through the cupboards. Cleverly engineered racks and shelves unfolded out of each other. Everything was as compact and space-saving as an RV. Here were packets and jars with labels from Aegypt, Palestine, Maroc, in Arabic and Cyrillic and alphabets that looked like Hindi but were different from any Indian letter forms Everett had ever seen. The packets were barely used. Many were unopened. Everett sniffed out a tin of Spanish smoked paprika.

"Your ma. The captain," Everett hinted, taking eggs from the refrigerator. "Eggs at room temperature, by the way. Always."

"She ended up with me. She had an amriya."

"A what?"

"Amriya. Like a promise, only you don't get to make it. Someone gives it to you. Like something you'll always owe someone and maybe they'll never collect, but maybe one day they will."

"She adopted you because of this . . . this amriya?" Just enough butter in the pan to grease it. And in with the lightly beaten eggs. "So, your parents . . . are they . . . what happened?"

Sen gazed out the window. Her eyes were blank, like white ice.

"See that? That's the *Lady Constanza*. That's a sweet ship, her. See that coat of arms on the prow? Lions and unicorns and all that palaver? That means she's a Royal Mail Liner. Specially licensed by

His Majesty's Government to carry His Majesty's mail. That's what Annie wants, that crest on our nose. Bonaroo, that. Get that and you're sorted."

Everett turned the scrambled eggs out onto a plate. A dust of the paprika and he slid them to Sen.

"Mine are never that colour." She tried a forkful. The look of ecstasy on her face was so naked Everett almost laughed. This he had learned about Sen in the short time he had known her: she let her feelings shine for all to see, good or bad. "Oh, Everett Singh, those are the best . . . How did you do that?"

"No milk. Milk makes them tough. Take them off the heat just as they start to set and let them cook in their own heat. And a little Spanish smoked paprika to finish." Everett ate from the pan, leaning against the hob. The narrow galley table would have put him almost forehead to forehead with Sen. "Annie, that's the captain?"

"You don't call her that. Only I gets to call her that," Sen said. The ice-blank eyes were angry now. Ice one moment, sun the next, storm the moment after.

"What do I call her?"

"You calls her 'ma'am.'"

"So if the *Lady Constanza* carries the mail, what do you carry?"

"Machine parts from Leipzig, kidneys from Prague; asparagus from Danzig, lace from Den Haag; glassware from Oslo and jewels of Tangier; wodka from Moscow and silk from Algiers. We got Seattle circuitry and Jerusalem jam; we got Jakarta gemstones and De Beers diamonds and porn from Nippon would make your eyes water, Everett Singh. If it walks or talks or crawls or shits or makes a noise or is like really, really shiny, we've carried it. I been everywhere, Everett Singh. All the way round this little round world."

"We have aeroplanes carry freight, but nothing like this."

"Seen 'em. Most worlds have 'em—we're the exception, it seems. The oil thing. Wouldn't feel safe in one of them things. I mean, how do they stay up?"

"Physics."

"Ain't natural."

"Most things in the human world aren't natural. It's what makes it the human world. I'll tell you what is natural: bad dentistry and dying of the least little infections. That's natural."

"Oooh. Get her," Sen said. Her eyes went wide at Everett's small rant.

"I'm sorry. I just get annoyed when people argue that if a thing's natural, it's right. Natural wants to kill us. Science saves us. Science keeps our planes flying and this airship up."

"Okay. Whatever you say. Science is bona. But all the same, I don't like those things with wings. You get in, you whizz up whee right over the world, you come down again, you get off, someone else gets on. That's not a home. That's not a—"

Everett saw Sen catch the word "family" in the back of her throat, and saw that she knew he had seen her do that. She looked ashamed and angry. Then her face went from cold to bright, hard to curious.

"Say, Everett Singh, you're the guest on my ship. You tell me about your family. Fair play. First, though . . ." She pushed the empty plate at Everett. "Is there any more of them eggs?"

"I could make more." Even as he said the last word, the idea arrived, big and entire and well-shaped and brilliant. "But there's something else I'd rather make. A treat. For you—and the captain. Your ma."

18

"Let me get this straight. The Plenitude has kidnapped your father and brought him to our universe." Captain Anastasia lifted another piece of suji halva from the plate. Everett had seen the fine semolina, the rosewater, all the necessary ingredients tucked away in the infundibular recesses of the galley cupboards while trawling for Sen's breakfast eggs. He had thought nothing of them until Sen's raptures showed him the way to make himself more than excess baggage aboard *Everness*. The way to the heart is through the stomach. All those post-match Saturday cuisine nights came good in the end. If you went insane over scrambled eggs, just wait until you get some good old-fashioned down-home Punjabi cooking. Grandmother Ajeet had celebrated the least family event with tooth-loosening sweets. And semolina, rosewater, sugar said one thing to Everett. *Halva.* He watched Captain Anastasia take a polite bite out of the sweet semolina cube. "And now you are in our universe, what do you propose to do?"

"Find him. Rescue him."

Anastasia Sixsmyth could dominate any conversation by the width of her eyes. They looked directly at Everett, and they were huge with disbelief. Put like that, it did sound to Everett like the most stupid idea a guy with his IQ well into the gifted level ever had.

"I got this far on my own, didn't I?"

Captain Anastasia finished her piece of halva. She greedily eyed the final sweetmeat.

"Why should the Plenitude kidnap your father?"

"He's a scientist. A physicist. A quantum physicist. He worked on our Heisenberg Gate project—Einstein Gates, you call them."

"It's not a subject I'm particularly well versed in, but we do have our own Einstein, Heisenberg—whatever you want to call them—Gate scientists, and, no disrespect to your father, but they seem at least as good as yours, and possibly a lot better. I wasn't even a gleam in my father's eye when they opened the gate to E2, but we do have a few decades' head start on you. Unconvinced, Mr. Singh. Try again. Perhaps this might help your memory?" She slipped Dr. Quantum out of the drawer in the fold-down desk, then froze, eyes wide. She lifted a finger to her lips, then banged her fist loudly on the wooden bulkhead beside her. "Sen! Stop eavesdropping on confidential conversations." The captain's ready room was as neat and clever and airship-shape as the galley. Wood folded and unfolded into desks and chairs and closets and writing tables. Lamps swung in and out and around on hinged brass concertinas. Everett could see no bed, nor any place a bedroom could hide itself. He imagined that when the desk flipped up into the wall, a berth flipped down. All was immaculately clean and tidy. The tiny cabin smelled of sandalwood and mothballs. Captain Sixsmyth turned the tablet faceup. Everett thought of Sen turning up the Everness tarot on the Hackney-bound train. Somehow she had opened up the Infundibulum. It shimmered with the auroras of other universes. "She's a magpie, my daughter always having her eye caught by something new and zhooshy, always picking up something bright and shiny and bringing it back to the nest. Can't move in her cabin for shiny. That and posters of rugby players. Now, this here is just the sort of pretty toy'd catch her eye, but I don't think you'd have brought it across the planes just for a fancy lightshow. What are these, stars?"

"They're not stars. They're universes. Planes." Now was the moment of trust. Now was the moment of risk. Captain Sixsmyth would have happily thrown Everett off her airship if he'd been an agent of the mysterious Iddler. Here she was in her ready room eating his grandmother's halva. She had already taken the Infundibulum from him once. She could as easily hand it—and him—over to Charlotte Villiers. So Everett Singh, do you trust this airship captain? "It's a map of the multiverse. Not the Plenitude; the Panoply. All the planes. All the parallel universes."

Captain Anastasia's eyes were the widest yet.

"It's a set of coordinates. With this—and a Heisenberg Gate—you can go to any point in any universe. Not just gate to gate. That's how I got here. I didn't come through your Heisenberg Gate. I arrived on the second deck of the airship tower at Sadler's Wells."

"That's quite an achievement, Mr. Singh," Captain Anastasia said. "And this is quite an object for a young man of your years—excuse me sir, how old are you, thirteen, fourteen?—to have in your possession."

"My dad discovered it. He found a way to take all the coordinates and make sense out of them. That's why they took him, because they thought he had it. That's why he gave it to me, to separate the information from the intellect. They had him, but they didn't have the data. And he knew I could work it out. I could see the pattern, and I used the information to come and get him."

Captain Anastasia took the last piece of halva, a precise pincer movement of thumb and forefinger. She precisely bit the top off the little cube of sweetness. Her eyes narrowed in delight.

"How do you propose to do that?"

"I find out where they're holding him. I get in there. I . . . I . . ."

"Make it up as you go along, perhaps?"

"I got here."

"Yes, you did. You could have made your life—and mine—so very much simpler by just giving them this . . . device."

"The Infundibulum."

"That's a good, mouth-filling name." Captain Anastasia took a second bite of the halva. "Give it to them. A simple swap. You have what they want; they have what you want."

"I can't," Everett said.

"Why not, Mr. Singh?"

"My dad said not to give it to anyone. Not to trust anyone with it." *For you only, Everett.*

"I've got it," Captain Anastasia said. "You gave it to me."

"You took it from me." Everett leaned across the table, holding her gaze.

"You took it from me, *ma'am*." Captain Anastasia ate the last bite of the last cube of halva. "It seems to me, Mr. Singh, that you haven't a lot to thank your dad for. He never asked you if you wanted to be part of this. He dumped it on you. He left it to you to work out what that thing you're zhooshing around is, and what it can do, and who wants it. He left you to deal with the likes of the Plenitude and its sharpies. He left you to the danger. He left you to come and get him. What else could you do? I'd've done exactly the same. I know where you're from, Mr. Singh." She wiped her fingers on an old lading bill. "Space is tight on my ship. No passengers, no freeloaders. But this is bona manjarry. You're a good cook, Mr. Singh. For a man. Sen tries, but she has the attention span of a gnat. Mchynlyth is a good cook—for a chief engineer. I could use a temporary cook and assistant deck-hand. Mr. Sharkey will weigh you in, Mr. Mchynlyth will show you what you need to know not to get killed at the first load out. Me, I require the finest comestibles available to humanity, on my table, twice a day. Lunch is a moveable feast."

"I can stay?"

"You can work." Captain Anastasia banged on the bulkhead. "Sen. Take him out and tog him up proper Airish." But Everett did not leave. Captain Anastasia raised an eyebrow. "Yes, Mr. Singh."

"My computer. Ma'am."

She smiled as she handed Dr. Quantum to Everett.

19

Bona Togs, was the sign above the dingy little shop. *Bona*: good shiny enviable cool must-have sweet, Everett said to himself. *Togs*: posh togs. Swimming togs. Togged up. Clothing, clothes, gear. Same word in both Londons. They must have a common root in both worlds. In this one it had become the private language of the air freight people: Airish. In Everett's world it had gone underground, like water vanishing into a limestone landscape, leaving a few residue words behind. Airish was easy to pick up, with its almost-Italian vocabulary. It was all about listening for patterns.

The shop looked very far from Bona. Off Morning Lane, in the shadow of the airship hulls, was a warren of alleys and arcades. Tiny stores, no wider than their front windows, huddled under rain-dripping canvas canopies that almost touched in the centre of the alleyway. Narrow but deep: Everett peered into the gloom past the gleam of the neon signs: FARRIDGE: CORDWAINER; LEDWARD AND OBOLUWAYE: EXCISE AND TAX; ADE: GUNSMITH; WRAY ELECTRICAL; FAT TARTS AND HOT FAGGOTS. Electric lights flickered deep in interiors that went back farther than the architecture of the streets should allow. Everett and Sen's progress through the crowds—steaming, smelling of hot oils and the unmistakable tang of electricity—that thronged the alleys was slow. Everyone greeted Sen, and she stopped to return the greeting, hail an acquaintance, share a joke, pass a compliment or a compliment or good wishes for the season. At every one she riffled through her deck of Everness tarot and showed a card. The people would smile, or laugh, or frown, or kiss their knuckles. Sen scooped up a bag of roasting chestnuts from a brazier.

"Hey!" the chestnut-monger cried.

Sen pulled a tarot card out of her jacket. She frowned at it.

"I see dinari for you. Very very soon."

"You said that the last time! And the time before that, and the time before that! Go on, freeloader!" The chestnut roaster aimed a kick at Sen, but the banter was good-hearted. As the Airish slang words flew around Everett's head like birds, he gathered the impression that Sen was like a mascot to the people of Hackney Great Port, a charmed child, a street saint, their own Ice Angel. If things went well for Sen, the captain's beautiful daughter, they would go well for them.

"Here."

"Here?"

Some of the neon tubes outside the dark little shop had failed. ONA OG. Clothes hung on cheap wire hangers with people's faces cut from magazines and catalogues stuck on the handles. The idea was presumably to make the jackets and tops look as if someone was wearing them. To Everett they were more like a display of grinning shrunken heads. Sen pushed through swaying swags of hanging clothes. The shop was cold and smelled of mothballs and damp wool and that same spicy, earthy smell he had caught from Sen. On her it was mystical and electric. Here was it claggy and creepy.

"Olly olly Dona Miriam! Brought a cove."

A shadow detached itself from the gloom in the back of the shop. A small, dumpy shape waddled up between the ceiling-high glass-fronted drawers and the chipped, horror-movie-eyed dummies, setting the hanging togs swinging. The light of the sputtering neon revealed a squat, frog-mouthed woman, sharp black little eyes beneath an unruly mass of greying curls. She wore a pair of harem pants and a grey woollen cardigan pulled tight around her. Gold half-glasses hung on a chain around her neck.

"Omi needs zhooshing up," Sen said.

"Oh, the Dear Lor. Where do you find 'em, Sen?" Dona Miriam put on her glasses and peered at Everett, then over the top of them, then took them off to see if it made any difference. "Oh he does, dorcas, he assuredly does." She turned on Everett so fast he jumped. "Any handbag, chicken?"

Everett proffered his backpack, Dr. Quantum locked inside. Riding down the drop-line from *Everness*'s hold to street level, Everett had felt safer with the Infundibulum at his shoulder rather than leaving it on the ship. Every bump, every jostle, every nudge in the alleys made him less sure of his decision.

"Handbag. Metzas, dinari, gelt. *Money*, honey."

Everett fumbled his wallet open. Sen seized all the cash and spread the notes before Dona Miriam.

"He needs you, Dona Miriam. Help him."

"I need that," Everett shouted. Dona Miriam was already flicking through the notes.

"You're on the company," Sen said. "You get paid."

"Dorcas, with me." Dona Miriam crooked a finger and summoned Everett to the back of the shop. "Stand still, will ye?" She measured him with an eye and thumb-and-forefinger held at arm's length. Then she left Everett among the changing booths, tall and dark and ominous as coffins, and went hunting through the musty stock. She stripped bald-headed shop dummies. She hooked shrunken-head coathangers down with a long stick. She went up ladders and rummaged in glass-fronted drawers. She hummed and tutted and threw away twice as much as she kept. Sen cavorted among the hanging costumes at the brighter end of the shop, emitting squeals of joy with every jacket she felt or pair of boots she lifted up into the wan winter light. This for Everett was what clothes shopping had always been; standing about by the changing rooms while others drew an incomprehensible—and inexhaustible—joy from looking at clothes they had no intention of buying.

"Try these." Dona Miriam presented Everett with a double armful of clothing.

"There's leggings. I don't wear leggings."

Dona Miriam looked over her glasses and rolled her eyes.

"Dorcas . . ."

"In my world . . ."

"What?"

"He's not from round here," Sen shouted quickly. "Foreign cove."

"His accent's very good."

"He's got an English ma," Sen called. Everett meekly took the pile of style into one of the changing coffins. It was almost as small and difficult as the toilet at the Sadler's Wells skyport. And the leggings ultimately were no different from his compression sports gear. While he pulled on the shirt, and the long shorts with lots of pockets in fantastic places, and adjusted the jacket lapels and the collar and drew the waist in tight, he heard Sen and the shop owner's conversation.

"Now where did you find that dolly dilly? Don't lie to your Dona. My ogles may be buggered, but even I can varda that omi ain't *so*."

"Can't say, Dona Miriam; 'cept that it is *so*, so."

"Are you alamo?"

"Bona lacoddy. Bonaroo lallies. Fantabulosa dish. Had a varda when he was in the shower, didn't I?"

"And the chicken? Alamo?"

"Nante."

"The more fool. Have you considered, dorcas, whether the dally chicken alamos polones at all?"

"You mean, omi-polone?"

"Dorcas, this is Hackney."

"I do like girls," Everett interrupted. "Sort of."

There was a moment of silence; then two female voices exploded in laughter.

"Parlamo palari," Dona Miriam said.

"Hama saba apanē nijī bhāṣā'ēṁ," Everett said in Hindi. He emerged from the changing coffin.

"Bona," Dona Miriam said. She clasped her hands in delight.

"Fantabulosa," Sen said. Dona Miriam spun a full-length mirror. Everett beheld himself. The cavalry-style jacket, gold at the collar and at the cuffs and on the lapels, was very very good on him. The baggy shorts, all pockets and D-loops and zips and places to attach things, were pure street biker. Even the leggings underneath the shorts were an acceptable anonymous grey. He was hot.

"I just need one of those bandanas."

Sen and Dona Miriam looked at each other, aghast.

"No no no bandana," Dona Miriam said. "It's not *so*."

"You need these," Sen said, and plonked a pair of boots in Everett's arms. They were fantabulosa boots. Calf-length, complex, black, bad-ass. Everett pulled them on, did up the lacings and strappings and tightenings and made a turn in front of the mirror.

"Can I afford these?"

"No need," Sen said. "From Sen." Dona Miriam cleared her throat loudly. Sen walked slowly around Everett, so close he could feel the warmth of her breath, looking him up and down.

"Do I pass?" Everett said. "Do I look *so*?"

"Yes *so*," Sen said. "Indeed *so*."

She seized his lapels and pulled herself closer still. For a moment Everett thought she might kiss him, but she whipped a card out of nowhere and slipped it into the waistband of his pants. Dona Miriam shook his hand and palmed him a small wad of notes.

"Soft air, sweet voyaging, and a kind wind at your back," she said.

After the smelly dinginess of Bona Togs, shaded and shadowy Churchwell Alley was blinding. Everett stepped out in his new togs, and for moment, just a moment, Hackney Great Port belonged to him. Well, perhaps not Hackney Great Port, maybe this bazaar of streets off Morning Lane. Well, maybe not the whole warren, maybe just this alley. Maybe not even this alley; just the few square centimetres of wet, greasy cobblestones under the soles of his new boots. Or even just his own skin. If you can say that much space belongs completely and utterly to you, that is a big say. He fished the Everness tarot card out of his waistband. An old line drawing of a peacock, squaring up and spreading its tail against its image in a mirror. The name of the card was *Pride*. And what's so bad about pride? Everett thought. Away from the fusty mustiness of Dona Miriam's shop, his togs recovered their new clothes smell, which is the greatest and rarest of perfumes because it only lasts until the first laundry.

With a shock he bumped into Sen.

"Everett Singh, do you think you can run in those new boots?"

"Why?"

"Because you need to in three, two, one!" And Sen was off like a bolt of ice from a crossbow.

Everett paused to pull the backpack safe and tight up high across his shoulders rather than down across his ass where he usually wore it, and in that hesitation he almost lost her. God, she was quick! He saw her look back. Her eyes went wide. Everett glanced back. The man with the Dutch accent, who had threatened him the night before: bearing down so fast and so close Everett could smell his breakfast on his breath. Everett spun on the heel of his new boot and ran. Sen? Where? All he could see were people, slipping and twisting out of his way.

A hand shot out from a dark opening in the shop fronts, grabbed Everett by the lapel, and hauled him into an alley so narrow his shoulders brushed brick on each side. Sen ran light and fast as a pale greyhound. She sensed every turn and twist, every discarded crate and cardboard box, every treacherous piece of fruit peel or slippery chip wrapper. Everett skidded on an orange skin, banged into the wall. He looked back. The Dutchman was behind him, so huge he filled the alley like a storm. The confined space had not slowed him at all.

"With me!" Sen yelled, vaulted a crate and, as Everett cleared it, pulled down a pile of crates and boxes piled on top of a big commercial trash bin. She grabbed the end of the bin and let her momentum spin her round and through an open doorway Everett would otherwise have missed completely. He grabbed the edge of the bin and spun round and through the door. Sacks with Chinese lettering on them, crates of soy sauce, pallets of noodles. Blocks of dried fish, massive and solid as concrete; a golden Maneki Neko cat, waving his paw. Sen plunged on, through a tiny, steamy, oil-stinky kitchen where chefs leaped up from their work, waving cleavers and shouting. Through a tiny tin-table restaurant, the day's newspapers from around the world pasted on the walls, men in long coats and leather caps with the earflaps folded down looking up from their bowls of noodles. Kids. Back to slurping noodles. Out the front door into the crowds.

"Out of the way!" Sen yelled. The crowds parted. She ran like a wild deer, but Everett's body-awareness was returning, his goalkeeper sense of spatial awareness. He had caught up. He was right on her shoulder. He saw her looking for alleys and rat-runs, clever twisting ways of escape.

"Left!"

She jumped over a beggar lolling in the mouth of an alley, warmed by steam venting from a kitchen extractor. One step behind, Everett hurdled the old beardy man in the coat tied with string, down another alley. He was still there, the Dutchman. He cleared the baffled old tramp. He moved well for a big man.

Ahead, a solid brick wall.

"Dead end," Everett shouted. Sen darted in towards the wall, slapped a switch, then grabbed Everett and pulled him in to the wall. With a noise like the sky falling a ladder rattled down from the darkness above.

"Hold tight," Sen whispered. The Dutchman bore down on them.

"Right, you little bastard!"

Sen kicked a latch on the ladder. The Dutchman looked up at the clang and clatter of moving metal above his head, then leaped back as the counterweight fell to the ground and the ladder shot up, snatching

Sen and Everett out of his grasp. Everett saw the Dutchman's big, white face looking up at him, like the moon fallen to earth, dwindling as the emergency ladder lifted them away from him.

"Jump!" Sen shouted. She leaped into darkness.

"But—" No time for buts. Everett jumped into the unknown. He landed heavily on a metal gallery, invisible from street level, attached to the side of the building that formed the right wall of the alley. "Ow!" He had grazed knees and hands on the metal mesh. Sen was already away, so fast and light she seemed to be flying along the wall. She went up a zigzag staircase without breaking step. Everett followed her up onto the roof. Amazement stopped him. Above him, so close he could almost touch them, were the bellies of the great freight ships. He stood a long moment, turning, reading the names and the mottoes and the heraldic crests and the pin-up characters and the dragons and wyverns and angels and demons and gods and mythological creatures that adorned the hulls.

"Oi! Don't dillydally. We's not out of it yet. The Iddler always sends his bassards in twos, coz on their own they so stupid they can't even find their own asses."

Everett reluctantly broke away from the wonder.

"You'll get used to it," Sen said. She noticed the blood on his grazed wrists. "Oooh, your poor hands. Want me to kiss 'em better?"

Everett quickly thrust his hands into his armpits.

"So are you?" Sen asked.

"What?"

"Homy palone. It's okay if you are. I know loads of HPs."

"Like I said, I like girls . . ."

"Sort of. You said 'sort of.' Is you bibi? I's cool with bibi too."

"I like girls. Okay?" Everett said. "Were you watching me in the shower?"

"Might have."

"Well, you shouldn't. That's like . . . infringement of privacy."

"No privacy on an airship, omi. And the water's rationed as well.

Had to make sure you weren't using too much." She smiled. "You're pretty fit for a comptator kind of guy."

"I play football."

"Do you? What position?"

"Goalie."

"Oh, the other game."

"Why, what's the game?"

"Rugby footie; now there's a man's game. Soccer, well, that's for posh boys and fruits, ain'it?"

"Not where I come from. On my world, soccer is a toff's game played by thugs, rugby is a thug's game played by toffs."

"Don't much like the sound of your world, Everett Singh. Sounds awful soft. Well, come on then, posh boy. Keep up if you can."

She turned and set off across the rooftops at a gentle lope. Everett followed two steps behind, easily falling in with her rhythm, up one side of the sloping roofs, down the other, past smoking chimney pots and steaming vents that smelled of garlic and ginger and fish, ducking beneath spiderwebs of fizzing, sparking electrical cables. Rickety wooden gangways had been built over the alleys. Sen, who had grown up in the three-dimensional world of the airships, where up and down were as easy and natural as left and right, ran heedlessly across them. Everett looked down. Far below his feet were the canopies and stall umbrellas of Morning Lane bazaar. Heads, hats. Dizziness pulled at him; then he felt a hand grab his and pull him onto the next roof.

"Rule number one: don't look down," Sen said. "Trust your feet." Two blocks over they came to a gap between the roofs where the bridge had rotted and fallen.

"Think you can make it?"

Everett sized up the distance, the weight in his backpack, the unfamiliarity of his footwear. He had passed two tests already: at Bona Togs when he trusted Sen and Dona Miriam to dress him; in the chase through the lanes and tunnels, when he had to trust that Sen could get them out of a blind alley.

"I think so."

"Bona. Remember—"

"I won't look down."

Sen seem to fly over the gap in slow motion. She landed light and agile as a monkey. Then it was Everett's turn. The only run up was down the steep pitch of the roof; the only space for takeoff the width of a gutter. Miss the footing . . .

"Trust your feet," Everett muttered. Four strides, Dr. Quantum slapping hard against his back. He hit the takeoff spot. And he was up. And over. He landed hard, soles and fingers scrabbling at the slippery slates, sending dislodged tiles slithering down into the street. The voice of an angry stall-holder roared up at them, furious at ripped canopies and smashed wares.

"Not bad," Sen said.

"Is there much more?" Everett panted.

"Nah. See that stair head over there? That'll take us down to the Downs Arches and we're home and hosed." The metal stairway zig-zagged down the side of an old red brick warehouse. BORDEN'S STEEL-MILLED PORAGE OATS was painted in two-metre-high letters on the wall, faded with years of east London weather. The elevated railway ran above the street, the staircase connected with the platforms, but Sen led Everett down under the dripping steel. A train roared overhead. She pushed open the street gate. A figure stepped into the space.

"How now," a guttural man's voice said. Everett recognised the voice's owner: the Dutchman's partner of the previous night. Everett saw Sen tense herself, as if she might charge him, head butt him. Guttural Man read the move too. He clicked his tongue; his hand jerked. There was an ugly black gun in it.

"Hey ho," said a voice above. Everett looked round. The Dutchman leaned over the railings at the el station. He was out of breath but grinning.

"Well, I can only assume that you didn't deliver my boss's message to your captain," Guttural Man rasped. His lungs rattled with phlegm. "Now that's very unprofessional, and a bit of a personal insult—that you think so little of my boss that you don't even pass on important messages. Well, we shall have to send a clearer message this time. Polone, you come with us. You, omi, you tell Captain Sixsmyth that if she wants to see her dear daughter again, come and talk to us at the Knights. And tell her not to fanny about coz we might just start deducting interest, you know? With a knife."

"You touch me, you die!" Sen spat.

"'And the King shall answer and say unto them, Verily I say unto you, Inasmuch as ye have done unto one of the least of these my brethren, ye have done unto me,'" a voice suddenly declaimed in Southern States, preacher's drawl. Guttural Man half turned. Sharkey was behind him, close enough that his breath stirred the hairs on the back of Guttural Man's neck. Everett couldn't see how he had got there, or where he had come from, but the American took a step back into the street and flicked back the tails of his long, half-caped coat. Light glinted from metal concealed in clever pockets in the lining. Sharkey's hands moved faster than thought. An ivory handled sawn-off shotgun appeared in each fist. He gestured with a gun for Guttural Man to step aside. Guttural Man looked at his own weapon. Sharkey clicked his tongue in disappointment.

"'Verily, a fool hath no delight in understanding.'" He raised the guns and levelled them at Guttural Man's head. Guttural Man cleared the gate. Sen and Everett clattered down the steps to join Sharkey.

"Now, sir. Your piece. Set it down now. On the step." Guttural Man let the gun dangle from his finger by the trigger guard. He bent slowly, never taking his eyes from Sharkey and his ivory shotguns, and set it down on the metal step. "And step away, sir." Sharkey swung one gun up to draw a bead on the Dutchman on his platform. The other he kept trained on Guttural Man's face. "Miss Sen, if you please."

Sen scuttled in and retrieved the ugly black gun. Everett noticed that she seemed comfortable with it. She undid the front of her jacket, buttoned closed against a Hackney December, slipped in the gun, and closed it up again.

"Thank you, gentlemen," Sharkey called out. "Our business is concluded. Good day to you both." He tipped the brim of his hat with the barrel of his shotgun.

"We'll get you, with your fancy-dan fiddle-dee-dee accent and your Bible quotes. Your captain owes us. You owe us."

"'Though I speak with the tongues of men and of angels, and have not charity, I am become sounding brass, or a tinkling cymbal,'" Sharkey proclaimed. But he kept a shotgun sloped over each shoulder until they had all reached the end of the road. As the crowd thickened, Sharkey slipped the guns back into the lining of his coat.

"Do you generally go around with two guns in your coat?" Everett asked. He'd stowed away on an airship; jumped through a Heisenberg Gate; conned his way through a strange, parallel London; evaded Charlotte Villiers and her goons; but this was the coolest thing he had ever seen.

"Consistently, sir. 'Redeem the time, because the days are evil. Take ye heed every one of his neighbour, and trust ye not in any brother: for every brother will utterly supplant, and every neighbour will walk with slanders. For I will surely deliver thee, and thou shalt not fall by the sword, but thy life shall be for a prey unto thee: because thou hast put thy trust in me, saith the Lord.'"

"Do you know all the Bible?" Everett asked.

"Every bit of it," Sen interrupted. "Old Testament best. It sounds better."

"'Thy word is a lamp unto my feet, and light unto my path,'" Sharkey quoted. "'Hear the word of the Lord, ye who tremble at his word.' Psalm 119, verse 105, and Isaiah 66, verse 5. We have not been properly introduced sir. Our previous meeting was a tad strained. I am Miles O'Rahilly Lafayette Sharkey, citizen of the Confederated States of America; weighmaster, soldier of fortune, adventurer, gentleman: Atlanta is my home and Heaven my expectation." He swept off his hat. His hair was long and streaked with silver, though Everett guessed him to be in his mid thirties. Everett took the offered hand firmly.

"Everett Singh, sir." Sharkey's way of talking was catching. "Goalkeeper, mathematician, traveller, planesrunner."

Miles O'Rahilly Lafayette Sharkey's left eyebrow lifted a millimetre. He bowed.

"Honoured, sir."

20

Everett rode the lift line up through the inner organs of *Everness*. Beneath him, the loading deck where Sharkey was in careful negotiations with a stevedore over a consignment of containers bound for St. Petersburg. Above him, like clouds, the ranks of gas cells, and Sen, a body-length above him, riding the line high with the grace and ease of an angel. She grinned down at him. Thinking in three dimensions was easy—he had had to think in seven dimensions to fold Tejendra's random Heisenberg jump addresses into the Infundibulum. Living in three dimensions—effectively on the inside of a huger, hollow object—that was much less easy. But he was getting the feel of it, learning the timings and the orientations and to think that the shortest distance between two points was often *across*, not around. He thought of it as minding a goal the size of an ocean liner. Sen swung in over the central catwalk and dropped lightly to the mesh. Everett was right behind her.

Sen wanted to give him a tour of the ship before the weigh-in—the second time he had heard that faintly ominous phrase that day. She took him round the crew quarters first—*galley you know, captain's ready room you know*; showed him his own little cabin—*latty* was the Airish-speak; helped him sling his hammock and showed him how to use it without rolling straight out again. She had even graced him with a glimpse into her own latty. Everett got an impression of tubes of cosmetics crowding every surface, strewn underwear (rather small, it seemed to Everett) and posters of rugby players with their shirts off. The bridge: the heart of the ship. It was smaller than Everett had thought; with all the crew at their stations it would have been crowded. But the view from the floor-to-ceiling window was compelling: a winter afternoon in Hackney Great Port, airships drifting across the purple-and-gold December skyline, plumes of steam and smoke rising from along the edge of the world. Everett barely noticed the instruments and tools of airship command; the steering yokes, the lift levers, ballast pumps, the joysticks that trimmed the attitude, the binnacle, the computer displays glowing behind their magnifying monocles, the banks of closed-circuit monitors keeping eyes on all of *Everness*'s huge body, inside and out. Then down a spiral staircase, bent double in the crawlspaces beneath the cargo deck, among the batteries; banks and banks of them wedged so close Everett could hardly squeeze between them. They were warm and humming and filled the claustrophobic crawl-ways with the thrilling, spicy smell of electricity. *Everness*, like all airships of her class, ran on electricity. In dock at Hackney Great Port she was recharging from the port grid, but she was configured to charge up from any available electrical source.

"Worst comes to it, we could even hook up to a thunderstorm," Sen said. "Bit dodgy, though. If you gets that wrong . . ." She left the sentence unfinished. She looked uncomfortable, as if she had said too much.

Everett tried to calculate the amount of energy stored in the plates of batteries. There was technology here decades beyond anything on E10. These seemed to use the same carbon nanofibre as the ship's skin, skeleton and lift-cells. Yet their computer technology—their comptator technology—was how Victorians would build computers. Different worlds, different techs.

"I's taking you to the COG," Sen said.

"Centre of Gravity," Everett said, thinking aloud. "Of course, the cargo and the ballast all has to be equally placed around the centre of gravity to keep the ship stable."

"Smart, aincha?"

"Thank you," Everett said. His new boots clicked on the spindly spun-carbon catwalk, delicate as spiderweb. That was it. *Organic.* This was a body. He was inside a living thing, a whale-machine.

"Tell me about Mr. Sharkey."

"What about him? He's first mate and weighmaster."

"I mean, those were pretty cool-looking guns."

"Cool, were they? Impressed you, did he? Charmed you, didn't he? He's a real charmer, all that Southern gentleman stuff, and the manners, and 'sir,' and 'ma'am,' then gives them a big hunk of that hokey Old Testament stuff and they just roll over and let him tickle their bellies. Weighmaster, soldier of fortune, adventurer, gentleman my arse. Miles O'Rahilly Lafayette Sharkey's not even his real name. And he ain't no gentleman. No natural gentleman. Oh he's Miles Sharkey, all right, his da was Reverend Jasper Sharkey, preacher and Bible salesman. He ran travelling tent missions all over Georgia and the Home States—that's where all that Word of the Dear comes from. Soon as he could he bailed and took himself off all over the Confed. That's where yer O'Rahilly Lafayette comes from. You get farther down there if you're a gentleman. The story he tells is that he shot his own da in a duel because he slapped Sharkey's mum at the Peachtree Ball in Atlanta. Now, I reckons he did shoot his da, but it weren't over his dear ol' ma. Reckon the old bugger got hammered on the mint juleps and started mouthing off. Don't like anyone looking cleverer than him, our Sharkey. Been all around the world, he says: debt collector, art dealer, con man, bodyguard, pearl fisherman, barman, diplomat. That's what he said he were when we picked him up in Stamboul. Spun us some tale about working with the tsarists against the Ottomans and the Ottomans against the tsarists, but he knew his way around a lading bill and he can negotiate anyone up. That was back in oh seven; I was a kid then. He's good, our Sharkey; love the omi, but he wants you to like him and sometimes, well, that's not good in a person."

"In my world, the Ottoman Empire ended a hundred years ago. And we've got one America: the United States."

"Gor, that's dull. We got three. There's the Confederated States of America; that's Sharkey's home. It's a rich rich place. It's all land, you see. No one ever went broke buying land. So now they got all these genetic-whatchermacallit crops and they're making a fortune. They even got this new genetically-thingied bean can produce oil—like your oil. Liquid fuel. Revolutionise the world, they say. 'Cept I reckons we's gone too far in one direction to be able to turn back and head another direction. Sort of like turning an airship. Needs a long run up and a lot of airspace. Atlanta's beautiful, though, that wall of glass towers all gleaming and goldie in the morning light. Then there's the United States. Which is like what you have, I reckons. They think they're the real America coz they don't recognise the Confed, so they gets really angry if you mention the CSA or Atlanta or anything like that. They was the original and the best, they says. I mean, it's a hundred and sixty years. Get over it. Then on the other side of the Rockies it's Amexica. That's the bit that broke away from Mexico in the last civil war. Now that's a doss. Los Angeles, haciendas and orange trees and cool pools and everything. I could stay there forever. Beautiful. I likes a bit of sun on me back. Oh, and there's a fourth. I's forgetting Canada. Funny how you do that."

Sen's toe tapped on metal. Everett looked down to see a small steel medallion set into the mesh. It was engraved with three triangles, superimposed on top of each other.

"The centre of gravity," Everett said, looking up around him at the spaces and strut and stresses of the huge airship, all focused here, all balanced in equilibrium around this one point. He touched the little metal medallion. He felt he could balance *Everness* on the ball of a finger.

"'Tain't much. Come and see outside," Sen said. Lateral walkways joined the main spine at the centre of gravity. Sen took the right catwalk. They walked between the gas cells, held in their nanocarbon nets.

"So, who is this Iddler?" Everett said, and remembering Sen's answer the last time he had asked her that question, said, "And don't give me that stupid rhyme again."

"What's wrong with that rhyme?" Sen said. "I made it up."

Everything she said was a question or a challenge. It was infuriating, it was fascinating.

"You could just tell me."

Sen relented.

"You know everywhere there's always some big fat bugger who don't exactly run everything, because if he did that, he'd draw attention to himself, but can like, sort things, knows people, makes things go away. And in this business, sooner or later you runs into something you wish you could make go away. Annie, now she tells me things she won't tell another living soul, not even Sharkey—and there was this time, early on, just after we got the ship, and she got this tax bill she couldn't pay. New captain with a bona ship: the only kind of loan she'll get is from a bank wanting to foreclose on *Everness* and sell her on. So she goes to the Iddler and he makes it go away. Like that. Gone. 'Cept instead of owing the bank, now she's owing him. So every so often, and it's not that often, he asks her to run a little consignment for him on the QT. Extra special like—there's always some cove of his at the other end to take receipt in out-of-the-way places, kind of off the normal landing sites. 'Coz we may be big, but I can drop her on the head of a pin.

"So it's all dally until two months ago, when the Iddler's sharpies come calling and ask her to take a consignment over to St. Petersburg. Annie's not in a position to say no, so she does, but up over Reugen she gets hailed by an Imperial Deutscher Customs cutter. They order us to stand to, drop anchors, and make ground. These consignments, they're not exactly as you might say, bijou. The moment they comes aboard, it'll be in their faces like a dog's bollocks. We daren't outrun and we can't outgun it. So Annie orders me to take her out over the Baltic like we haven't heard, and then on the third hail, as they're getting above us to force us down, we turn and drop the consignment into the sea. In the drink. Oh, sorry Mein Kapitan, radio problems; of course we'll comply. We make ground at Stralsund, they come aboard, and we're clean as a nun's fanny.

"The problem is, the Iddler don't like it when he loses a consignment. He's out of pocket. He wants compensation. Hard dinari. And our captain, she's not one of the bigger families, like the Gallacellis or even the Bromleys. They got relatives and deep pockets. Us, we got ourselves, and *Everness*. It's about cash flow—so Sharkey tells me. Dinari coming in quicker than dinari going out. Problem is, it's other way round too much of the time. So, the Iddler's sending his sharpies to give us little reminders."

"Would they have cut you up?"

"Them fruit-boys? Like to see 'em try. Hey, you're in luck, Everett Singh."

The crosswalk ended at a hatch in *Everness*'s skin. Sen peered up through the porthole and waved at something Everett could not see. Sen spun the hatch wheel; lugs unfastened; the hatch swung inwards.

"Come on then, Everett Singh."

Everett stepped out onto a balcony as delicate and elegant as a spider's nest. He resisted the temptation to glance down at what was beneath his feet. He looked out. A hundred metres away lay *Everness*'s neighbour, nosed in at the docking arm. She carried—airships, Everett had learned, are always female—a crest of three golden crowns on a blue shield and the name *Leonora Christine*. She was offloading; pallets and containers running down on hoists from her cargo holds into the receiving arms of busy, scuttling forklifts and loaders. The last of the small fast clouds had been cleared from the sky; the wind had dropped; the air was intensely clear and still. The smoke from the eternal chimneys rose straight up, a palisade along the edge of London. Everett shivered at the promise of deep winter cold. It was only six days to Christmas.

Next he looked *along*. The balcony was on *Everness*'s exact centreline. To Everett's right were the forward impeller pods and stabilisers. The windows of the bridge and the crew quarters were hidden by the forward curve of the hull. To his left were the aft impellers and the elegant sweep of the tail fins. *Everness*, you are a beautiful girl, Everett thought. He gripped the railing. This was real. This was here.

"Look up," Sen suggested, smiling wickedly. Everett almost went back over the rail with surprise. Mchynlyth's face grinned down into his from a distance of a few centimetres. He was standing on the hull; facing a peeled-back flap of ship-skin a metre on a side. A harness buckled over his baggy orange flight-suit connected him by a line to the rail that ran the length of *Everness*'s back. Mchynlyth was abseiling on the outer hull of an airship. As Everett watched, Mchynlyth rolled down the skin to cover the exposed ribs and then ran what looked like a knife along the edges. Wherever the knife passed, the join vanished. The skin was whole and entire. Mchynlyth noticed Everett and Sen beneath him, grinned between his legs at them, then jumped off the hull, paid out line, and dropped lightly onto the balcony beside them.

"How did you do that?" Everett asked. "The hull, I mean, it's nanocarbon."

Mchynlyth held up his tool. It was indeed a knife, curiously curved. The edge of the blade seemed blurred, like a heat-haze.

"Skin-ripper," Mchynlyth said. He held the blade up before his eyes and gazed at it with delight. "Only thing'll cut nano is nano. Cut her open and sew her up again sweet as a wee nut." Then he folded the blade into its handle and slid it into one of his many pockets.

"So are we still air-shape and Hackney-fashion?" Sen asked.

"Sure, she's the sweetest ship running out of this town, and that's including that great nancy Swedish bird over there," Mchynlyth said, disconnecting the line from his harness. His accent was so thick and his voice so soft Everett had to concentrate fiercely to make out what he was saying. "So, you're for the weigh-in then?"

"I wish everyone would stop going on about it. It's making me nervous."

"Ach, away with your nervousness, you jinny. Sure it's just a formality." A flick on the line activated a winch high up on the ship's back that reeled it in. He stepped out of the webbing harness and threw it over his shoulder. "Right then, son."

They were scales, proper scales, down on the loading dock. Two metres high, two metres across, brass and wood and rivets: scales like the ones the figure of Justice held high above the courts of the Old Bailey. On one side was an antique buttoned leather chair, so old that stuffing sprung through the cracked upholstery. On the other, counterbalancing it, a large glass cylinder. Above the cylinder was a brass tap connected to a run of hose that snaked out of sight among the containers and crates. The whole of *Everness*'s crew had turned out: exactly four. Sharkey stood by the scale.

"Take a seat, sir."

Everett gingerly hauled himself into the leather armchair. The tilt mechanism had been wedged so it only gave a few millimetres beneath him. His feet swung.

"One moment, Mr. Sharkey." Captain Anastasia held out her hand. "Mr. Singh, your shush-bag, please." Everett reluctantly handed Dr. Quantum over to Captain Anastasia. "It is mandatory that all prospective crew members be mass-rated. Mr. Sharkey."

Sharkey kicked a lever, the scales clanked and Everett's feet hit the ground.

"'Thou hast been weighed in the balance,'" Sharkey said ominously, and turned the wheel on the metal faucet. Water gushed into the glass cylinder. The sound of gurgling pipes and surging water was the only noise in the huge cargo deck. Faces were grave. Then Everett felt his knees stretch and his feet leave the deck. He rose into the air, bobbed up and down a few times while Sharkey fine-tuned the inflow, then came to rest.

"What is the displacement, weighmaster?" Captain Anastasia asked. Sharkey ran a finger along the brass scale.

"One hundred and two pounds, twelve ounces of ballast,"

Sharkey announced. There was a small round of applause. Everett understood now. Airships were not balloons. They couldn't heat air to ascend and vent it to descend. Every gramme of lift was sealed in those gas cells above him. *Everness* flew by neutral buoyancy. Her mass equalled the mass of air she displaced. Basic physics. She naturally neither floated nor sank. The impellers and the steering vanes would lift her to cruising height; she would float there as readily as at ground level. Every gramme of mass that came aboard Everness affected its buoyancy. A fourteen-year-old boy would not send *Everness*'s two-hundred metre envelope crashing out of the sky, but his mass would still need to be accounted for, to the gramme.

"Release the ballast, Mr. Sharkey."

"Aye, ma'am."

Sharkey released a catch, and the brass bottom of the ballast cylinder fell open. The rush of water vanished through the floor mesh and splashed away down drains and channels. Everett banged down hard on the deck. He imagined the water jetting from a waste vent in the hull, like a big dog having a tiny pee.

"Welcome to *Everness*, Mr. Singh," Captain Anastasia said. She offered a hand. Everett took it. Her grip was very firm and her eyes were true and unwavering. "Now, what's for supper?"

21

They had been watching the tower for two days. There was a sweet spot behind a pillar in Rumbold and Sachs's department store café, a little table for two among the potted palms with a clear view of the entrance to the Tyrone Tower. A place where you could see but not be seen. A place where you could sit all day, watch and take notes, and not be disturbed.

"Have you not got enough by now?" Sen complained. She was not a good staker-out. She got bored and fidgety sitting, watching, and taking notes, from opening hour to closing time. She looked around her or went off on extended expeditions around the store—"bona togs in here"—or tried to engage Everett in conversation when he was concentrating on syncing the photographs he had taken on his phone with Dr. Quantum.

"What?"

"I said, do you want some tea?"

"I've just had tea."

"I know. Do you want some more?"

"No thanks." Everett had drunk so much tea on the stake-out that his bladder felt like it was turning to leather. What, who might he have missed on his too-frequent trips to the bathroom?

"Are you sure?"

"I'm sure."

"I'm having some."

"You have some."

"Would you like a bijou bun?"

"No!" Everett snapped. "I would not like a bijou bun."

Sen sat up and bristled in offence.

"Well, I'm having a Viennese whirl," she declared, and got up noisily.

"Sen, sorry . . ."

She was as quick to forgive as to anger.

"Are you really really really sure you don't want one?"

She went to the self-service counter without waiting for his answer. For all its discreet view, the table in the third-floor coffee nook was second-best. When Everett had scoped out places to spy on the Plenitude headquarters, he had quickly sussed the sweetest spot of all: a bay window table in the Sweet Afton Tea Room on the second floor. It was closer to the street, closer to the faces, better positioned, and better concealed among the London ladies with their ribbon-bound boxes and striped bags of Christmas shopping. Everett had no sooner hidden Dr. Quantum behind the menu than a waiter, apron gleaming white, matching napkin folded over his arm, came up to the table.

"I'd like some coffee," Everett said. "A cafetière of the Sumatra please."

"Tea," Sen said. "And buns. Could you bring that there trolley over?"

"I don't think so," the waiter said.

"Pardon?" Everett said.

"I don't think so. You two, out."

"I want to order some coffee."

"Out," the water repeated, leaning close so as not to be overheard by the other tables. "We don't serve your types in here."

"What?" Everett said, loud enough to make the morning coffee ladies look round.

"Don't serve Airish, you mean," Sen said.

"You'll have to leave," the waiter said.

"No, this is not right," Everett insisted. "This is racism. You're a racist. I want to speak to your manager."

"It would be better if you didn't make a scene," the waiter said. The rest of the waiting staff had drifted away from their positions into a vague semicircle, only a click of the fingers away. Some of them were big men. To be physically thrown out would be humiliating. Worse, it would draw attention.

"Don't matter what you call it," Sen said. "I won't stay where I'm not welcome. Come on, Everett Singh." Everett tucked Dr. Quantum under his arm. He thought about pulling off the tablecloth, sending the silver creamer and sugar bowl and rose vase and cutlery embossed with Rumbold and Sachs's crest ringing to the floor, toppling the so-neat Christmas trees with their twinkling blue lights. That would be petty. That would certainly draw attention to him. But every step out of the tearoom blazed with humiliation and rage. He could feel every eye on him. *Airish.*

"It's all right, it happens all the time," Sen said, with a fine, final toss of her head to the two penguin-suited waiters on the door.

"It's not all right," Everett said tightly.

"So, it's not, but we're not the ones to change it."

"Why not? We've changed things in my world."

"Have you? I's impressed."

"Did you see his face?"

"He had a naff 'tache."

"His face was the same colour as mine."

"So it was." Sen's surprise was genuine. She recognised the similarity, then let it fall from her attention. You couldn't do that in my world, Everett thought. "Come on, Everett Singh. There's a self-service caff up on the third. I'm sure the view's as good. They won't care who drinks their tea there." She fluffed up her hair, stood tall, and put on a swagger. "I may be dirt, but I's class dirt."

So for two days Everett and Sen had occupied the table behind the pillar in the third-floor cafeteria and not a soul had disturbed them apart from the waitress who came around every hour to clear away the cups and cutlery, and the robot sweeper, like a cross between a trilobite and a rat, that scurried around the tables feeding on fallen cake crumbs. It was a machine, so it didn't count as a soul.

Sen set a mug of tea and plate with two Viennese whirls on the table. "I got you one anyway." She took a slurp of tea, then ate the pale, crumbly pastry with both hands and wiped her mouth. She had the sweetest tooth of anyone Everett had ever known. He had hardly been able to keep Sen supplied with Indian sweetmeats over the last three days. She looked at the remaining Viennese whirl. "Do you want that other one?" Everett waved it away.

"I think I've got almost enough photos now." Everett tapped up the images he had loaded into Dr. Quantum. First up: Charlotte Villiers, ten shots over two days and a morning, all time-tagged. She was dressed for winter: fur stoles, fur hats, gloves, brocade coats. He ran the pictures as a slideshow. "This is Charlotte Villiers. Do you recognise her?"

"Bona hats," Sen said.

"She's plenipotentiary from E3 to my world. I believe she had my dad kidnapped. She wants to get her hands on the Infundibulum. She's clever—very clever. She took one look at Dr. Quantum and almost worked it all out there and then. But I don't think she's operating on her own. Colette said my dad thought there was a group inside the Plenitude, working to their own plan. I don't know who they are yet, or what they want, but when I met her, I also met this man." Everett flicked up a photograph of Ibrim Hoj Kerrim getting out of a sleek black electric car. He had a leather briefcase in his hand and wore an elegant jewel on his headgear. He looked hurried and worried. An aide in E3-style clothing held the door open for him. "This is Ibrim Hoj Kerrim. He's the plenipotentiary from E2 to my world. I don't think he's with Charlotte Villiers. I don't know why I think that. I just get the feeling he can be trusted."

Everett pulled up another picture, of a fair-haired man in the type of business suit familiar to him from his own world.

"I don't know who this is."

Sen scowled. "Could be your world, or E4, or E8. Any number of Es. Not everyone dresses as good as us."

"Look at this." Everett opened up one of the images of Charlotte

Villiers and slid it alongside the picture of the unknown man. "Take away the hair and the hat. Do you think they look kind of alike?"

Sen peered closer at the screen.

"I suppose."

"Suppose? They're like twins. But much closer than twins. I think he is her, from another universe. Or she's him. Or they're different versions of the same person."

Sen looked again at the picture. Her mouth twisted in distaste.

"Nah . . ."

"Why not?"

"That's wrong. Wouldn't they, like, explode if they met each other?"

"No, no reason at all why that should happen. I might be out there, for all I know."

"In Hackney? In Stokie? I'd know, Everett Singh."

Everett added four more photographs and slid them into a circle. Two women, two men.

"These are the ones who have been in and out most; the same number of times as Charlotte Villiers and Charles Villiers."

"Is that his name?"

"It is for me. I think these six are all working together. I think they're the group behind my dad's kidnapping."

"That's very good," Sen said. She sounded unconvinced. "And so?"

"And so, phase two. This is a bit more tricky. I need to see inside."

"Oh now, Everett Singh, you can't be doing that. They knows you're here, that posh palone has sharpies out looking for you, and you'd go strolling in through the front door? They'd have you in there with your dad quicker'n you could say 'knife.'"

"I've got the maps and the general layout of the place from the library this morning."

"Oh, so that's what you were doing."

In the aftermath of their expulsion from the Sweet Afton tearoom, Everett understood the librarian's cold stare at him, chillier by far than her glare at his first visit. Everett had grown up in multiracial, multicultural Hackney, the child of mixed-race parentage, and he had never known the prejudice he attracted as an Airish. Everett went to the architecture section and called up the database of plans. Sen sat flicking through fashion magazines, rocking back on her chair and humming to herself loudly enough to attract attention, not so loud as to get them thrown out. He had photographed the floor plans and elevations of the Tyrone Tower exhaustively. The huge Gothic spike, thrust into the heart of Bloomsbury, was only twenty years old. They liked their gods and gargoyles in E3.

Everett swept away the circle of conspirators and called up the plans. He stacked them one on top of the other, called up an image-manipulation application and took away the paper, leaving wire-frame floor plans: the Tyrone Tower in cross-section.

"Bona," Sen said.

A few transformations and Everett had a three-dimensional model of the Tyrone Tower. He dragged a finger across the screen and flew through the wire-frame corridors.

"The problem is . . ."

"They're just pretty patterns," Sen said. "You don't know what they mean. That there room could be where they got the Ein . . . Heisenberg Gate, or it could be the gents' carsey."

"That why I need to see—"

Everett started in surprise as Sen touched a finger to his lips.

"Ssh Everett Singh. All you need to do is see. . . . I'll go."

"But you're—"

"What, Everett Singh?" She had a tilt of the head and a sideways smile and a way of looking out from under her mop of white hair that turned her words into armour-piercing missiles. She was simply irresistible. "You mean I's Airish?" She slapped her leather satchel—her shush-bag as she called it. "Parcel for Mr. Hoojamaflip. We runs special deliveries—courier services, documents, body parts for hospitals—all the time. I'll not be the first of us in that there tower. Some people values us, you know. Special delivery! Oh, and I needs a signature."

"But what if you get caught?"

"Everett Singh, they don't know me from Aunt Nell."

"I need pictures."

"I needs some of your tech."

Everett opened up the phone and set up the camera and the bluetooth. He handed it to Sen. She took it as if it were a living creature that might die if she dropped it.

"This'll stream pictures back to me through a radio link. The best thing to do is start it when you get in and leave it running."

Sen mounted the camera on the strap of her shush-bag.

"It's a bit obvious," Everett said.

"Not half as obvious as me flashing it round all over the place. You forget, Everett Singh, people here ain't ever seen anything like this, so they don't know what they's looking for. So, what is I looking for?"

"Someone who looks like this." Everett turned Dr. Quantum to Sen. The photograph was of him and Tejendra in their Spurs shirts, in the North Stand, pies in their hands, mouths open to take a bite. Everett remembered Vinny taking it after the 3 to 1 defeat of Inter Milan in the Champions League. The prickle in the corners of his eyes, the catch in the back of his throat took him by surprise. "Anything, really. Get as far in as you can."

"I can be very persuasive," Sen said. "Okay." She shivered. "Oooh. Exciting. Well, I's offski." But she hesitated a moment. You're scared, Everett thought. You jumped up and said I'll do it because you're the kind of person who wants to be first to do anything and now you realise that this isn't a game, this isn't a chase across the rooftops with Sharkey and his shotguns to save you if it goes a bit wrong. You are on your own and you are scared. But anyone would be scared. Anyone should be scared. "Everett Singh, pick a card." She fanned out the Everness Tarot, facedown. Everett half pulled out a card. Sen turned it up. The old man on crutches stepping through a stone gate in a stone wall into darkness. "Death's Door. Lovely."

"Maybe it's not death," Everett said. "Maybe it's a door into another universe."

"Kiss for luck, Everett Singh." Sen leaned forward, expecting. Everett brushed her lightly, shyly on the cheek. Her silly, wonderful hair got in his eye. Her skin was very warm. What was that perfume that reminded him of so many things?

"That'll do, Everett Singh." And she was gone. Everett took his seat by the window. He poured some coffee. It had lost its heat and freshness. No one did good coffee in this universe. He checked Dr. Quantum's batteries. They were good. He opened the bluetooth. Nothing. Too early. He looked down at the traffic on foot and on wheel hurrying past the intimidatingly grand entrance of the Tyrone Tower. A deep, clear cold had set in over London after the rain and the wind. The shoppers pouring out from Rumbold and Sachs's revolving doors with their hands full of liveried paper bags seemed to relish it. Proper Christmas weather. Breath steaming, faces bright, collars up, scarves pulled tight.

As he watched, high above the people and quiet cars rolling along the street, Everett became aware of a knot, huge and hard as a fist, twisting in the pit of his stomach. It felt as if the bottom were dropping out of his life. It felt like old poison. It took him a moment to name it. Loneliness. His Christmas, his shopping, his present-buying should have happened in another world. He should have been piling bags into the back of the car at Brent Cross Mall, going to the school Christmas dance, getting something for his dad—whatever Divorcedads.com suggested was the ideal present for a first-time-post-breakup Christmas present. He tried to think of his mum and Victory-Rose doing all those things without him. He couldn't. They wouldn't. He had killed Christmas. First his dad, then him: vanished without a whisper. He hadn't thought of the ones he left behind. All he had thought of was his plan, the insane plan that was the most sane of all the possibilities Everett could think of. He had been looking at the moment he got them all back together again, safe, somewhere else. He hadn't thought of the moment he didn't come back from the school, the moment she had called his phone and left a message, and left a message and left a message, then called his friends, then the family, then last of all the police. He hadn't thought of her in another police station filling in another missing persons report, of Leah-Leanne-Leona and Moustache Milligan in her kitchen *again* drinking her tea and eating her toast and offering their sympathy. He hadn't thought of her alone and scared and crying and not knowing what was happening, who would disappear next.

He thought of it now and it was like a fist in a glove of frozen iron tearing out his heart.

"I'm sorry," he whispered. A movement in the corner of his eye: Sen, dashing between the traffic with her usual lack of heed and respect. As she went up the long flight of steps, between the stone lions and the pillars that supported the portico—big enough to play a football match under—he saw her touch the little device hooked onto the strap across her shoulder. Don't look back, Everett thought at her. You're too smart to look back.

She went in through the massive revolving doors. Dr. Quantum came to life. The picture was grainy from the poor camera lens, jerky from the slow bluetooth link, lurching in time to Sen's footsteps. Random people moved through the shot: phone cameras were wide-angle by default; the lobby seemed kilometres across.

Stand still, will you? Everett thought at the screen. As if she had heard him telepathically, Sen stopped. She turned very slowly. Everett took screen grabs of her panorama. The lobby of the Plenitude tower was built to awe, on the scale of the ancient world:

Karnak, Petra, the Pantheon of Greece, the ruins of Imperial Rome. He could not see the tops of the pillars. They were as massive and tall as redwood trees. The black marble floor was wide as a dark ocean. At a vast distance was a bank of reception desks. Behind them hung a banner. It must be thirty metres on a side, Everett guessed; black as the marble floor, bearing nine silver stars. A star for each world of the Plenitude. You're going to have to change that, Everett thought. It's ten worlds now.

"Seen enough?" Everett started at the voice from Dr. Quantum's speakers. Sen had worked out how to use the audio.

"Bona polone!" Everett shouted. The patient maid, on her rounds clearing tables, looked up.

"I'm going in now."

"Wait," Everett said. He'd seen a low fence across the lobby, a gate, two big men in uniforms. Beyond reception was another layer of security. He couldn't risk Sen getting caught. But she couldn't hear him. The stream started to jerk as she walked towards the desk. Wait. Everett called up a messaging app. *Sen, if you get this, say okay,* he tapped. Send. Notice the buzz. Notice the buzz on your breastbone where the phone sits in your shush-bag strap. Notice and look. He re-sent the SMS. *Sen, if you get this, say okay. Sen, if you get this, say okay. Sen, if you get this, say okay.*

"Okay."

We're in contact, Everett texted. Then he saw a motion in the street that distracted him from the tension in the lobby. A long line of children was walking down the street, past the façade of the Tyrone Tower, up the steps, under the porch towards the revolving door. Everett estimated there were forty, fifty of them, a big train, adults every ten kids, all muffled up for winter. It could only be an end-of-term school trip. A school trip to the Plenitude. Why not? Everett had been on school trips to the Houses of Parliament and Greenwich Observatory. The United Nations in New York took school parties. NASA showed school trips their rockets. This was

E3's equivalent of both: exploration and administration. To the schoolchildren it was a mildly interesting afternoon out—the highlight would be if they actually saw someone go through the Heisenberg Gate—with souvenir eraser and pencils in the gift shop and home early. To Everett, it was opportunity.

Big crowd kids coming in, Everett texted.

"See 'em," Sen said.

Join them. The picture jogged again. Faces flushed with winter filled the screen, hats and scarves and hoods and gloves. *Don't get too close.*

"Trust me, Everett Singh." The group moved past the camera towards the reception.

Doing???

"They're getting tags."

Danger, Everett thought. One of the teachers would spot Sen as an intruder. But no tag, no entrance. *Can U get close to tag?* he texted. Sen mingled with the milling mass of school kids as they fitted guest passes to their coat lapels and pockets. Everett hissed through his teeth in concentration as he tried to drop the screen-grab frame onto a clear, solid shot of a tag. They were moving too quickly. A badge drifted into frame. Everett dragged the frame around it, tapped. Got it. It took Everett thirty seconds on the image-processing app to sharpen the photo, resize it, and change the name.

Picture 4u. And it was through the bluetooth link and onto the screen of his smartphone on Sen's chest-strap. It wouldn't survive even a moment of detailed scrutiny, but for a back-marker in a crowd of noisy, restless, bored early-teens it would pass a glance. Sen dawdled along at the back of the tour group as it approached the uniformed security men. And through without even a nod. The camera showed Everett a woman with a clipboard and a tag and a very sharp suit and shoes. He guessed she was the tour guide. Better and better. Everett waited until the tour had left the lobby before buzzing Sen with a message.

Get close enuf 2 hear guide.

This was a last-day-before-Christmas-holiday tour. The guide was as bored and distracted as the schoolchildren. But she was gold to Everett. This is the Chamber of the Council of Worlds. Each world sends twenty councillors. The presidency rotates between the members of the Plenitude. Up this escalator. Please keep shoelaces and straps away from the edge of the treads. On these levels are the embassies of the Nine Known Worlds. One embassy per floor. Please hold the handrail. This level is currently being refurbished to be the Embassy of World 10. Sen turned the camera to the left, to the right, and Everett went snap snap snap snap. He almost laughed aloud with glee. Everything, she was giving him everything. He tagged the images as he dropped them into his wire-frame model. Council chamber. E2 Embassy. E4 Embassy. E5 Embassy. The Hall of Plenipotentiaries—a circular pit of ten leather-backed seats facing each other across a round table. Recessed lighting threw shadows up into the wooden ceiling. It looked like a set from a James Bond movie.

"Now we're going to go up to the gates," the guide said. Everett could see excitement ripple through the tourists. Something happening! Not just rooms. Everett loved the rooms. His father was in a room, somewhere in this building. "We operate twenty Einstein Gates on this level," the guide said as she led the party along a curving corridor. Glass windows on the inner curve gave views over the gate chambers. Sen, dawdling at the back, made sure Everett got a good shot through each window, once the press of curious boys had moved on to the next one. The operation was much more slick than the ramshackle setup hidden in the abandoned Channel test-tunnel. A single curved desk with three seats faced an empty metal ring four metres across. That was all. Nothing could have looked more like a gateway to another universe. "You're in luck," the guide said, barely audible over the chatter and calling. "We've got a scheduled jump in Gate Twelve." Sen did not need the hint from Everett. She pushed up as close as she could among the heavy coats and hoods and angled the phone camera through the window. Between the backs of the heads Everett saw the backs of other heads, of the three technicians at their workstations. Light flooded the camera lens. The gate opened. A man in an E3-fashion greatcoat and suit stepped out of the light into the room. The gate closed. The technicians shook his hand, checked his passport, and presented him with paperwork to sign.

"That was a scheduled return jump of one of our diplomatic staff from the embassy on E7," the woman said. She sounded very pleased with herself, as if she had just performed a great conjuring trick. Make a man appear out of thin air. "And with me, please." She led her tour group on. Sen lingered to video the diplomat leaving the gate room, entrance formalities completed.

It was a terrible plan. A ridiculous, impossible, foolhardy plan. Sen had told Everett that to his face, on their first stake-out of the Tyrone Tower.

"What, you find where they've got your dad, get into the building, get him out, get to a Ein—Heisenberg Gate, plug in your Infundibbiedabbiedoo, get home, pick up the rest of the family—while someone keeps the gate open—and then use the Infundamentalist to take everyone off somewhere the Plenitude can never find you?"

"Yes," Everett had said.

"That is the worst plan I have ever heard."

"Can you think of a better one?"

"No."

But she had been right. It was a terrible plan, apart from all the others. But it was working. Little by little, clue by clue, it was working. It looked a lot more reasonable than taking the Ring to Mount Doom. Everett giggled. This was his very own dark tower.

The tour guide was saying something about exiting via the gift shop. "Everett Singh," Sen whispered. "I's trolling off on my ownio. Have a varda round."

Where? Everett sent.

"Back down to that new embassy they're building for your world."

Careful . . . Everett typed. His hand hovered over the send button. Sen didn't need him to tell her what to do. She dawdled behind the tour group until the last one had disappeared round the curve of the corridor. They were happy. They'd seen a minor civil servant make the jump from another universe. Then Sen turned back and headed for the elevator lobby. Everett followed the descending floor numbers on his model of the Tyrone Tower. Sen stepped out into the noise of power drills and nail guns, saws and screwdrivers. The corridor was littered with cardboard packing and discarded fabric wrap, the air thick and grainy with dust. Two construction workers sat on a pile of plasterboard drinking tea.

"You lost, love?"

"Parcel for Alan Pardew."

"Never heard of him."

"This is Level Twenty-two?"

"Certainly is."

"I'll find him."

Sen continued past them. When they looked away, she ducked into a set of rooms off the corridor. The suite was under construction: lighting fittings dangled unfinished from the ceiling, the power sockets hung from the walls, ducting was exposed, cables ran up the pillars. The Tyrone Tower was a thoroughly modern skyscraper under its Gothic skin. Beyond the incomplete suite was a second, in the middle of fitting out. Sen walked across a newly laid wooden floor, leaving footprints in the sawdust. The walls were wood-panelled; chandeliers hung from the ceiling. She stopped and turned to shoot a panoramic.

"You getting this, Everett Singh?"

U think he's here?

"Best place to hide a thing is right under everyone's noses. Now what's behind those?"

The camera came to rest on a curtain of heavy, translucent polythene. "Let's have a varda."

Sen pushed through the hanging plastic. The sheets of polythene obscured the lens; then Sen breathed, "Everett." He could see. This section of Level 22 was complete; complete and fully furnished. Potted plants, paintings on the walls, comfortable chairs and occasional tables in the alcoves, concealed lighting, and soft, fresh deep-pile carpet. Tasteful lifestyle magazines, fresh flowers. It looked like a corridor in a five-star hotel. Everett found he was holding his breath. He remembered to breathe. He remembered to capture images. Sen tried a door handle. Locked. The short corridor ended in a T-junction. Sen shot left, then right. To the right was a service trolley, of the kind chambermaids pushed up and down hotel corridors. Sen was onto it before Everett could hit the keys. On the cart were folded sheets and blankets, pillows and bed linen, a small tray of hotel-style toiletries. Behind the handle hung a grey linen refuse sack. The camera peered inside. What it showed Everett was so ordinary, so everyday that he missed the significance for a moment. A discarded newspaper and a plastic water bottle.

A plastic bottle. Plastic, made from oil. On a world without oil.

Everett's heart turned over. *Paper*, he texted Sen. She hauled it out and unrumpled it for the camera. REDKNAPP FIELDS MATCH-FIT BALE AGAINST CHELSEA. A Tottenham Hotspur story. In a world where the big stadium sport was rugby. Where Gareth Bale wasn't one of the players and the manager certainly wasn't Harry Redknapp. Sen turned the paper over. The *Daily Telegraph*. Tejendra would hate that. He was a dedicated *Independent* reader. She brought the paper up so Everett could read the date. December 21st. Today's date.

Sen put her hand on the doorknob and twisted it. Everett hit the keys.

No!!!!

Sen froze, hand on the doorknob.

The cart. Someone in there.

Her hand drew back from the door.

Go. Now.

Sen was walking away when the phone's tiny microphone picked up the sound of a door opening. She turned. Two figures stood by the service cart. One was a small woman with an apron and a headscarf. The other was a tall, thin, shaven-headed man. The lens's resolution was terrible, but it could not disguise Thug-in-a-Suit.

"Yes?" Thug-in-a-Suit asked.

"Parcel for Alan Pardew?"

"How did you get in here?"

"The workmen—"

"You shouldn't be here."

"Sorry."

"You can't be here."

"Bona. Going now. Gone."

He's there, Everett thought. He dragged images across to the map of the Tyrone Tower. Level 22 southeast. End of the corridor. He was there behind that door. Like a hotel room you couldn't check out of. A five-star cage. They'd built this entire sector just for him. They brought water and a copy of the *Daily Telegraph* in from another universe every morning. You're there, Dad. If only the cart hadn't been there, if only he could have got Sen to slide some message under the door. But if the cart hadn't been there Everett would never have known that that was the room where Tejendra was being kept prisoner. I know you're there. I'm coming.

"Whoa!" Everett shouted aloud at a movement in his peripheral. On the feed screen a door had opened ahead of Sen. A woman stepped out. An immaculately dressed woman in heels and a tall fur hat and matching stole, a tiny bag clutched in one of the grey gloves that matched her finely cut suit. Charlotte Villiers.

Sen breezed past. Charlotte Villiers didn't spare her a glance. But at the end of the corridor, where another plastic curtain covered the entrance to the main elevator lobby, Sen glanced back. From the end of the corridor, Charlotte Villiers studied her. Her face was puzzled. She frowned. Then she stared straight into the lens of the camera phone. She remembered. She remembered where she had seen this piece of alien technology.

Go go go! Everett texted Sen. The phone buzzed urgently. Look at it, Everett thought. Look at it. *She knows.* Sen ran. She burst out of the plastic curtain. A final backwards glance through the thick translucent polythene showed Charlotte Villiers walking purposefully towards her. She did not hurry. She seemed to be talking into the lapel of her jacket. At the end of this stretch of corridor was more plastic sheeting. Sen flung herself through and found herself face-to-face with the startled builders.

"Did you find him then, love?"

"Who?"

"The man you were going to give the parcel to."

"No. Wrong floor after all." The camera came to bear on the elevator lights. There was nothing even close to this floor.

"Where are the stairs?"

The second workman jerked his thumb over his shoulder. A door swung in Everett's view. For a moment he peered down a bottomless stairwell; then Sen was hurtling down the concrete steps. The speed was extreme and terrifying. One false step and she would tumble and not be able to stop. Round and round and round. The stairs were featureless; the stairs were endless. Down she pounded. God, she was fit. Everett could hear her breathing. Down and down, round and round. Where was she now? Everett had lost count of the turns and landings. There were numbers on the doors, but Sen moved too fast for Everett to read them. With every floor groundwards, a dread grew inside Everett. Charlotte Villiers would have alerted security in the lobby. They would pick her up there. He had to let her know. She was running headlong into danger.

They're waiting for you, he typed. He kept his finger poised over the send key. Round and round, down and down. Suddenly there were no more steps under her. She was on concrete facing a door with GROUND FLOOR written on it. Send. Sen froze, hand on the door.

"Is there another way out?"

Everett did not need to look at his model of the Tyrone Tower. He was out of options. All he could do was warn.

Sorry Sen . . .

"Doesn't matter. I got a bona plan," Sen said, pushed the door open and strode out.

"Whoa no!" exclaimed Everett across the street in the warmth of the coffee-and-Christmas-scented cafeteria. He wrapped his arms around his head in dread. He could clearly see on the screen the men in suits at the checkpoint in the middle of the big black marble lobby. There were more of them at the revolving door. They were discreet, just a glance and a nod at the people streaming out of the Tyrone Tower. They knew what they were looking for. Sen's first advantage was that they were looking at the elevator lobby and the escalators. They hadn't thought someone might come galloping down twenty-two flights of stairs. Her second advantage was that she wasn't moving in the expected direction. She wasn't heading down the lobby to the doors. She was moving across—to where? All the jolting camera showed was brightly lit windows. Now her destination was in clear focus. The gift shop.

"You clever girl," Everett said. He could have hugged himself. The school party was still in the shop. Sen slipped in, slipped off her conspicuous jacket, and stuffed it into her shush-bag. Quickly, confidently, she slipped a bobble-hat off a display and over her big hair. She found the middle of the crowd and blended in. Everett heard the voices of the teachers calling. The bus was waiting. Buy what you're going to buy or you'll get left behind. The stragglers quit the tills; the teachers herded their charges, Sen hidden in the middle of them, out of the gift shop and toward the security post. Like a big noisy rugby scrum the school party bowled past the men in suits. They did not even look twice. Across the lobby, past reception, under the huge wall-sized black-and-silver banner of the Plenitude of Known Worlds, out through the revolving door and on to the street. Everett reeled back on his seat, gasping with relief.

"You got what you need?" Sen said into the phone.

Everett texted a thumbs-up emoticon, then typed: *OMG OMG. I thought U were dead.*

"Nah," Sen said. "Sharpie's not born can catch Sen Sixsmyth." Everett could see her now, coming down the steps, pulling on her jacket, pulling off her bobble-hat, and shaking out her great hair. Down on the street she threw the stolen hat out into the traffic. The school kids headed right. She headed left. "Everett Singh, get your stuff and meet me at the taxi rank on Cleveland Street. I hope you got some dinari left, coz I's cruising back to Hackney tonight."

22

In the quiet-running electric taxi Sen was still high on adventure. One moment her face was pressed to the condensation-misty window, watching the traffic, the trains, the people on the streets. The next she was fidgeting in the seat, buzzing with adrenaline, hitting Everett with question after question after question after question. *Do you think they's following us? Did you see what I did back there? Wasn't I fantabulosa? Do you really think your dad's in there? When are we going to go and get him out? That was easy.*

Everett didn't want to say what he feared: that it had been easy because it had been meant to be easy. The game of his enemies—and he still didn't know exactly who they were or what their strategy was—had always been to get him to bring the Infundibulum to them. He had played along every step. They had even got him thinking like them now.

Sen picked up Dr. Quantum and turned the plastic slab over in her hands with a sense of familiarity and ownership that made Everett bristle.

"I mean, it's just a map, what's so special about that?"

"It's a map to anywhere and everywhere. And it's much more than a map, it's a phonebook. You can programme a Heisenberg Gate to connect to any point in any of the universes in there, not just another gate. Do you know how many universes there are in here?"

"A lot?" Sen said. "More than thirty?"

"Ten with eighty zeroes after it. And think about what you could do if you had that power. For a start, if you can jump to any point of any universe, that includes any point in this one. I could dial it up and I could step out of the gate on a planet a billion light-years from here. Well, I could if I had the full working Infundibulum, but that'd be way too big for this computer, or maybe any computer. I mean, every point, everywhere in every universe . . ." He had worked it out in the privacy of his latty, late when the ship had closed up and he had cleaned the plates and cutlery and put everything away in the galley, rocking in his hammock, lit by the glow from Dr. Quantum, the battery recharging sweetly on the adapter Mchynlyth had built with a few grunts and passes of the soldering iron and glue gun. It couldn't be everything. Everett had once worked out that there were ten to the power eighty atoms in the universe—this universe—no, *that* universe. A code for each atom. That was a huge quantity of information; much more than Dr. Quantum could hold. Lying in his hammock, quilt pulled up under his chin, listening to the great airship creak around him, Everett had run the numbers in his head. It wasn't an exact science; it was back-of-envelope science, getting-an-idea-of-the-scale-of-the-question science. Say a billion universes, and a code for every point within a thousand-kilometre radius of Imperial College's Heisenberg Gate. All of the British Isles, much of continental Europe, some way out into the Atlantic. That was still a staggering amount of space. The Infundibulum held inside Dr. Quantum was a passport to a trillion alternate Britains. The full Infundibulum, if a machine could ever be built to contain it—Everett's mind had reeled, spinning out from his tiny cabin, little longer and broader than his hammock, through infinities of infinities.

"What I could do is dial it up and step out into your latty in *Everness*. And I could assassinate you and step back again and no one would ever know who did it. Or maybe I wouldn't have to assassinate you. I could just take you. No one would ever know where you had gone. Our I could just replace you with your double from another universe and no one would even know you had gone at all."

"Nah," said Sen. "I mean, another me? Nah."

"You think so? Ten to the eighty is a lot of universes. The chances are almost certain there'll be another Sen Sixsmyth out there somewhere. And that Sen Sixsmyth mightn't think like you at all.

She might be rich and powerful or she might be homeless. She might have a load of reasons to be you."

Sen fidgeted in her seat. The adrenaline burn was fading and the realisation that you weren't the unique, fantabulosa person you thought you were was chilling. Everett remembered how he had felt when he understood—properly understood, with his heart and emotions and empathy—what Tejendra had been telling him. Billions of Everetts. It had felt like the bottom was falling out of his world. You're not so special. He learned to live with it by convincing himself that those other Everetts were so far away, so inaccessible, sealed up in their other universes, that he would never know of them, much less meet them. That could never happen. Right.

Sen pulled her feet up onto the taxi's leather upholstery and hugged her knees to her. "But maybe I am the one and only, Everett. There are all those worlds where there are other yous, right? But there are ones where there aren't any Everett Singhs. There's someone else—lots of someones else. And there could be billions of some of those someones elses, and maybe a few thousand of some others, and maybe a hundred of other ones, maybe a handful. And in all those worlds, there have to be some one-and-onlies. That's me. I know it, I feel it. There's no one else like me. I am the special one."

A loud bang. A chair bounced off the hood of the taxicab. Sen was thrown against the back of the driver's seat as the driver braked hard.

"Okay, end of the ride," he announced. Everett winkled shillings out of his backpack as Sen got out of the car. She stood, hands on waist, mouth open.

"Fantabulosa!"

The street was full of people. The street was full of *men*, jammed together, backs turned, oblivious to the taxi, straining to see past each other. All their attention was given to some major event farther up Mare Street. Men were pouring from the warehouses and stores. They abandoned forklifts and goods trains, loaders and trucks, and came running. They came streaming from the Knights of the Air. There wasn't an intact window in the pub. Smashed furniture lay in the broken glass. It was easy to read that the altercation had started there and spilled on to the street. Hands brandished pieces of smashed furniture. Bottles and cobbles flew. There was a huge wordless roar like Cup Tie Saturday at White Hart Lane, a wall of sound.

"Fiigght!" Sen yelled. "Come on, Everett Singh!"

"Here, what about my hood?" the car driver demanded.

"Invoice me," Sen said, blowing him a kiss as she spun on her heel and headed for the action.

"Every bloody time I go up to Airish Town," the driver grumbled as he backed away and turned the cab.

Everett could make out words in the wall of voices, a huge chant; *a ring, a ring, a ring!*

"What's going on?"

"A ring," Sen shouted. "Fisticuffs. Gloves off. No rules. A fight, Everett Singh. Come on!"

Everett had seen a fight, a big fight, a street fight. It had been the easiest thing in the world to get into, just come up from the underground at Westminster Tube Station to get tickets for a Water Music and Fireworks New Year spectacular on the river, and without asking to be or wanting to be he and his dad had found themselves in the middle of a student protest. Ten thousand angry people not going anywhere. The police had this tactic where they got everyone into one small place, surrounded them with riot shields and horses, stationed helicopters overhead, and kept everyone there for hours. "Kettling" they called it. Everett knew what a kettle was for. You put things in it and brought them to a boil. Boil the students had, boiled over. A roar had gone up somewhere towards Parliament Square; then bodies had surged hard against Everett and Tejendra. There was action somewhere, but who, where? Everett was disoriented, afraid, exhilarated, aware something big was going on but not able to see it or know how near it was, whether it might break over them at any moment. He had known crushes and surges at football games; this was a different order. It was incredible and terrifying. For a few moments he had glimpsed police hi-viz jackets and black riot shields above black body armour; a mounted policeman head and shoulders above the crowds in a hail of sticks snapped off from placards. The fighting had died down as police squads had snatched and dragged out rioters, but he and Tejendra and ten thousand others had been kept there until nearly ten o'clock and then only released after the police had checked ID and photographed them and stored them on a database. This was a Hackney Street fight, not police and demonstrators, but Everett smelled that same gunpowder whiff of uncontrollable danger. This was raw, thrilling, scary, unpredictable; a mob: a fire that might blow back in an instant and engulf them. Everett had learned in Parliament Square to know and fear mob violence, its allure and how infectious that could be.

"No, Sen. I can't risk Dr. Quantum getting damaged."

He saw the disdain in her face. Then a sudden uproar from the crowd distracted her as the ring of bodies heaved and parted and a man came reeling out. He was a hulk; shoulder-length black hair matted with sweat, face livid with exertion beneath his thick brows and muttonchop whiskers: exertion and bruises. His left eye was swollen shut; his mouth leaked blood from each corner. His shirt hung in tatters around his waist. He looked dazed but ready for the fight, eyeing the world as if any part of it might attack him, and he would be ready, his fists clenched hard like iron cannonballs.

"Aw, did you get your dish kicked again, Seth Bromley?" Sen shouted.

"Don't annoy him," Everett said. "He's very big. Who is Seth Bromley?" A group of hard-faced men pushed their way out of the crowd. They took the big, groggy man over to the front of the Knights of the Air, set up the one intact chair, and sat him down in it. There was steam coming off him.

"Who's Seth Bromley? The biggest fruity-boy in Hackney!" Sen shouted cheerfully at the big man. "Did your mummy put you up to it, Seth Bromley?" He looked up, stung, and glowered out of his one open eye.

"Don't you sully my mother with your dirty breath, you little ship rat," he growled.

"Seth Bromley Seth Bromley, the big fruity omi; he does what his dear mama says," Sen chanted. Everett had seen Sen's verbal aggression several times now, but it always surprised him. She could be bitingly cruel with deadly accuracy, but Everett wondered if her taunts and nasty little rhymes were thought out in advance, to be drawn like knives when she needed weapons, or if she was like a wasp that stings by reflex.

Now Seth Bromley pointed a finger. "I don't fight polones."

"That's because this polone'd boot you in the basket, Seth Bromley."

"But in your case, you meese little feely . . ." He surged up from his chair, fists raised. The rear part of the crowd turned, attention seized, then opened. Sharkey walked slowly out. His hat was battered, the jaunty feather broken and dangling. Otherwise he was unmarked.

"'Take heed that ye despise not one of these little ones,'" he said to Seth Bromley.

"I can look after myself, Sharkey," Sen said.

"Is that so, miss? If you'd half the facility for getting out of trouble that you have getting into it, I might be disposed to believe you. Come on, out of here."

"I want to see it. It's Mchynlyth again, isn't it?"

"Mr. Mchynlyth, unlike you, donaette, can look after himself," Sharkey said.

"So what was you doing then?" Sen asked defiantly. "Wouldn't be like you to stand around with your arms the same length when the captain's honour's insulted."

"And what honour would I have if the captain's daughter got her charming features redesigned by one of the Bromleys?" Sharkey said, but Everett could see that Sen had scored a point and that he was eager to get back to the fight. "Here's the deal. Find a safe place and watch and say nothing to no one and I'll say nothing to no one."

Sen solemnly shook hands. "Deal." The same hand took Everett's and led him at a run to the steps of a container loader. As they clattered up to the gantry by the driving cab, Everett saw Sharkey break into a run. He launched himself into the pack roaring, "For Dundee, Atlanta, and St. Pio!" and a battle cry like a yip with a twittering fox yelp that was the most uncanny thing Everett had ever heard from a human throat.

"That old Confed yell," Sen said. "I still don't know who or what Dundee is. Or was."

From the gallery they could see the whole of the action. Every man in Hackney Great Port, and some of the women, had turned out to watch the spectacle. They formed a jostling, shouting ring of bodies ten deep. The empty space at the centre changed shape constantly, spectators reeling back or surging forward as the men in the ring reeled and charged at each other. The noise was incredible. There were three men at the centre of the voices. Two of them were big, dark haired, cast from the same mould as Seth Bromley. They moved slowly, heavily, circling round the third man. He was Mchynlyth. His orange flight coveralls were unbuttoned to the navel and tied around his waist. His body was bruised and bloody; he shone with sweat under the streetlights of the cold December evening, but his eyes were on fire. They never stopped looking from one Bromley to the other, one to the other, one to the other, and he was skipping, dancing, dodging, ducking, slipping under their blows, bouncing out of their reach. He had the maddest grin on his face as he glanced from one to the other.

"Come on you bassards, no fair no fair . . . I can whup any one of youse, but two? Make a proper fight of it, ye bassarding Bromleys."

"Who are they?" Everett asked.

"Albarn Bromley and Keir Bromley," Sen said. "Seth's bijou brothers. Younger and thicker. Not Kyle. He's the kid of the family. It's his fight, but Kyle Gorgeous Bromley'll never risk his eek in that ring."

The two Bromleys came to a nonverbal agreement and charged Mchynlyth. He ducked under their combined assault easily and came up dancing like a butterfly on the other side of the ring. The crowd cheered. Everett had fought this kind of fight hundreds of times. It had been on the Xbox, against Ryun, in the warmth of Ryun's room, not on the cobbles of Hackney Great Port with the frost settling out of the air, but the principle was the same. It was the classic of speed versus power. Everett's analysis favoured speed. It was how the great Ali had won all his classic fights, back in the '70s, when boxing was cool. Keep moving, that butterfly beat, tire them out, take their best shot and survive and then come back. One two, out. But the Bromleys were a lot bigger than Mchynlyth, and he was looking almost as tired as they. And there were two of them.

"How did Mchynlyth get himself into this?"

"Oh, he'll have started it. He gets a meese fighting head on him when there's drink taken. Or when there isn't drink taken, now I come to think of it. He'll have seen them all down the Knights and told them Annie'd sooner marry a ground-pounder than Kyle Gorgeous Bromley."

"Captain Anastasia's engaged?"

"Ma Bromley thinks she is," Sen said. "It's all sorted, according to her. Kyle Bromley marries Anastasia Sixsmyth, thus bringing *Everness*—which as everyone knows is the sweetest ship in all Hackney Great Port—into the family fleet. Rejoice rejoice! Only problem is—"

"No one's told Captain Anastasia."

"Correct, Everett Singh. Well, they have told her. Proper proposition and everything. I heard Annie's reply. I 'spect Ma Bromley heard Annie's reply all the way over at Pylon 22. Those Bromleys, they reckon they're right Hackney aristocracy, and no one can say no to them. It's an insult. Noblesse oblige and all that. Insult Kyle, you insults 'em all."

Sen's knuckles went white on the rail as Mchynlyth walked into a sly rabbit punch to the ribs. He went down on one knee, wincing, winded. The Bromleys grinned at each other and closed. Then Sharkey forced his way out of the press of spectators. He crossed the ring in three steps and with a well-timed kick tripped up Albarn Bromley and sent him crashing to the ground. The big man roared and rolled and found himself looking up at Sharkey's face along the barrel of a shotgun.

"'The bows of the mighty are broken, and they that stumbled are girded with strength,'" Sharkey said. "First Samuel chapter two, verse four. Let's fight nice." He held Albarn Bromley under the gun as Mchynlyth picked himself up, straightened his neck, popped his knee joints, flexed his shoulders, and dropped into fighting pose. Again the crowd roared. Keir Bromley came at him. Mchynlyth blocked a hook, spun away, and planted a Thai-boxing kick firm in Keir Bromley's ribs. Bromley reeled.

"Kill him, Mac, kill him!" Sen yelled. Mchynlyth pressed his advantage, driving Keir Bromley backwards as the big man blocked and dodged. The crowd moved with them, moving blow by blow, ooh by aah up Mare Street. Sen beat her fist on the rail. Everett found her naked bloodlust alien and hateful. Hackney Great Port was hard, and applied its own rules quickly and harshly; the Airish way of life was more immediate and passionate than anything Everett knew in his contained, concerned, middle-class London, but girls shouldn't call for blood. They shouldn't enjoy physical violence. Everett wondered again about Sen's background. When he had asked her she had dodged the question, but he had seen the look in her eyes at Seth Bromley's parting jibe. If she could have clawed his lungs out, she would.

"We're missing it!" The fight had moved under the shadow of

the airships and out of the line-of-sight from the crane. Sen grabbed Everett's hand and dragged him off the gantry. "Come on!"

"What's with the 'come on's?" Everett muttered. "Everyone's always telling me to come on." He came on anyway. Sen found a fine vantage point on a gallery that encircled the second floor of the Acheson and Muir Bonded warehouse. Everett felt the rusting metal creak beneath him. The fight moved up the street, a mauling, rolling scrum of bodies. Both Mchynlyth and Keir Bromley were bruised, shambling, shiny with blood. The ring of spectators urged them on, though the combatants could hardly stand, let alone land a blow on each other. Everett felt sick. There was nothing noble in this, there was no honour, just two people ruining each other. The intention to harm, the rage, was the only thing that kept them upright. They stumbled out from under the shelter of *Leonora Christine*'s hull into the clear night air. They reeled; they staggered. The ring flowed and moved and re-formed around them. This was horrific.

"Stop it!" Everett yelled. "Stop it!" He was a scientist. He didn't believe in magic. But even as his shout flew over the heads of the crowd a jet of water blasted out of nowhere and knocked Keir Bromley and Mchynlyth from their feet. Down they went skidding and spinning under the torrent. Then the jet turned on the spectators, sending them falling and reeling, scattering them like a hose washing dead bugs from a car. Keir Bromley tried to get to his feet, but the water blast turned on him and pinned him to the cobbles. The fight had carried under *Everness*'s shadow. There on the cargo hoist, ten metres above the big brawl, was Captain Anastasia with a control unit in her hand, directing a ballast vent onto the mob. She moved a joystick; the jet of high-pressure water sent the spectators scurrying.

"Go on, get out of here," Captain Anastasia cried, sending stragglers scurrying with blasts from her water cannon. "What would your wives and girlfriends and partners think? Shame on you all. Go on, go home." She shut down the vent. Water dripped from the valve on *Everness*'s hull. Captain Anastasia said, "Mr. Bromley, tell your mother that my answer remains the same. You shall not have me and you shall not have *Everness*. Good day, sir. Mr. Mchynlyth, I neither need nor appreciate your gallantry. You have sullied the honour of this great ship. And Mr. Sharkey, don't think I didn't see your part in it. Report to the cargo deck. You have two minutes to make yourself spick and airship-shape. And you too, Sen and Mr. Singh. I'll be docking wages. Ballast water's not free, you know."

The cargo hatch touched ground. Sharkey slid his shotguns into the tail of his coat. He had somehow avoided the water. Even his hat had regained its proper shape, and he had found a new feather from somewhere. Keir Bromley dragged away, dripping. Mchynlyth wrapped his arms around his saturated body. The heat of the fight had gone out of him; a cold clear night was settling over Hackney Great Port. He was shivering uncontrollably, but he was grinning. Last of all Sen and Everett joined the group on the metal platform. Sen nudged Mchynlyth, a soft shoulder-charge. He winked back. Captain Anastasia pressed the hatch control. Winches whined; cables tautened. As the hoist drew them up into the vast belly of the airship, Captain Anastasia ordered, "Mr. Singh, private supper in my latty, at your convenience." Her words were stern, but Everett got the impression she was smiling.

23

The captain and her daughter were putting up Christmas decorations. Everett watched them through the open galley door as he whipped up seasonal hot chocolate, stirred with a cinnamon stick. There were wonders upon wonders tucked into the corners and crannies of the galley's cupboards. Sen was up ladders with lights and paper garlands; Captain Anastasia handed the decorations up and directed where to put them. They talked. They talked like no one was overhearing them. They talked about Christmas and who had got what for whom and the extra presents they had got themselves. They talked about the cargo that was being loaded and whether they might take time off after Berlin, which was its destination, and have some fun because Berlin was a great city; they talked about how the ship was feeling a bit rough, troubled by the weather; they talked about the news of Hackney Great Port and the stories from Dona Miriam and the other gossips. They talked not like captain and pilot, or even mother and daughter; they talked like two girls together. Everett had to constantly remind himself that Captain Anastasia was younger than he thought, maybe not even out of her twenties. The cinnamon stick stopped in midstir. Everett was overcome by a sudden wave of loneliness so crushing that he had to grasp the edge of the counter with both hands to keep himself up. His eyes filled. This was their home; this was their family. He had a latty, but not a life here. His family was in a room on the twenty-second floor of the Tyrone Tower, and two kilometres up the road in another universe. Broken into pieces. He had to break it to be able to put it back together, but they could not understand that. Tejendra was physically unable to understand; all he knew about the worlds was what Charlotte Villiers allowed him to know. His mum only understood that the two men in her life had vanished in less than a week. And he had to make his move soon, before *Everness* lifted for Berlin. Christmas was the time. Guards were dropped, vigilance relaxed, holiday moods prevailed. He had worked it out. There was a task for everyone aboard *Everness* with their different talents and abilities, and even for the ship itself. Before any of that he would have to make that appointment to see Captain Anastasia in her ready room, without Sen listening at the bulkhead, and say, *I need your help*. He would have to explain exactly what he intended to do, and how only *Everness* and its crew could help him. And he knew what she would say: *You're asking me to risk my ship, my crew, my daughter?* And he could only say, *I am.* And put like that, not even Everett would say yes to himself. The clock was ticking. Mchynlyth, confined to ship until lift-time along with Sharkey as punishment after the Bromley fight, had spent the day before buying in lift gas from the Gas Office, the government monopoly that controlled the helium supply. He would have to ask soon. He dreaded it. It ate at him. Everett resumed stirring the hot chocolate. He almost dropped the cinnamon stick at the sudden call of his name.

"Mr. Singh!"

Captain Anastasia beckoned him. He brought the steaming mugs. Dunsfold Air Traffic weather station reported a high-pressure cell anchored over southeast England with clear skies, low winds, and plummeting temperatures. Everett had cleared frost on his latty porthole when he woke muffled deep in his hammock that morning. Sharkey and Mchynlyth were in five layers but still shivered at their labours. Sharkey was supervising a squad of dockers, shipping containers onto the loading bay and operating *Everness*'s internal gantry crane to distribute them evenly around the ship's centre of gravity. Mchynlyth was under the deckplates, down in the power distribution system, with voltage meters and bypass cables and much of his individual style of language that always sounded as if he was swearing. The cold had even worked its way forward to the crew quarters. Sen was in thick grey woollen tights, a too-big pullover, sleeves stretched down to her knuckles, and a scarf. The only warm place was the steamy galley. Captain Anastasia took a sip of scalding, cinnamon-infused chocolate. She closed her eyes in bliss.

"Mr. Singh, that is damn fine chocolate. What's the little suspicion of heat?"

"Chilli," Everett said. "A pinch. I once had it in this coffee place in Seattle."

"Mission for you, Mr. Singh. Christmas is coming and we must have bona manjarry. Does your Punjabi granny have any recipes for turkey? Away down to Ridley Road Market and see what you can rustle up. Get plenty of vegetables. Sen would eat nothing but meat and carbo if I gave her the chance."

"I would not," Sen protested. "I like veg. Sort of."

"Fresh, green, and seasonal, Mr. Singh." Captain Anastasia counted a wad of pounds from her wallet, which was a marvellous magician's box of a thing, folding this way, that way, turn it over and it opened a third way, revealing new layers and levels and flaps and pockets, more and more the farther in you went. Infundibular. "If it comes to more than that, my credit is good with all the retailers in Hackney, but I'd prefer you kept to the budget. Do you know what the first law of the Airish is?"

"Neither a borrower nor a lender be?" Everett said.

"No, Mr. Singh, though that is a wise saying. Much more prosaic than that. Cash is king."

Leeks, long and straight and dusty blue-green. Italian kale, its leaves so dark a green they looked almost black. Potatoes—waxy ones, which were better as part of a dish with other vegetables, rather than floury ones for roasting. Already he was developing a cooking plan. Onions—cooking was inconceivable without them. He picked over a dozen types of onion, from ones as flat as a turban to tiny pickling onions the size of his thumb. Everett settled for two pounds of small, dark-skinned Polish onions that he could smell through the paper bag.

"These are bigger for the same price," Sen said, holding up a pale-skinned Spanish onion the size of her fist.

"Too big. They're all water. No flavour. Big isn't always best."

"It is with me."

Garlic. Lots of it. Root ginger. Everything was available at Ridley Road Market. Every day, every hour there was something new to discover about this Hackney. Ridley Road Market—go past the boarded-up Knights of the Air pub, go through the tangle of pipes and valves and gas-cylinders where the Gas Office stored its helium—was one of the bigger discoveries. Not because it was a market, but because it was a market in both the universes that Everett knew. In his home London it had been a street and a half of mostly Caribbean stalls and lock-ups opposite Dalston Station. In this London it was a bazaar of ethnicities and skin colours tucked into the arches and culverts and narrow alleys of a complex railway exchange. Laneways led to tunnels to vaults and church-sized halls built inside red-brick railway viaducts. Food and clothing and books and dodgy electrical goods, ironmongery and kitchen ware and suspiciously cheap tools. Crockery and household goods. Toys hung like a mass execution from the fronts of stalls; bolts of cloth stacked high, the lower ones flattened by the weight of those above them. Women drinking tea at stalls beneath high brickwork domes. The trains that passed regularly overhead shook the market to its core, shook the cups and tea sets on the china stalls, shook drips of rainwater that formed at the tips of the stalactites leached from the arches' cement joints, dripping down on the heads of the shoppers. Here Hackney Great Port and greater London met and mingled and haggled. City fashion mixed with the most piratical Airish dress; standard English, in a dozen accents, with palari. Everett went from stall to stall, asking, sniffing, holding in his hand, checking for blemishes, haggling, passing on.

"Hows can you tell the difference? It's all just spuds and onions," Sen complained. She was restless and bored.

"Well, it's all just lip gloss and makeup, but that doesn't stop you taking the lid off every single one."

"That's different. That's shopping."

"So what's this?"

"This is buying." Sen thought for a moment. "Do all the omis in your world know how to cook?"

"I think the question is the other way round; do none of the omis in your world know how to cook? My dad taught me."

"Your dad."

"And?"

"Nothing. Just. Well. You people are weird."

"It's a basic life skill. Are you going to starve to death in the middle of a market like this because you don't know what to do with basic ingredients?"

"Not me," Sen said. "I has grace and charm. That's what everyone says. Tell me about your dad, Everett Singh. We's supposed to be rescuing him and all I know is he's a scientist and bad guys want him and he supports some fruity-sounding team called Tottenham Hotspur. Oh, and he taught you how to cook."

"My dad's called Tejendra."

"See? You didn't even tell me that."

"You haven't told me your dad's name," Everett said. Or anything else about him or any of your family, or if they are alive or dead.

"Uh uh. This is your dad we're talking about." Sen didn't miss a beat as they walked on, stall by stall, into the depths of this Earth's Ridley Road Market. "You see, if I'm supposed to be helping you rescue him, I's entitled to know a bit about what I's rescuing."

"It's a Punjabi name. *Singh* means lion. It's a really common name in the Punjab. *Punjab* means 'five rivers': it's up in northwest India; in my world it's split between India and Pakistan. A lot of people died when they split Pakistan from India. Millions. It was a bad time;

the worst time. I don't know what India's like in your world. My dad's family comes from a village right at the centre of the five rivers. Right in the middle. They all moved to Ludhiana before my dad was born—he was born in India, but he moved before he was five so he doesn't really have the accent—well, you can hear a bit of it when he gets excited about stuff. He had three brothers and two sisters, and they grew up over an Asian supermarket in Walthamstow. So that was eight of the immediate family, then a couple of unmarried aunts and an uncle who'd just got married, all in this one house. You see, the Punjabis are like the Airish of India. They're always shouting and rowing and making up and celebrating and fighting. They all live with the volume up at eleven. Now, if you met my dad you wouldn't know right away he's Punjabi, because he's not big and noisy and he thinks about things, but you should see him at White Hart Lane at the North London Derby. And when he talks about physics, when he talks about those things that no one else understands but mean so much to him, you can see it in him like fire.

"How could I make you understand my dad's side of the family? Okay: I'll show you how my bebe and my other uncles and aunts would celebrate Christmas—which they all do even though they're not Christians, because Punjabis like nothing better than a good party. You wouldn't be sitting down to dry old turkey. No no, that's not proper manjarry for a feast. It'd be something for a real celebration, like royalty was coming. Always entertain as if you entertained princes, my bebe Ajeet says." Everett looked around the meat and poultry stalls; the turkeys plump and round as buttocks, the geese with their heads tucked under their long bony wings, the rounds of spiced beef filling the air with the scent of cinnamon, the clove-studded hams. His eyes lit on the pheasants hanging by the neck, male and female in pairs, from the game stall.

"How long have your pheasants been hanging?"

"In this weather, about nine days," said the stall holder, a square-built man, cheerful with salt-and-pepper hair cut into a stiff brush. Everett lifted a cock pheasant and sniffed it. "We get them from Lord Abercrombie's estate," the stallholder added.

"How much for four?"

The stallholder named a price. Everett haggled him down, parted with some of Captain Anastasia's banknotes and left with two paper bags with long, beautiful tail feathers sticking out of them.

"My bebe, she'd be thinking now, what's the most luxurious, wintery thing I can do with pheasants, what's royal and extravagant, and I'd be thinking, like murgh makhani, but with pheasant: pheasant makhani, with maybe a bit of edible gold leaf over the top; and she'd be thinking that's kind of goldy red and I'd need something green with that to show it up but I already have my leeks and my kale; and you'd need rice, a pillau that's so rich it has jewels in it, and bread because there's no Punjabi meal without bread; and then she'd be thinking, oh, let's eat sweet and talk sweet, so she'd be looking for things like sesame seeds and cardamoms and rosewater and clarified butter . . ."

As he talked, Everett moved through the market, filling the bags ingredient by ingredient, haggle by haggle, moving out from the subterranean stores into the alleys that opened on to Dalston Lane. Here were the clothing and fabric stalls, the hats and bandanas and scarves for winter, the bolts and bales of print cottons and chiffons and worsteds and taffetas.

"There's one last detail," Everett said, looking up and down the lines of stalls, their owners muffled up in coats and scarves and hats and fingerless gloves, huddling over mugs of tea. "You can't serve a meal for a prince on a table for a beggar, so I'd need to dress the table. But I'd know that everything on an airship has to justify its weight, so I'd be looking for something that's beautiful but light as a feather. Like *that*."

The sari shop was at the Cecilia Road end of Ridley Road Market, where the market's interzone became Hackney Great Port proper. The owner was an elderly, bird-thin Tamil lady. She wore one of her own saris, with a heavy Icelandic-style knitted cardigan over and fleece boots under. She put her hands together in a namaste. Everett returned the greeting.

"Bona," Sen said. The stall owner flicked out sari after sari, the feather-light fabric unfurling like a banner before settling over Everett's arm for him to inspect. Sen picked up a sheer white sari trimmed with gold and held it up against herself. The Tamil woman showed her how to turn and drape and fold and tuck it around herself. Sari-clad, Sen posed and pouted in the full-length mirror. "Bonaroo." Everett decided on a black sari patterned with silver. In the bag it went. The Christmas shopping was complete. Pheasants, kale, spices and ghee, a sari, and basmati rice. There were still fifteen shillings left from Captain Anastasia's purse.

"You're wondering what a Punjabi Christmas dinner has to do with my dad," Everett said. "This is him. This is me. You've never met him, but you might think he was quiet and geeky, and I know you don't think I'm a proper omi, whatever a proper omi is, but my people, well, we just can't help doing the big things, whether it's Christmas dinner, or multiverse physics. And that's why I'm here, in your world. Because I couldn't stay away. Every drop of my blood made me come here."

For once Sen had no smart, slangy answer. She stood chewing her lip, twisting one foot in the discarded orange peel and handbills for a Christmas variety show in the Hackney Empire. She couldn't look at him. Then she hugged Everett in an embrace of grey wool and musk and kissed him hard on the cheek.

"You are a proper omi, Everett Singh. You are so *so*." Sen pushed him away. She had felt Everett tighten against her. "What's with you? Don't you like me?"

"It's the Iddler." Over his days among the peoples of Hackney Great Port Everett had glimpsed the godfather figure sufficient times to recognise him. He didn't doubt that the Iddler, with or without his minders, on his rounds of Hackney Great Port, had glimpsed him and Sen in return. The incident with Sharkey had taken the edge off his aggression—word passed quicker than influenza around the port—and he had lurked and skulked for a time. He did not lurk or skulk now. He was open and bold. It was because of the woman beside him. "He's not alone."

"They're a joke."

"It's not Evans and Van Vliet." Everett had learned the names of Guttural Man and the Dutchman at the same time he learned his enemy's face. "Move!" Sen looked behind her.

"Oh the dear . . ."

Beside the Iddler, tall and magnificent in silver fox fur, high-heeled boots, dove-grey gloves, her lips vampire red in her winter-cold face, was Charlotte Villiers. Nothing could have made the Iddler look more like a squat, hopping toad in a bad suit. At her killer heel were ten uniformed Missionaries. Their helmets looked a joke on Hackney's streets; the riot sticks in their hands did not. Charlotte Villiers strode down Cecilia Street as if no force in the universe could swerve her. People cleared from her path as they would from a tidal wave.

"You're going to tell me to come on," Everett said.

"I am. Come on." Sen darted behind the sari stall and into the archway where the stall owner kept her stock and equipment. Everett, bags of pheasants and Christmas groceries in his hands, was two steps behind her. He saw the Missionaries break into a run. Charlotte Villiers kept the same steady, implacable, heel-clicking pace. Sen led him between metal racks stacked to the arch-top with sweet-smelling cottons and silks. A door at the back led to a corridor, washrooms, a tearoom where chilly-looking women sat looking up at a tiny television with a huge magnifying screen on a swivel arm set high on a wall. They ran along the backs of the other stallholder lock-ups on Sandringham Road. "These all connect," Sen said. "They'll never find us here." She dived through a lock-up full of cones of hairy, dusty, itchy knitting wool and out into the street.

"Piece of piss," Sen crowed. They had come out on the small square where Amhurst Road met Dalston Wharf on the Lea Valley Navigation. Water behind them. More Missionaries between them and Andre Street. At the head of this detachment was Charlotte Villiers's mysterious clone; the more her double in every detail under the low winter sun slanting in across the electrical yards on Amhurst Road. "I hate sharpies!" Sen yelled in defiance. "Okay. Up now."

She must know the location of every fire escape and its release switch in the East End, Everett thought. The staircase swung down from the third-floor gallery of the warehouse that enclosed the three sides of the canal basin. She stopped halfway up the metal stairs.

"What are you carrying them for?" she yelled. "Leave 'em down!"

"I'm not going to get four pheasants for four pounds again," Everett said. He held up the shopping bags. Sen shook her huge mop of bleached curls. They ran on. Two sharpies followed gingerly, the old iron creaking under the weight of grown men. The rest of the squad, led by the man Everett thought of as Charles Villiers, followed at ground level.

"It's a pity you don't have a website called TV Tropes," Everett panted, clanging along in Sen's footsteps.

"Wasting 'is breath on shopping and now palari-ing," Sen said.

"It's about plot devices in stories and movies and comics that get used over and over again. There's one called 'Treed.' It's where the good guys on the run go up onto a roof and then all the bad guys have to do is sit around and wait for them to come down, like a cat up a tree."

Even Sen could see Charlotte Villiers with her Missionaries come round the corner of the warehouse on the far side of the dock. The Iddler was nowhere to be seen. His job was done. He had led the police faithfully; the one person who knew Hackney Great Port as well as Sen. Charlotte Villiers spoke into her fur collar and three sharpies took up position at the other swing-ladder, by the Andre Street end of the wharf.

"Cat up a tree, Mr. TV Tropes? Well, follow this polone." She hopped up onto the railing next to the wall, then scrabbled up over the guttering onto the roof slates. One bag clenched in his teeth, the other slung over his elbow, Everett followed her up. Sen pointed out over the roofscape, squeezed between the railway viaducts of Ridley Road Market, to some scaffolding erected against the side of the canal warehouse. "Come on." It was inevitable, Everett supposed. The scaffolding was a roofer's elevator, a simple platform on a winch. Escape.

"How did you know?" Everett asked.

"Airish always look up. Ground-pounders never do. That's our secret."

The winch creaked loudly. The platform jolted. Sen ran, but the elevator had descended out of reach by the time she reached the scaffolding. She looked down at the Iddler. He winked up at her and tipped his forelock.

"TV Tropes?" Everett said and immediately felt petty and mean. Don't snark and snipe. Think. There is always a way out. Always. Charlotte Villiers and her sharpies arrived at the foot of the scaffold tower.

"Have the good manners to come down," she commanded. "I'm not risking a heel going up to get you."

"How did she know to come to Airish town?" Sen whispered.

"She saw you, remember?" Everett said. "In the Tyrone Tower. The jacket, the leggings, the boots, and my phone. She doesn't need to be a genius to work that out."

"Will you come down, Mr. Singh?" Charlotte Villiers called again.

"Sorry, Everett," Sen whispered. Then Everett heard the noise. He heard it at the precise moment it changed from disorder into order; from dozens, scores, hundreds of Airish leaving their business and going into the street to their feet falling into rhythm and step. People. Marching. The sound echoed from the viaduct walls, rolled around the piers and stone barge basins of Dalston Wharf. Marching.

This was Hackney. This was Airishtown. This was where City and Civil and Customs law ended. This was where people lived by their own laws and justice, harsher and more immediate than the laws of police and courts and excise, but no less effective and no less just. The agreement had been made generations before, when the air-freighters first built a port on the edge of polite London, among the roughs and the toughs and the scofflaws, between the two justice systems. It was a handshake agreement, a gentleman's contract, but strictly and successfully observed for the century that the airships had been arriving over the great bazaar of Hackney. Ridley Road Market was a buffer zone where Londoners and Airish mingled, each observing their own laws and customs. Either side, the border was sharp as broken glass. Charlotte Villiers and her metropolis police had broken the unwritten law, and Hackney was rising to defend itself.

The crowd turned into Canal Place. Even icy Charlotte Villiers was taken aback for a moment. Men stood ten, twenty deep; barrel staves, bottles, cobblestones, pieces of furniture from the Knights of the Air fight in their hands. That fight had not ended properly. It had not been resolved, not the Hackney way. Its energy still hung in the streets like smoke. It clung to the fists of the mob. At their head was 'Appening Ed, a small, squat terrier of a man—a union rep, a barroom lawyer (even if his barroom had been smashed to matchwood by the Bromley/*Everness* brawl), a troublemaker, a man who had to be at the centre of everything. He was the closest thing Hackney Great Port had to a politician. He had anger management issues.

"Stop," Charlotte Villiers said. The mob stopped dead. 'Appening Ed's mouth fell open, such was the tone of command in Charlotte Villiers's voice.

"You don't tell us what to do, polone," 'Appening Ed shouted. "This is Hackney." The mob murmured its agreement.

"Silence," Charlotte Villiers said. And there was silence, by that same absolute authority. She stepped forward to confront 'Appening Ed. "This is a Plenitude affair. Do not interfere."

"Don't care if it's the Dear Almighty's affair, you don't march in here with your sharpies like you own the place. You don't have the jurisdiction."

"I would strongly advise you not to obstruct us in the execution of our operation," Charlotte Villiers said. But all the people heard was the word "execution," and a ripple ran through the crowd that turned into a mutter, into a surge of voices. Fists punched the air, waved cobblestones and clubs in the direction of Charlotte Villiers. A bottle smashed at Charlotte Villiers's feet. She did not flinch. In a flicker of movement, a gun was in her grey-gloved hand. This was not the elegant, decorative piece she had pulled on Everett to try to stop him from jumping through the Heisenberg Gate. This was small and black and alien.

"Oh, now we see the violence in the system," 'Appening Ed said. "Well, polone . . ." He strode toward Charlotte Villiers, a head and a half shorter than her, chin jutting, finger jabbing, bristling fury. "I'm going to take that little toy pop-gun and I'm going to shove it—"

There was a high-pitched whine in Everett's ear, sharp and painful, like a needle up his auditory nerve. He saw a disc of light engulf 'Appening Ed. And he was gone. Vanished.

"Oh the Dear oh the Dear," Sen said. "I didn't think they were real."

"What's real?"

"A jumpgun. Oh the Dear. Oh my God."

Whatever a jumpgun was, the moment of shock passed. The crowd gave a deep, animal roar and surged forward. Charlotte Villiers calmly levelled her weapon.

"I can set the focus as wide as I like," she said. The crowd stopped.

"Where's Ed?" a voice shouted, and another: "Bring him back. Right now, you bitch!"

Charlotte Villiers smiled.

"Even if I wanted to, I couldn't do that. You see, I've absolutely no idea where he is."

Sticks and bottles came arcing from the back of the crowd. Cobbles crashed and rolled around Charlotte Villiers's feet. Bottles exploded like grenades. Nothing touched her. She held a steady aim.

"Leave now. I will shoot. Do you want to see your children, your lovers ever again? Leave us."

"What is that thing?" Everett whispered, up on the catwalk.

"It doesn't kill you. It just sends you away and you can't get back."

Then a bottle spinning through the air broke the standoff. It struck Charlotte Villiers hard on the cheek. She staggered. The crowd cheered, deep in its throat. Charlotte Villiers touched her fingers to her cheek and drew them back red. She stared in amazement at the blood. The police rushed forward, batons raised to charge, and surrounded her. Under a hail of missiles, they withdrew around the corner of the warehouse back on to Andre Street. A few of the younger, bolder Airish gave chase, then remembered the power of Charlotte Villiers's little gun and stopped at the corner to throw stones and jeers after the retreating sharpies.

"Let's get back to *Everness*," Sen said. She didn't wait for the elevator but tracked back across the warehouse roof to the gallery around the canal wharf.

"I still don't know what she did there," Everett called after her. "I still don't know what a jumpgun is."

Sen stopped up on the roofline, silhouettes against the hard winter sky.

"It's a Plenitude weapon. It's supposed to be kind. It doesn't kill you. It just sends you into the same location in a random parallel universe. Biff boff gone. And you don't come back again. That's the story. Some kind of kind, that is. 'Coz it ain't just one of the Nine—sorry, Ten Worlds. It's any of 'em, all them what you got in your comptator, Everett Singh. It could be like, no air, or the middle of the ocean, or all ice, or in a war, or the Dear knows what. But hey, it's not like she actually shot you or anything."

Everett's imagination raced as he followed Sen over the rooftops and dropped down onto the gallery, then down to street level and into the bustle and throng of Hackney Great Port. Charlotte Villiers knew he was here. Through the Iddler she knew exactly what ship at what berth. Her retreat was only temporary. She would be back, cleverer, more powerful. She wouldn't stop. She'd come straight to *Everness* next time and she would come with strength, that no one could humiliate her again. He had to move now. That talk with Captain Anastasia; that would have to be now. The Iddler, the Bromleys, now Charlotte Villiers and her secret organisation. Everyone was after Anastasia Sixsmyth. He had to tell her she would never be safe in Hackney Great Port again. Berlin: he'd overheard her talking with Sen about how much she loved Berlin, the fun they had there. Get out to Berlin. Even Berlin might not be far enough. Soon, very soon, sooner than he had planned, he had to get Tejendra, get to the gate, get Laura and Victory-Rose, and get out of the Plenitude altogether. Get somewhere they could never find and could never follow, like being hit with a jumpgun. Except that it wouldn't be random. It would be carefully picked, oh so carefully. The jumpgun. What kind of insane weapon was that? E3's jump technology was advanced, but this was a handgun-sized Heisenberg Gate, one you could slip into a pocket or a clutch-bag. This came from somewhere else. Was it purely random, or could it be programmed? What if he connected it to the Infundibulum? A gun that could shoot you anywhere in the Panoply? Mad stuff. Mad ideas. Think about Captain Anastasia. You're about to tell her that her world is over. How are you going to do that? Everett stopped in the middle of the street. His elbows and shoulders ached. What, why? He had been so tied up in plans and strategies and possibilities that he'd forgotten he was still carrying the shopping bags. Groceries for a Christmas dinner no one would ever eat. But if he dumped them, Captain Anastasia would ask questions before he had time to prepare convincing answers. She might never get the pheasant makhani, but she might like the sari.

24

Everett was at the sink, drying coffee mugs (no two of them matched, every one of them was chipped) when he felt the change. It was small, an almost imperceptible disturbance that didn't even throw him off balance or send much more than a ripple across the dish-washing water, but in the pit of his stomach Everett knew he was no longer connected to the ground. He went to the porthole. The slates and glass skylights of the warehouses were sliding beneath him. The service arm that had bound *Everness* to the docking hub swung in to the side of the gantry, dripping ballast water from the pipes. Sparks crackled around the electricity charge port. A dockhand in an orange high-viz, a leather helmet, and goggles spoke into a walkie-talkie and raised a hand in farewell as Everett drifted over him. Engine pods swivelled on their mountings. *Everness* turned as she lifted. She drifted over the back of *Leonora Christine*, gaining height all the time. As the airship spun around her axis, Hackney Great Port played in panorama across the galley's small, half-steamed-up porthole. From above, moored four to a docking hub, the airships looked like petals, Hackney Great Port a field of titanic flowers. Railway lines ran like silver veins on their viaducts and elevated tracks. The roofs went on forever; here was a glinting thread of canal, there the connecting weave of power lines. Now the great, monolithic mass of Haggerstown passed in front of his view. Higher now and the towers of London came into view, from the corporate blocks of the city, shouldering like thugs up to St. Paul's, bullying it with their cast of gods and angels and gargoyles, down the length of Fleet Street to the Strand and the river front to the government palaces at Whitehall. Highest of all, so slim and improbable it looked like a cut-scene from a Japanese RPG, was the spire of Sadler's Wells Skyport, heavy with docked airships. To the west were the clustered skyscrapers of Bloomsbury. Everett picked out the jagged spike of the Tyrone Tower. Exhilaration turned to horror.

"You can't lift now!" Everett yelled in the small wooden coffin of the galley. "You can't go now! I have to . . . Go back go back go back!" He banged his fists against the hull. The nanocarbon weave took his blows and did not even give back as *Everness* continued to ascend, smooth and stately, as if being airborne were the most natural thing in the world. Now he could see the reservoirs and marshes sparkling with frost, the loop of the river at Greenwich and the long run down to the sea. The engine pods swivelled into horizontal flight. But Sharkey had said he was a day from completing loading. This was an unscheduled lift. Everett burst from the galley onto the curving forward catwalk, took the spiral staircase up to the control level two steps at a time. The bridge door was open. Every screen was alive, every monitor glowing, green displays flickering through the magnifier screens. Sharkey glanced up from his station at the radio deck at the sound of Everett's approach. Sen stood at the helm, a control lever under each hand. Captain Anastasia stood at the great curved window, hands clasped behind her back, Hackney Marshes and the great silver bow of the Thames at Woolwich at her feet.

"What is this, where are we going? You can't go, not now," Everett shouted.

Captain Anastasia did not turn, did not even move a muscle to acknowledge the interruption.

"Mr. Sharkey," she said in an even, low, utterly dangerous voice. "Escort Mr. Singh to the galley. If he displeases you in any way, confine him there for the duration of the flight. Mr. Singh, I allow nothing on my bridge that I do not believe to be beautiful or know to be useful. Your unseemly language has failed you in the first part: I'm giving you a chance to comply in the second. Hot chocolate. On this bridge, quick smart."

"What's going on? I've never heard her like this," Everett said as Sharkey planted a hand firmly in his back and steered him off the bridge. The weighmaster did not reply until out of earshot, and then in a low voice: "'Beware of him, and obey his voice, provoke him not; for he will not pardon your transgressions.' Oh, I heard her like that. Not often, and always memorably, but I heard her, and I seen her." Sharkey opened the galley door for Everett and closed the two of them in the tiny cabin. "You better make the best damn hot chocolate in your life, sir. And I'll take one as well."

Everett melted chocolate, whipped in cream until it was thick and glorious, dripped in chilli-warmed sugar syrup. *Everness* was climbing steadily over the great docks at Silverton, a geometric waterland of wharves and basins and locks.

"So why are we flying? Where are we going?"

Sharkey sucked in his lower lip. "To Goodwin, sir. The Goodwin Sands. 'Why, yet it lives there uncheck'd that Antonio hath a ship of rich lading wrecked on the narrow seas; the Goodwins, I think they call the place; a very dangerous flat and fatal, where the carcasses of many a tall ship lie buried . . .'"

"Is that from the Bible?"

"No, Shakespeare. *The Merchant of Venice.* I know Shakespeare too, and Milton, and *Moby Dick*, but I generally stay away from them. Psychos and freaks and sociopaths quote Shakespeare. The Goodwin Sands, six miles off the coast of Kent. And it's as true for many an airship as for Duke Antonio's trading ships. They say you can see their ribs and spars, their spines and skeletons, sticking out of the sand at low water. And that's where we're going, friend. Amongst all those things Miss Sen been teaching you about the Airish way of life, did she ever mention the word *kris*?"

"I've heard of amriya." Everett poured Sharkey a tiny cup of thick, sweet, chilli-warm chocolate. Sharkey took a sip and closed his eyes in pleasure.

"That sir, is God's own chocolate. Kris, well you are partly correct; in some ways it's like an amriya, in that it can't be refused. Not with honour. A kris is a challenge to a duel. A duel of airships. No one's called kris in a generation, but Ma Bromley, the evil old bitch, she prides herself that she's the heart and soul of Hackney Great Port, the only one who remembers the old ways. She remembered that one well enough. She served the challenge right proper and pretty, all properly served by the youngest son. Master Kyle Bromley. Master Prettyface Kyle. Called out Anastasia's names three times, and the scroll all neatly tied with three red ribbons and all properly worded in the most formal and correct language. 'For the many insults, injuries, and affronts that I have endured from the hearts and hands and lips of the master and commander of *Everness*, I call and conjure Captain Anastasia Sixsmyth in kris: that it is meet, right and her bounden duty to offer satisfaction to the Master and Commander of the *Arthur P* in aerial combat, me and mine, thee and thine, thither and yon, ship to ship and hand to hand and heart to soul, in the time-honoured place at 3 o'clock this avvo. And if she sheweth herself not, then let her skin be pierced with many barbs and her gas deflated, her spine broken and her engines bent, and let her name be shamed and dishonoured, so that all flee from her very shadow, down all the generations.' Good mouth-filling stuff, and apparently correct in every detail. She's thorough, is Ma Bromley. If only her sons had inherited her spunk."

"When did this happen?"

"While you were out buying in our Christmas comestibles. Kyle Bromley in person, the little bastard, with a big grin all over his face. He can count himself lucky he still has a face, after the drubbing Mchynlyth and I gave his siblings. Of course, that does make me partly to blame. . . . 'For the many insults, injuries, and affronts . . .' You thought you saw the captain angry with you when you sassed her up on the bridge there—foolish, sir, foolish. You should have seen her when that snivelling little piss-drip handed her the challenge. Him, marry Captain Anastasia?"

"Duelling airships," Everett said, carefully pouring Captain Anastasia's cup of chocolate and wiping away a drip from the rim with a piece of kitchen paper.

"The rules are pretty simple. The victor either tows the defeated party back to port, or they lie broken and smashed on the Sands of Goodwin. How we work that is entirely up to us." Sharkey drank down the remainder of his chocolate. "Let's get back to Annie. She's going to need all hands, even yours, Mr. Singh."

Captain Anastasia was still standing by the window when Everett reentered the bridge, more discreetly this time. Once again she did not acknowledge him but put out her hand. Everett gave her the mug of hot chocolate and stepped back. Captain Anastasia took a sip. Everett heard her intake of breath.

"In your world, Mr. Singh, do you have anything to compare with this?"

Everness followed the line of the Thames, gliding over the frozen fields of Thamesmead and Erith, now coming up on the bright, silvery gap the river cut at Dartford in the wall of power plants and chimney stacks. Beyond it the river broadened to the sun-shimmer of the estuary. Airships flew lower and slower than aeroplanes; cruising height was a thousand metres. Everett tried to work out the speed from the gentle processing of fields and roads and villages under his feet. One hundred and fifty, two hundred kilometres per hour? He gave up. The slow stately flight was hypnotic. Aeroplanes lifted you too high; you couldn't read the details, you were disconnected from the earth. From *Everness*'s bridge Everett could see trains dashing along their lines, rails flashing as they caught the low sun. Cars and vans wound through the narrow village streets. Smoke rose from house chimneys; straight as a pencil line in the still air. A great steam-powered tractor puffed across a field; seagulls followed the plough as it turned the hard earth for early wheat. And *quiet*. So quiet: the electric impeller engines made almost no noise. He could hear the clack and clatter of a train, the cries of the gulls, the tolling of an iron church bell. This was how you flew when you dreamed of flying, when you just lifted your arms and because it was a dream, you lifted from the ground. Light as air.

"No, ma'am," Everett said. "Nothing like this."

Everett thought Captain Anastasia might have smiled.

"Miss Sixsmyth!"

"Ma'am," Sen called from her piloting station.

"Maintain heading. Standard altitude for crossing the Smoke Ring." To Everett, Captain Anastasia added, "Bad air, Mr. Singh."

"Standard six thousand feet, ma'am." Sen pulled back on the altitude control levers. The ground dropped away without any physical sensation of tilt or movement. *Everness* approached the great wall of chimneys and cooling towers. From this greater height Everett could see the curve; not a line across the world, but a wall. *Shutting in or shutting out?* he wondered. Sen took the ship through the layer of orange smog where the individual plumes from the smokestacks mingled and merged and exchanged chemicals. *Everness* trembled in the eddies of smoke and hot air from the cooling towers. Captain Anastasia's cup rattled on its saucer. She took another sip, daring Everett to reach for a handhold to steady himself. He looked down into the mouths of the chimneys, the gaping black maws of the cooling towers. *Everness* shook again; then they were over the Smoke Ring.

"Bona air, Mr. Singh," Captain Anastasia said.

"I have *Arthur P* on camera ten," Sharkey said.

"Screen six, if you please, Mr. Sharkey." A monitor hanging on a pivot arm above the window flickered to display a view out over *Everness*'s tail fin. A big airship was approaching head-on, flat and menacing as a shark. The crest on its brow was a dragon coiled around a crowned orb.

"She's gaining on us," Sharkey said. "Ground speed one eight five."

"Match velocity, Miss Sixsmyth. *Everness* will not be seen dawdling like a sow to market. Inform me of any changes in *Arthur P*'s speed, Mr. Sharkey."

"Aye, ma'am."

Sen turned to the throttles and gently pushed them forward until the readings on her green magnifier screens matched.

"Nineteen minutes to destination," she said. This was a Sen Everett had never seen before. Her focus and concentration were total. No flip answers, no casual palari, no look-at-me grandstanding. Everett had never quite believed her when she said she was *Everness*'s pilot—she was a natural exaggerator—but she was, and she was magnificent. She controlled *Everness* with every part of her being. They were over Kent now. To the left were the Isle of Sheppey and the wide expanse of the Medway and Thames estuaries, grey and dismal as cold iron. To the right and forward, Everett thought he could see the cross-shaped plan of Canterbury Cathedral; towers throwing long winter shadows across the rooftops. Dead ahead a line of cloud, dark and yellow-tinged as a bruise, ran from horizon to horizon. "What do you make of that, Mr. Singh?"

"I'd say it's a weather front, ma'am. Coming from the east, at this time of year, it could be snow."

"I would concur, Mr. Singh. Mr. Sharkey, weather report. Unlike your air-o-planes, Mr. Singh, we can't fly over the weather. We fly with it. A good captain can use the winds, and the pressure gradients, and the thermals, and the down-draughts, to her advantage."

"South Sandettie automatic weather station as of fourteen hundred hours," Sharkey said, one hand cupped to his headphone like a DJ. "Winds east-nor'east backing nor-nor'east, thirty knots, snow, visibility one hundred metres, pressure 105 millibars and falling."

"Excellent!" Captain Anastasia announced, rubbing her hands. "Maintain heading and velocity, Miss Sixsmyth. Take us down to standard cruise."

Everett stepped up to the window. He put his hands on the glass. Here, like a figurehead on the prow of a sailing ship, he could imagine he was flying free, borne up by winds and pressure, driven into the heart of the storm whirling in from the coast of the Low

Countries. They were coming up on the coast now; another horizon line. Flakes of snow whirled and smashed to cold grains of ice on the sloping window. Everett shivered; the cold was reaching into *Everness.*

"Our rival, Mr. Sharkey?"

"Maintaining speed and heading."

"Take us down to two hundred, Miss Sixsmyth. Engage autopilot."

Everness crossed over seaside Deal, its sea-front promenade and antique pier twinkling with wind-whipped fairy-lights. Everett saw dog-walkers look up as the huge dark mass of the airship passed silently over their heads. The size of a skyscraper, but light as air. And away, out over a greying, wind-whipped sea. The sun was gone. Grey above, grey beneath, grey flecked with swirling white snowflakes ahead. The snowstorm, curled, coiled, waited, then broke over *Everness* in a howl of whipping sleet. *Everness* quivered but drove on, deeper into the blizzard.

Captain Anastasia raised a beckoning finger. "Sen, Mr. Singh. It's important you see this and pray the Dear that you never see it again." Sen locked on autopilot and joined Everett and her mother looking out into the featureless, fractured grey of a blizzard at sea. Snow was building up in the corners of the window panels. Everett could feel the cold beyond the glass. He saw a lighter grey on the deep grey; a place where the waves were breaking white. There were shoals beneath the surface. The shallows was tinged green; Everett could map the shifting contours of the sandbanks. Here was a more regular pattern, the water flowing around a line of ribs that looked like the skeleton of a fish, buried like a dinosaur fossil in the sand. The whirling snow, the grey-on-grey, the white-flecked waves made it difficult to judge scale; then the wind eddied the snow away for an instant and Everett saw that it was huge, a hundred metres long. It was the skeleton of a long-dead airship, swallowed by the shifting sands. A second ship-skeleton drew a pattern in the sand, a third crossed it, ahead lay a fourth, a fifth; more obvious as the water grew more shallow and sandbars rose out of the sea. Tangles of ribs and spars, some broken like a snapped spine, some reaching up out of the sand like the fingers of a drowned airshipman, the running tide water foaming around them, scraps and rags of ship-skin fluttering in the snow-laden wind. Now the sands were exposed and gulls rose up and fled from *Everness*'s shadow, crying in their dead-soul voices. Dozens of airships had died here and been dragged down into the ever-moving sands. This was their graveyard.

"The Goodwin Sands," Captain Anastasia said. "The duelling ground of the Airish. Sen, the cards." Sen took the Everness tarot from the place next to her heart. Captain Anastasia shuffled the cards, then cut them one-handed, three times. She returned the deck to Sen. Sen's pale face was blank, her eyes dead as the dead ships down in the swallowing sand, as she laid out five cards in a cross on her command post and turned them, one by one.

The top card of the cross: A child in a seashell drawn by turtles. The child looked out of the card, beaming sunnily, oblivious to the lightning storm crackling in the background of the card. "The Cockle-child," Sen said. "Innocence under threat. Ignorance ain't bliss. Big peril."

Everyone on the bridge had gathered around Sen's station.

The bottom card of the cross: Two swans with crowns around their necks. The crowns were joined by chains. "Swannhilde and Swannhamme," Sen said. "A lifelong partnership or union of some kind. It could be broken. Swans mate for life. If one dies, the other dies not long after."

The left side of the cross: An old, bearded man, sitting with his knees drawn up to his chest, staring out of the card with wide eyes. Snow was piled up around him, to his neck. "The Winter Watcher," Sen said. "Cold. Hunger. Want. Will spring ever come? If it's November or February: death of an old person. They're the killing months."

Now she turned over the card on the right side of the cross. A man in eighteenth-century hat and breeches set out along a path that wound into the depths of the card, leaning on his staff, face serious with intent. Everett again wondered how Sen had come by these cards, who had taught her their names and interpretations, who had put them together. "The Traveller Hasteth in the Evening," Sen said. "The time is short and the hills is dark and I's got miles to go before I sleeps. It is no easy road."

Sen flipped up the corner of the final card, the card at the centre of the cross. She put it down again. Captain Anastasia reached out and boldly turned it faceup. The sun and its planets, in the jaws of an all-devouring wolf. "Season of the Wolf," Sen said. "The lowest throw of the dice. The bad guys win. The sun is eaten. The world is given for a season to the forces of darkness, and there is no light."

"So be it," Captain Anastasia said. "We make our own luck here. To your posts. We've work to do. Mr. Sharkey, our enemy?"

"Nothing on the cameras, ma'am. Then again, we can't even see our own tail in this weather. The radar's throwing up all kinds of spooks and false readings."

Captain Anastasia held up her hand. There was silence on the bridge. She held herself completely still. Everett held his breath. Slowly, slow as a glacier, Captain Anastasia turned to her left. Her eyes went wide. "Sen! Hard to starboard!"

Sen threw the wheel over as something huge, world-crushing, all-devouring loomed out of the storming snow. The wolf, Everett immediately thought. The wolf that ate the sun. No: worse. An airship, coming straight towards them at ramming speed.

"Take us to the floor," Captain Anastasia shouted. Sen pushed the levers to the end of their travel. "Brace!" Everett reeled into the window as *Everness* wheeled and dived. The whole of *Everness*'s two hundred metres shuddered as *Arthur P* grazed along her left flank. For an instant Everett imagined the whole structure coming apart, the lift cells breaking free and fleeing into the upper atmosphere, the skin unwinding like orange peels, the nose splitting off and spilling him towards the snow and the sea and the impaling ribs of the dead airships below. Then Sen brought them out of it into clear air. *It's as if she heard*, Everett thought, watching Captain Anastasia pull out the intercom. *Something in the air, some vibration, some pressure shift she felt through the skin. She heard them coming. If she hadn't . . .*

"Mr. Mchynlyth, damage report."

The engineer's voice came through a shriek of wind from down in the belly of the airship.

"Bassards took out number three and five impeller pods!"

"How long until we get full power back?" Captain Anastasia asked.

"Captain, I canna get full power where there's no engine. . . ."

"I have it on camera," Sharkey said.

"On my screens please."

The pictures were grainy and snow-smeared, but Everett could see the snapped spars, the spray of sparks from the severed power lines, the violation of the purity of *Everness*'s sleek lines. It felt like he had lost a finger for each engine. Captain Anastasia's face was grim. Her ship had survived, but she had been hit hard.

"Sen, shut down numbers four and six impellers. I'll not have her shake herself to bits. And bring us up. It's death down there. Mr. Sharkey, I want whatever sense you can make from the radar. I want to know where *Arthur P* is."

"There's nothing on the radar. It's like she's disappeared."

"Airships do not disappear, Mr. Sharkey."

"I'm getting nothing but snow and seagulls out there."

"On my screen." Captain Anastasia slid zoom lenses over the magnifier screen, looking deeper and deeper into the video snow that speckled the screen. *Arthur P* had come out of nothing, sideswiped *Everness*, and vanished into nothing again. Two hundred metres of cargo airship. Impossible. Irrational. This was a ghostly place, but there was nothing supernatural at work here. As goalkeeper for Team Red Everett had enjoyed a reputation of being spooky, superpowered, a Jedi. It was cool to be a goalkeeping ninja, but that was magical thinking. All he did was look at all the possibilities, the probabilities, look in three and more dimensions.

"Maybe it's not *out* there," Everett said. "Maybe it's *up* there."

Capitan Anastasia's eyes went wider than Everett had ever seen. "Mr. Sharkey, vertical scan."

The radar pinged, sending its beam down and up rather than forward and aft. At once Captain Anastasia's monitor showed the great shadow of *Arthur P*, directly overhead. Directly overhead, and descending fast. She meant to crush *Everness*, drive her down onto the spines and spikes of the wrecks beneath.

"Ahead full!" Captain Anastasia yelled. Sen rammed the drive levers forward. *Everness* moved, but she was big, and cumbersome, and slow slow slow with half her engines out of commission. Everett watched the shadow of *Arthur P* loom to fill the radar screen. Thirty metres. Acceleration in a machine the size of *Everness* was feeble. Twenty metres. So much inertia to overcome. Ten metres. Everett could feel the vibration of the straining impellers through the hull all the way into his molars. "Come on," he whispered. "Come on come on come on." Clear. Almost clear. A shock ran the length of the ship. *Everness* groaned in every spar, every nanocarbon fibre. The floor began to tilt. *Arthur P* had *Everness* by the rudder and was pushing her tail down, prow up. The empty chocolate cup rolled across the bridge and fetched up against the bulkhead. Everett grabbed for a stanchion.

"Hang on, It's bringing her nose up," Sen shouted, pulling back the attitude yoke. "I hope you strapped that cargo down, Sharkey." The impellers screamed again. *Everness* pitched up more steeply. The magnifying lenses swung free from their monitors. Mchynlyth's voice rattled on the intercom.

"That wee girl is killing my ship!"

Sen held the yoke, teeth gritted. Then *Everness*'s tail swung out from underneath *Arthur P* and she drove into clear air.

"Bring us round, onto *Arthur P*," Captain Anastasia ordered. "Hold station, fifty metres off her bow."

"Yes, ma'am."

"Mchynlyth!"

"We're still airborne, the Dear alone knows how. It'll take me a wee while to get back to have a look at steering."

"No need, Mr. Mchynlyth."

Sen swung *Everness* round, bringing her to bear head-on to *Arthur P*, levelling out from its crash-descent. Captain Anastasia went to the glass window, leaned against it, peering into the grey-scape.

"Kyle Bromley could never handle a ship like that," she said. "That's Dona Bromley herself on the quarterdeck. And she means to wreck us, leave our bones for the gulls and the squid and the cold Goodwin sands. If she cannot have *Everness*, no one will." Captain Anastasia pulled down the intercom again. "Can we fight, Mr. Mchynlyth?"

"Are you lallygagging? I doubt we can even keep aloft."

"I'll take that as a no. Well, you've fooled me once and you've fooled me twice but you won't fool Anastasia Sixsmyth again. Mr. Sharkey, hail *Arthur P*. Dona Bromley is not the only one knows the old ways."

Sen held station in front of *Arthur P*, moving *Everness* backwards in perfect synchronisation with its enemy's advance. Everett looked out at the heraldic crest on the prow, the strip of window beneath it, half-seen through the snow.

"*Everness*, this is *Arthur P*," said a woman's voice, harsh and crackling.

"Dona Bromley," Captain Anastasia said. "You fly bona."

"Captain Sixsmyth. I wish I could return the flattery, but, oh dear; your reputation greatly exceeds your ability. Perhaps not the wife I'd hoped for Kyle," Ma Bromley said. Everett saw Sharkey's jaw tighten, his lips twitch with anger. "As well then that I plan to drive you down in the dirt where you belong."

"I call on you, Dona Bromley," Captain Anastasia said calmly. "I call upon you and all here present, that you shall at this time and in this place, meet me in single combat."

Sharkey was on his feet. Sen's face was paler than her usual white. Everett heard himself gasp. He'd never thought people did that, gasp with amazement. Captain Anastasia raised a hand to silence her crew.

"Kris is old, but the right of single satisfaction is older. And I believe that once called, it can't be refused. Am I right, Dona Bromley?" There was a long static-filled silence. Everett thought he saw silhouettes move against the cabin light in the other airship. "Either you or your nominated champion. As I ain't in the habit of fighting old ladies, I'll accept your son in your stead." Captain Anastasia took her thumb off the transmit button.

"They'll kill you!" Sharkey shouted.

"I was taught La Savate by the legendary Maitre Gastineau of Marseilles," Captain Anastasia said.

"That's not gonna . . . I mean, Kyle Bromley . . . he's . . . he's . . ."

"A man?"

"Yes."

"As opposed to me, a woman."

"Polones shouldn't fight omis."

"I've always had a problem with that little word, 'shouldn't.' Ugly, snivelling little word." Captain Anastasia pressed down the talk button. "Have I an answer, Dona Bromley?"

"You know fine well we can't refuse you," Ma Bromley said, and Everett could hear the bile and loathing in her voice. She's got you, he thought. She's played you at Queen of Hackney Great Port, the heart and soul of the old ways, and trumped your old tradition with an older one. She's beaten you. But what exactly has she won?

"We'll meet aboard your ship in five minutes," Captain Anastasia said. "Then I shall have satisfaction." She signalled to Sharkey to cut the transmission.

"Of course, you're right. I can't win and they won't fight clean. Mr. Sharkey, Mr. Mchynlyth, did you get that?"

"Yer insane, woman," came the voice from down in the belly of the airship. "But I'm with ye."

"You fought what you thought was a fight for my honour once. I didn't need it then, but I need it now. I need all the fight you have, gentlemen. I'm there to buy time. You're there to do the maximum amount of damage you can to *Arthur P*. And I'd imagine you can do a lot. Mr. Singh!" Everett started. He had been half-hypnotised by the play of snow across *Arthur P*'s nose. "I need every able body. Sen, I'll need you to fly the ship. Mr. Singh, you're on the crew manifest; you fight for the ship. Mr. Mchynlyth will equip you. You feeling handy, omi?"

25

Two airships faced each other across ten metres of airspace, holding themselves in the chaotic heart of the snowstorm with delicate touches of their impellers. Ten metres, kissing distance. The docking gantries had been run out. Mchynlyth and *Arthur P*'s engineer were at work in the swirling clouds of snow, locking them together. From the out-port bay Everett thought the long, spindly bridges looked as crazy as butterfly tongues. Mchynlyth came scampering back into the bay. He gave Captain Anastasia a thumbs-up. Captain Anastasia turned up the collar of her coat. She picked up the intercom.

"Miss Sixsmyth, you have the con. *Everness* is yours."

"Yes, ma'am. Ma . . ." Everett thought he heard tears in Sen's voice. It could have been the intercom, the howling of the wind drawing notes from the stanchions and beams, piling snow against the bulkheads. Captain Anastasia quickly cut the connection.

"Gentlemen, raise hell itself."

Then she turned and strode out along the slender air bridge, high over the clashing waves of Goodwin. Her coattails billowed behind her. Then the snow swept in and Everett could see her no more. An amber light lit on a panel by the hatch. Mchynlyth thumbed a switch and retracted the air bridge.

"Clear." Mchynlyth swung the bay door to and dogged it shut.

"Hold on," Sen announced on the public address system. "This could get bouncy." Everett lurched towards the exit hatch as *Everness* kicked back and away from *Arthur P*. Sharkey and Mchynlyth were already halfway down the spiral staircase to the cargo deck. Everett reeled against the handrail as Sen spun the ship with what remained of its engines and steering. The cargo deck loomed; then Everett pushed himself back from the drop. Sharkey and Mchynlyth were already pounding across the cargo deck. Captain Anastasia had reckoned she could extend the formalities to five minutes at the most. Sen had that long to get *Everness* into position to drop a raiding party. Everett reeled again. The deck tilted. If he lost his footing he could roll the entire length of *Everness* to smash into the rudder mechanisms in the tail. The ship shivered. Sen had opened up the other two starboard side engines, trading vibration damage for speed. Everett smelled the ozone-y burn of straining electrical systems beneath his feet. He went in four different directions as he crossed the last dozen metres to the cargo hatch. Sharkey had already armed himself. Mchynlyth handed Everett a dozen cable ties and what looked like a pistol with a blunderbuss bell-shaped muzzle with a plush-toy stuffed in it.

"This is a thumper. You've been on the end of one of these," Mchynlyth said. "Hurts like buggery, don't it, but it don't put holes in the engineering. Nonlethal." With his gun he pushed aside the tails of Sharkey's coat. Shotgun handles gleamed. Mchynlyth tutted. "Oh, and one of these." He handed Everett an ornately curved plastic handle. A skin-ripper. "You got to get in to get out. Up to cut, down to bond." Mchynlyth flicked open a walkie-talkie. "We're ready and raring down here."

"Give me a code word so I knows it's youse for pickup, " Sen said. Sharkey and Mchynlyth looked at each other.

"Tottenham Hotspur," Everett suggested.

"I'm over *Arthur P*," Sen said.

"Hold on to your arses," Mchynlyth said, and pressed the control button. Winches whined. The solid deck beneath Everett's feet lurched. A crack opened. Icy air blasted in. The crack widened into open air, into naked sky. The blizzard screamed and shrieked around the descending cargo platform, setting it rocking on its winch cables. Beneath lay the snow-covered upper hull of *Arthur P*.

"'And I will strike down upon thee with great vengeance and

furious anger those who attempt to poison and destroy my brothers,'" Sharkey said as he descended through the whipping snow. "'And you will know I am the Lord when I lay my vengeance upon you.'"

"I know that one," Everett said. "*Pulp Fiction*. It's a movie in my world. Samuel L. Jackson says it just before he kills someone."

Sharkey grinned. With the wind streaming his hair out behind him and the light in his eye, Everett could believe every dark tale told of him.

"Thirty seconds," Mchynlyth said into the walkie-talkie. Everett wrapped an arm around a cable. *Arthur P* was so huge its hull dwindled into snow-blind invisibility forward and aft. The upper hull was wide and gently curving, but snow compacting to ice made it dangerous. Miss a footing here and you'd toboggan screaming all the way down to the sea below. The lift jolted against *Arthur P*'s skin. "The omis have landed," Mchynlyth said. "Everett, follow me and try not to get thumped."

Mchynlyth loped down the hull, bent low against the wind. Everett glanced over his shoulder to see the cargo pallet retract and *Everness* lift and turn away and vanish into the grey.

"Yah!" Mchynlyth flicked out his skin-ripper, stabbed it deep into Arthur P's skin and quickly cut a square. He peeled it back and peered inside. "Aye. She'll do. It's only a wee drop down." And he was gone. A hundred metres up-hull, Sharkey cut his own entry and dropped down into *Arthur P*'s interior. For a moment Everett was alone on top of the airship. Then he grasped the edge of the hole, lowered himself into the gloom, and dropped. He hit the upper catwalk hard, let his knees fold and rolled like he'd been taught in judo class. Mchynlyth beckoned him. They ran at a low crouch to the central staircase between the huge spheres of the lift cells, then sneaked down the spiral staircase to the central crosswalk. Everett felt something under his foot. The brass plate that marked the centre of gravity, the heart of *Arthur P*. Mchynlyth pointed down over the railing. A tiny figure in hi-viz orange patrolled the cargo deck. Everett produced his thumper.

"Too far," Mchynlyth whispered. "They're on a wee string, so you can get them back after. Economical. Here." He pulled over a couple of drop lines. Everett looped wrist and foot into the straps.

"What do you think the captain's doing?" Everett whispered.

"Fighting," Mchynlyth said. "That French kickboxing yoke's mighty fancy, but I wouldn't count on it to save you on a Saturday night on Argyll Street. Now, I don't have the controls for these, so it's a free drop. They're on an inertia reel, so it'll not be too bad. On one. Two. Three."

They leaped over the rail. Everett felt a moment of freefall; then the inertia reel caught the line and lowered him through *Arthur P*'s cavernous interior. He braced for impact and landed soft and sure as a cat. In two steps he was in cover among the containers. Mchynlyth was concealed behind the opposite container. He gestured for Everett to move. They closed up on the crewman, one container at a time.

Cover me, Mchynlyth mouthed, and moved into thumper range behind the crewman.

Two gunshots rang out from the forward section of the hull. They echoed from *Arthur P*'s spars and struts. The crewman looked around, startled. He saw Mchynlyth and shot in the same breath. The thumper bag hit Mchynlyth in the stomach and knocked him flying into the side of a container. The crewman stepped forward to immobilize his victim. Everett stepped out of cover, aimed the blunderbuss muzzle at him, and pulled the trigger. The bag took him in the face. He went straight down. Everett darted in and swiftly cuffed him to a railing with cable ties. He went to Mchynlyth, who lay winded against the container.

"You okay?"

"No, I am not sodding okay." He tried to sit up and bared his teeth in pain. "Ah the Dear ah the wee man. My ribs . . . Look, Everett, Sharkey's shooting the place up like he's refighting the

Battle of Bull Run. You need to do it, man. Take her down. Bugger the *Arthur P*."

"How do I do that? I don't know what to do. . . ." And as Everett was looking around at the batteries beneath him, the cargo containers around him, the catwalks and the gas cells above him, he did know. It all began with the forklift truck. Everett had watched Sharkey during the loading of Everness and knew how to hit the latches to unlock *Arthur P*'s containers from the deck. Now, the forklift. It was easy to start; it was never designed to work anywhere but on ship so there was no security to unlock. It was easy and fun to drive. Everett backed up to get a good long run.

"What the sweet suffering are you at, wee lad?" Mchynlyth shouted, struggling to his feet.

Everett rammed a container. It shifted a few centimetres. He backed up and rammed it again. A few centimetres more. Again, and again, and again; each time, a few centimetres. A few centimetres was all he needed. A few centimetres would kick it off. Physics would do the rest. The *Arthur P* deckhand had recovered, and he lunged at Everett on the forklift. The cable tie snapped him up short. He reached for a walkie-talkie. Mchynlyth trained his thumper on him.

"Now, behave."

But Everett was done down on the cargo deck. He hooked on to a drop line and jerked, triggering the inertia reel. High above in the roof of *Arthur P*, smart-metal springs flipped to an alternative shape. Everett was snatched into the air. He hurtled up past the central spine. He heard Mchynlyth's call from far below among the unsecured containers.

"This had better be pretty damn brilliant, Mr. Singh."

Timing. Goalkeeper timing. Everett jumped from the line as it whisked him past the upper catwalk and dropped onto the carbon mesh as neatly as if he'd just scooped in an in-swinger bound for the top right corner of the net. Net. It was all about nets. Nets and containers, and that tiny brass medal at the centre of gravity.

More shots, flat and fast and closer to where he had left Mchynlyth now. He should have taken the walkie-talkie. No time for that. Look. Work it out. Think in three and more dimensions. See. There. The third gas cell up from the CoG. Everett climbed up on the railing, jumped, and grabbed two handfuls of containment netting. He wrapped his left arm through the weave and freed the skin-ripper. Up to cut. Carbon nanofibre was carbon nanofibre, whether it was ship skin or gas-cell netting. He slid up the switch and in one move cut a metre-long gash in the netting. The gas cell, as huge to him as if he were a fly on a football, creaked and shifted. Everett crab-walked across the net and cut another gash behind him. Again he scrambled across the netting, again he cut, again and again. The gas cell strained against the weakness in the netting. Cut and cut again. The cell bulged from the split. A few more cuts . . . The nanofibre netting was tough, but the pressure the gas cell exerted was enormous. The net tore with a sound like multiple gunshots. Everett clung for life as the torn net, with him on it, peeled away from the cell. He hung from the shredded net thirty metres over the cargo deck. The gas cell forced itself out of its confinement and found a new position squeezed into the gap between the two forward cells. It was a movement of a few metres, but it was enough. The centre of gravity shifted. *Arthur P* went prow up. It was only a degree or two, but it was enough to set Everett's carefully positioned cargo container sliding. It slid into the next container down, one Everett had unlatched from the cargo deck locks, started it sliding. Container struck container. From his web high above, Everett watched the slow avalanche of cargo containers. The deckhand, lashed to a railing, gaped in amazement as containers slid past him. The farther they slid, the more *Arthur P*'s nose pitched up as she became more and more unbalanced.

Everett felt the netting lurch. He clung tighter. Then, slowly, jerkily, he began to move upwards. He looked up. Mchynlyth was on the upper catwalk, hauling in the torn netting. His smile was huge and shining.

"Yah wee stoater!" he shouted. "Yah wee stoater!"

Everett presumed that was a good thing. Mchynlyth hauled him up to where he could grasp the railing and clamber onto the catwalk. The world sloped.

"How are the ribs?" Everett asked.

"I'll live."

"Next two?" Everett said. Mchynlyth nodded breathlessly, and produced his skin-ripper. He slid the switch up. "You go right; I'll go left." Everett crawled under the free gas cell—it had wedged itself across the catwalk—and climbed up the netting of the next cell forward two-handed, the skin-ripper in his teeth. He glanced across to see Mchynlyth plunge his skin-ripper into the net and slide down the outside of the gas cell, leaving a long gash behind him. *Arthur P* groaned as the net snapped and the gas cell burst free. Everett's followed. The huge airship lurched. From below came a shriek of metal on metal and a series of loud bangs as latches snapped and the log-jam of containers gave way and they all slid at once, catching on other containers farther aft.

"When they go," Mchynlyth yelled. *Arthur P* hung at an angle of thirty degrees, tail-down. Everett dangled from cell-netting over a fifty-metre drop. He hauled himself up to the catwalk, now more like a ladder.

"Two more," Everett said. Mchynlyth nodded. They climbed the catwalk, using the handrails as rungs. Every muscle in Everett's shoulders, upper arms, forearms, hands, thumbs screamed in pain. He clung. He climbed. He cut. He could do nothing else. To admit the pain, to relax, meant the long fall to sharp steel death on the containers below. But it hurt; it hurt like nothing had ever hurt before. With the last of his strength he dragged the skin-ripper down through the net. With the pressure of three gas cells piled behind it, the net gave way. The net gave way and dropped Everett on the end of a three-metre strip of webbing. He swung out across *Arthur P*'s interior. The catwalk and safety were out of his reach. He tried to swing, but he no longer had the strength. He couldn't hold it. He must hold it. And every second, *Arthur P* swung towards ninety degrees. Forty-five degrees, sixty degrees. Eighty degrees . . .

"Oh the dear God," Mchynlyth shouted down from his handhold up on the catwalk. There was pure awe in his voice. *Arthur P* was vertical. The piled containers finally spilled free in a booming, clanging roar of steel. They smashed into the steering gear, tearing away walkways and gantries, rebounding from ribs and spars.

"Mchynlyth!" Everett shouted. "I can't—"

Then a figure dropped from between the wedged gas cells overhead, a man on a drop line, coattails flying, a jaunty hat on his head.

"'Out of the depths I have cried unto thee, O Lord, for with the Lord there is mercy and with him there is plenteous redemption,'" Sharkey cried. He dropped down level with Everett, grabbed a fistful of net and started to swing. "Hold on with every fibre of your being, sir." With each swing Sharkey brought Everett closer and closer to the catwalk. "Now!" Everett loosed a hand and grabbed the railing. "The bonder, use the bonder," Sharkey said. Everett understood at once. He looped the dangling tail of the strip of netting around the railing, slid the trigger on the skin-ripper down and with the last of his strength sealed the loop onto itself. Secure, tied to the catwalk, which had become a vertical ladder. Mchynlyth had climbed down and extended a hand to Everett. As he took it the skin-ripper fell from his fingers. He watched it tumble down through the huge cylindrical pit *Arthur P* had become.

"I'm impressed, Everett Singh," Mchynlyth said. "You have rightly buggered this wee ship."

"Did you see the captain?" Everett asked Sharkey.

"She can look after herself." He released the brake drop line and sailed down to the crosswalk, now turned ninety degrees on its side.

"And that's our ticket out of here," Mchynlyth said. "Right sunshine, down and out."

They climbed down the handrails. It was an easy climb, but

Everett's muscles were trembling with strain and fatigue. He wasn't safe yet. Put one foot beneath the other, one hand beneath the other. *Don't look down*, Sen, Queen of the Rooftops of old Hackney, had said. He looked out, at the world-turned-sideways inner architecture of the capsized *Arthur P*. Sharkey was waiting for them down on the crosswalk. Mchynlyth took out the walkie-talkie.

"*Everness*, *Everness*. Our job is done."

"Fantabulosa," Sen crackled on the radio. "Oh man, you should have seen it."

"We saw quite enough," Mchynlyth said. "You've young Mr. Singh to thank for all that. Ready for pickup, port-side gallery." He passed the walkie-talkie to Everett.

"Tottenham Hotspur," Everett said.

They made slow but steady progress out along the crosswalk, stepping carefully from rung to rung, holding onto the stanchions overhead, a monkey-walk over the big drop to the smashed tail section below. Mchynlyth opened the hatch. The wind howled in, blinding Everett with snow and cold. The gallery was turned on its side, the gap between the hull and the far railing enough to be intimidating. But then the snow parted and out of it came *Everness*, dead ahead. Everett could see Sen in the lighted strip of the control room, her hands feathering the controls, dancing *Everness* in on its damaged impellers. Nearer. Everett clung onto the gallery rail, blinded by snow, buffeted by wind, aching and shivering. Behind him the hull of the upended *Arthur P* rose like the tower of a dark lord. Sen swivelled the engine pods and gently dropped the airship until its nose was level with the gallery. The nose hatch undogged; the boarding ramp extended. It came to within a metre of the gallery. No farther. Two jumps then—one to the rail, then the other, over open sky, onto the boarding ramp.

"Come on, Everett," Mchynlyth said. "It's a doddle, see?" He went from hatch to gallery rail to boarding ramp. He beckoned Everett on.

"'But they that wait upon the Lord shall renew their strength; they shall mount up with wings as eagles; they shall run, and not be weary; they shall walk, and not faint,'" Sharkey said. And Everett leaped. He caught the rail, caught his breath, caught his courage. He had battled the Bromleys and beaten them. He had wrecked their flagship. He had crossed universes. A metre of air was just that; air. He swung around the edge of the rail, positioned himself, and jumped. He landed soft as a cat on the ramp, and in twenty steps he was in *Everness*'s docking lobby. Sen was backing *Everness* away from the stricken Bromley airship when he made it up onto the bridge.

"The captain?"

"Annie's all right," Sen said. She nodded at the window.

Arthur P stood upright in the air, equilibrium fatally disrupted, as tall as a skyscraper. Her docking ramp was extended from her nose like a radio aerial. And there was a figure climbing that spike, a figure in tan breeches and boots and a white shirt, hauling itself up the rungs, lashed by storm winds and ice but dauntless. Captain Anastasia Sixsmyth saw her ship appear out of the blizzard and waved.

"Mchynlyth, open the cargo bay doors," Sen said into the intercom.

"Aye, ma'am," came the reply. Sen looked at Everett.

"You hear that? *Ma'am*. Bonaroo."

Captain Anastasia had made it to the end of the boarding ramp. She stood upright, daring the wind and the winter, arms spread wide, welcoming in her ship. And Sen brought *Everness* in so sweet, so light and gentle and precise, that all she had to do was step from ramp to cargo bay.

"Captain on the deck!" Sharkey cried as Captain Anastasia strode onto the bridge. She was grazed, bruised; her white shirt was bloody. Sen almost skipped with delight.

"Miss Sixsmyth, I relieve you of command. Stand by for orders. Mr. Mchynlyth, make her airworthy. Mr. Sharkey, hail *Arthur P*. Inform her commander that she is to be taken in tow as lawful salvage. Those Bromleys owe me a coat.

26

The snow came in from the east. It drove across Kent, dropped ten centimetres of white on the promenades and piers of Deal and the towers of Canterbury Cathedral, the towns and villages of the Medway, the commuter trains flashing along their lines carrying office workers and civil servants and shoppers to home and hearth. It sent flakes whirling round the vortices and thermals that boiled up from the stacks and vents of the Smoke Ring; it sent forerunners out to dust the Albert Docks and the Isle of Dogs with silver and a promise of whiteness to come.

In the heart of the snowstorm *Everness* was coming home. A slow passage it was, limping on four of her eight engines. She towed a heavy burden. Half a kilometre astern lay the hulk of the *Arthur P*, ghostly in the storm; sometimes visible, like a skyscraper at the end of a fishing line, sometimes hidden so that *Everness*'s tow cables seemed to dip into nothingness. The Bromleys' shame could not be hidden from radar. Air-traffic control picked up the anomaly coming in from the Channel instantly and within seconds it had gone out across the Airish community, from Paris to Copenhagen, Aberdeen to Amsterdam. Even the snooty and superior passenger liners, who never soiled themselves with the doings of the disreputable merchant fleet, heard the news and threw their smart caps into the air. Anastasia Sixsmyth had defeated the mighty Bromleys. Not just defeated. Wrecked ruined crushed humiliated the Bromleys. Hackney Great Port readied fireworks and train hooters and loud music to welcome back *Everness*. There would be the mother of parties. Until engineers restored equilibrium, *Arthur P* would hang tail-down over Hackney like a giant exclamation mark. The custom was that the crew of a defeated ship be hosted by the victor. Ma Bromley spat at the very idea. They would stay with their ship, in discomfort, turned ninety degrees, and be damned.

The airwaves crackled with the deed of Anastasia Sixsmyth, but she was not celebrating. She sat in her ready-room, a cup of chilli-warmed hot chocolate to hand. Her face was grim and heavy as the storm outside her window. She was marked, darker bruises on dark skin. Her ear was stuck all over with bright yellow plasters where two of her earrings had been torn away in the fight. She had refused to say anything about her hand-to-hand duel with Kyle Bromley. All she had said was, "I did not disgrace the ship." Kyle Bromley would certainly never speak of it. Fought to a standstill by a woman. That was the greatest shame of their shameful defeat. The wounds, visible and invisible, the heavy damage her ship had sustained, were not the causes of her grim face. The cause was Everett Singh, standing before her, more nervous than he had ever been in his life.

"So this Madam Villiers is holding your father prisoner in the Tyrone Tower," Captain Anastasia said.

"Yes."

"A plenipotentiary of the Plenitude."

"Yes."

"With almost limitless authority and access to resources."

"Yes."

"And a jumpgun."

"I saw it myself. Ask Sen. . . ."

"Who went into the Tyrone Tower."

"She volunteered."

"And now this Charlotte Villiers has traced you back to this ship, and she will stop at nothing to get her hands on your comptator—your Infundibulum."

"Yes."

"So I am involved whether I wish to be or not."

There was no answer Everett could give to that. Captain Anastasia continued.

"And now you ask me to risk my ship, my crew, and my daughter to help you get your father back."

"Yes."

"And you go off with your dad and your family to some plane far far away and live happily ever after while we're left in this world facing the anger of the Plenitude."

"Yes," Everett said. It was a terrible deal.

"I could hand you over. I could take you down to the Tyrone Tower and tell the man on the desk who you are and what you've got. I could do that, and my ship would be safe and I would be safe and Sen would be safe. Why shouldn't I do that?"

"There is no reason in the world."

"Sit down, Mr. Singh. I'm going to tell you a story. It's a good story, and a true one."

Everett unfolded a seat from the wall and sat down.

"Long ago, or not so long ago, in the blue yondering, I was pilot on a ship called the *Fairchild*, as bona a ship as ever lifted out of Hackney Great Port. Her captain was Matts Hustveit, a second-generation Norwegian; his people came over during the Russo-Swedish War. His wife Corrie was the weighmaster; she was proper *so*—Hackney Airish back all the way to when they first put gas in a bag and flew. They were like family to me. They *were* family to me. My own family . . . well let's say that family is what works. I'm not from here, I'm not a Hackney polone; I'm Western Airish; I was born in Bristol Great Port, within the sound of the bells of St. Mary Redcliffe. You should see the ships, lined up nose to nose along the Floating Harbour, all the Transatlantic Fleet. Quebec, Boston, Atlanta, Miami; Havana and Caracas and Recife and Rio; Montevideo and Buenos Aires. I knew what ship flew where, and who flew her. My dad was the flyer, a pilot on the Montevideo run. My mum, she worked in the Gas Office, but she was proper Airish. My dad, he always promised he'd take me up, take me flying down to New York or Savannah or Salvador. But he walked away, so I walked away.

What it's like to find someone not there, to not know why, to know that what you're being told isn't the truth and maybe wasn't the truth for a long time—I know that, Mr. Singh. I left them, so I could fly. I'm not proud of it; it was what I had to do.

"So there I was, fresh out three years at Skysail House—the piloting academy—looking for a job on the ships. I owed. I owed a lot. I still do. Piloting jobs are few and far between; it's like dead men's shoes. The ships are close. Like family. Captain Matts had just lost his pilot—Hugh Bom Jesus. Hackney mother, Lisbon father. Good pilot but terrible drinker. *Fairchild* was due to lift for Dresden, but Hugh had been on a three-day bender. Someone, thank the Dear, locked him in the cellar at the Knights and refused to let him fly. He'd have wrecked that ship. But Captain Matts had a consignment; and in I walked. Luck? No such thing, Mr. Singh. You see patterns, opportunities, moments, you take them. And you make them. I took the commission and weighed in. I'll always remember it: one hundred and twelve pounds three ounces of ballast. I took the helm, we lifted and we made Dresden quick-smart.

"I was pilot of *Fairchild* now, and I was hot, Mr. Singh. I was the talk and toast of Hackney. There wasn't a sinner wouldn't buy me a drink; there wasn't an omi in Hackney, and a fair few polones, didn't want me. And it was good; we were a tight crew. Captain Matts and Corrie had a daughter—I'm sure you can guess who she is. She was six when I came onto *Fairchild*—even more of a spoiled little brat than she is now. She could wrap anyone round her finger then as well—buy and sell the whole of Hackney, could Sen Hustveit. Good tight crew. Family.

"I'd been piloting two years when we made the Sargasso run. We were primarily a Baltic line ship—Deutschland, Polska, the Empire of All the Russias, what was left of Scandinavia. But this was a government contract; they needed it done quick-smart and airship-shape. The regular ship was in for an overhaul. We were being touted for the Royal Mail, and I think they wanted to see how we could handle a tight deadline and a government contract. It was fast and simple, a resupply to a Royal Geographical Society Oceanography survey ship out in the blue Sargasso Sea. Fly drop, back home again. We wouldn't even have to wait around for a return consignment.

"We lifted. It was August. The weather was hot and fine and clear. A great anticyclone had settled over Europe; people remember it as one of the great summers. We flew through blue skies over blue seas and not once did we see a cloud until we had recharged at Madeira and headed out west into the open ocean. August there is hurricane season, and if there's a high over Europe, there's a low over the central Atlantic. Not any low either; three low-pressure systems were spiralling together into the mother of lows. But our weather radar was tracking it, and Captain Matts made sure we kept wide steerage from what was brewing out there. The barometer was dropping towards lows I'd never seen before; the horizon was black from edge to edge. Even two hundred miles out, we could feel the wind shake us. The headwinds were ferocious. We made our drop, turned and headed back to recharge at Madeira. But sometimes things, when they get big enough, they become monsters, things no one can predict and no one can prepare for. She deepened, that storm, she deepened and she deepened, feeding off the heat in the Sargasso Sea; she deepened into nothing anyone had ever seen before. The survey ship cut and ran before it. We turned. We ran—we tried to run. But we'd used too much power battling the headwinds. We'd didn't have enough power to make it back to the Isle of Madeira. Without power, without impellers, that storm would have tumbled us across the sky like a leaf.

"Matts made the decision. It was a terrible decision; it was the only decision he could make. So in the end there was no decision. He ordered me to turn the ship and head into the storm. It's not done often—but all ships come with the equipment: recharge from a thunderstorm. I turned the *Fairchild*. I set course for the heart of the hurricane." Captain Anastasia glanced at her porthole, where wind-whipped snow was piling up. "You think this is a storm. This is not a storm. That was a storm. Renfield, our engineer, rigged the lightning-catchers. The sky looked burned and boiling; crazy with thunderbolts. Then the buffets caught us and I felt the steering yoke whip. I fought it. I fought that ship in among the lightning bolts. I held her steady, head-on into the eye of the storm. And we drew the lightning. When a ship hooks in the lightning, everything comes alive with electricity. Every rail and handle and lever sparks. Your hair stands on end. The glass crawls with St. Elmo's fire. Ball-lighting goes skittering across the decks. I held her there; I held her in the heart of the storm drinking down the lightning. When the meters read full charge, I turned her for Madeira.

"I still can't get rid of the idea that it was the turn that did it, that I was responsible. We'll never know. There was an arc from the dorsal lightning-catcher to the rudder, hot enough to ignite the carbon fibre. Nanocarbon doesn't burn easily, but when it does, it burns with an incredible heat and hunger. It consumes everything: skin, the struts, the skeleton. The very bones of the ship burn. We were on fire. You've never seen an airship burn. Few people have. Pray you never do. Have you ever seen a house burn? It's the most wrong thing in the world. It's someone's hopes and safety and all the things they love and cherish, burning up without any thought. The fire has no thought and no conscience. A ship's like that, but in the sky, like an angel burning.

"*Fairchild* was burning, and we were a hundred miles from land. Corrie put out a distress call to the RGS survey ship. Captain Matts gave me Sen and told me to take her to the escape pods. Get to the pod. Get out of here. She was only eight then. And she saw her home, her ship, burn.

"She burned from the tail. I picked Sen up and I was running with her, and ahead of me I could see the tail end a mass of white flame. Nanocarbon burns hot as magnesium, and it goes straight to soot, no ashes, no cinders. I saw the fire crawl along the hull, and the skin just vanished. It was like a disease or something, skin turning to gas and blowing away. I saw the ribs glow white-hot and then disappear.

"I didn't see another pod come off the ship. I think they had a desperate plan to vent the helium; it would have snuffed the fire out. But nothing else came off the *Fairchild*. I was terrified until the parachutes blew, and even then I was terrified because bits of burning ship-skin were whirling down, and if they caught the chutes, we were dead. I can still see her there, half-consumed by fire, in the sky, glowing from the inside as the ribs burned inside the skin. Then the skin would catch and vanish in flame. The wreck of the *Fairchild* must have been visible for hundreds of miles, if anyone but us had been insane enough to be out in that storm. Last of all the gas cells broke free. I saw them go bowling off, blazing, in the hurricane winds. Nothing else came off that ship. Then we splashed down and I had too much to do to think about what I'd seen. I blew the parachutes so we didn't get dragged, and deployed the sea-anchor and the emergency beacon. And we held on, tossed about in the middle of a storm in the middle of the ocean. Ocean scares me. It's bigger than anything. Even a great ship the size of the *Fairchild* is nothing compared to the ocean, a match struck in the dark. Poof. Gone. And ocean hates us. It always has. Maybe not hates us, but cares nothing for us and our achievements. It's not human. I stabilised the pod, got the radio working, and we ran with the storm all night. Just us, a young woman and a child, in an escape pod on the ocean.

"And the ocean is strange, Mr. Singh. The strangest thing there is. I think that's what scares me most. We slept, I don't know how, and the great storm flicked its tail and turned back into the west again and left us bobbing like a cork. I woke to calm waters and clear skies and the sun shining on my face through the porthole. And there was a ship out there. But it wasn't the RGS survey ship, which had been tracking my beacon through the night. And here is the part I know you will have difficulty believing, though the evidence is staring you right in the face, Mr. Singh." She rapped the table with her bruised knuckles.

"Not a watership at all, an airship, lying about three miles south of us at about three hundred metres, trailing landing cables in the water. Just hanging there, engines dead, nothing on the Common Channel. A ship, Mr. Singh, in dead air. This ship. *Everness*. I could tell you long about how I caught her by the landing line, and shinnied up in a climb-cradle, and found her empty—not a soul, Mr. Singh. I could tell you about how I brought her home, and the mysteries at Jane's Airshipping Registry, and the Court of Salvage, and how I came to be the owner, master and commander of an airship that didn't exist. I could tell you, Mr. Singh. I don't need to. The evidence is all around you. What you need to know is that I watched the *Fairchild* burn and fall from the sky, and Sen's mother and father with her, and in that moment, I became Sen's family. I'm not a superstitious or particularly religious woman—no more or less than any Airish—but I feel in my bones that *Everness* was given to me to be a home for her.

"Sen's never told you about her family. I know you've been asking. She tells me these things. She never will tell you, Mr. Singh. The nightmares have gone—it's been a couple of years now—for both of us, but they're never far. I've done my best for her; I'm not her mother, I'm not a mother. But Matts and Corrie, they gave me a family and a home, and I've given her a family and a home. As I said, Mr. Singh, family is what works.

"And that's why I am going to help you. You might have heard around—maybe even from Sen—that I have an amriya; an unbreakable vow in our palari. If I do, it's one I've taken on myself. I promised myself that I would give as I had received. I'm nowhere near the end of that yet. I will help you. My ship and crew are at your service. There's an accounting to be had as well, for poor bugger 'Appening Ed. We may bicker and fight among ourselves, but if anyone offends one of us, they offend all of us. Madam Charlotte Villiers needs to learn that we are not her servants. And you helped me. You saved my ship, I hear. *Arthur P* would have left us out there on the Goodwin Sands, another broken wreck. Now I help you."

There was a great singing noise in Everett's head. It was different from the great singing noise when he was laying out his big ask to Captain Anastasia. That had been the high-pitched noise you get in your head when you are doing something you absolutely must do but absolutely hate doing, when you hear yourself saying the words and hate the words and hate your voice saying them and hate the hateful way they make you feel. This was the noise—very different—you hear when you have convinced yourself that they are going to say no, that everything you have said can only lead up to a no: and then they say yes. Yes: so small you miss it, and then trip over it like an unseen crack in the pavement and have to go back and actually see that there is something there that sent you sprawling. Yes. Everett rocked on his feet. Yes. He could feel the bones in his eye sockets. His face was flushed. He thought he might cry. She had agreed. She had said yes.

"You could thank me, Mr. Singh," Captain Anastasia said.

"Thank you."

"Thank you what?"

"Thank you, ma'am."

"You're welcome, Mr. Singh. The bridge, sir. Call the crew to posts. I shall follow you up shortly. I need to put on a bit of slap first. We arrive in Hackney in short order, and by the Dear, we'll look airship-shape and *damn* hot. Away with you."

"Yes, ma'am."

27

"Lift to holding altitude," Captain Anastasia said.

"Aye, ma'am."

Sen slid forward the elevation levers, and *Everness* rose soft and silent as a prayer from her docking cradle. Snow from the east and the season of the year had driven Great Hackney indoors. This was Christmas Eve, when people close their doors and pull down their shutters on the world and turn to the lives of others. Those few out—the chestnut sellers, the coffee stalls, the brass band of the mission to the Airish playing carols by the Clapton Viaduct, the late revellers heading out with their party clothes under their heavy winter coats, the early drunks reeling home from the corner pubs and the half-repaired Knights of the Air—looked up at the hum of impellers, the slight displacement of air as something huge passed through it. No matter how commonplace, no matter how many ships lifted and landed each day, there was no soul in Hackney Great Port too small to look up at the touch of an airship shadow, and smile. Everett knew he would never tire of standing by the great window of an airship and seeing the world laid out at his feet. Never tire and never forget, because after this night, after this flight, he would never do it again. He would never come back to this world—he could never come back to this world. In a short time—less than an hour—he would see his dad. That was an excitement so huge it was almost a dread. It made him feel sick. It seemed so long—weeks, months—since he had waited outside the ICA on the Mall in another London and seen Charlotte Villiers's agents knock him off his bike and take him away to this world. It was little more than a week. It was so easy to mix up space with time: a few days became mixed up with the distance of whole universes. Excitement he felt, and anticipation, and dread, and also loss. His reunion with his dad would be his farewell to the crew of *Everness*, Mchynlyth and Miles O'Rahilly Lafayette Sharkey, Sen and Anastasia Sixsmyth. They would go back to their ship and take flight for a safe port beyond British extradition treaties. He and his dad would go their way, out across the worlds, to a place they could never be found. Everett wished he could bring the crew of the *Everness* back to his Stoke Newington. How much easier would it be to explain to Laura that they would have to flee to another universe with a two-hundred-metre airship hanging over Roding Road. It couldn't be. Only individuals could jump between worlds.

Sharkey at his station, one earphone pushed up on top of his head. Everett didn't doubt that the shotguns were still tucked into the lining of his coat. Sharkey the talker, quick with the word of the Lord and the manners of a Southern gent. And how much of those were true? When you're far from home, when you're an exile, you cover yourself with stories. *Weighmaster, soldier of fortune, adventurer, gentleman*, he'd called himself. *Goalkeeper, mathematician, traveller, planesrunner*, Everett had replied. Say it enough and it will come true.

Mchynlyth: out on the hull under this crystal sky, swinging on his line high above the spires of London, laughing like a devil as he worked the engineering trickery they would need to fool Dunsfold Air Traffic control. Mchynlyth: Glasgow-born but not Scottish; Indian DNA but not Punjabi. *Airish*. You are what you choose to be.

Captain Anastasia: grace, power, and dignity even with half her ear ripped off. Sassy, classy, daring. She terrified Everett; he adored her. He could bring her hot chocolate with chilli forever. You are everything I admire, Everett thought. I would love to be like you. I would love to *be* you.

Sen. He couldn't look at her. So light and frivolous, decking *Everness* out in Christmas decorations—lights blinked from every hook and nook on the bridge. So serious and focussed at the helm, guiding the ship over the Christmas lights of London. Her sulks that broke into grins; her cunning and her spontaneity; her pride that spun on its heel into offence. Her delight in everything shiny and bona.

Family is what works, Captain Anastasia had said. Would his family work when he pushed it all back together again, on some world that looked enough like the one they came from for some version of the life they had to be possible? But that life hadn't worked. His mum and dad had split up. Who was he to force them to try again, in a whole new world? Would they split again? Would Laura even want to come with them? Would he just cause the ultimate split: Mum and Victory-Rose, Dad and Everett, forever apart in separate universes? It was a deep, dark shock, a fist clenched around the heart, for Everett to realise that every decision he had made, every action he had taken, had caused someone to pay a high and terrible price. It was never like that in the action movies. There were never any consequences.

"Mr. Sharkey," Captain Anastasia ordered.

Sharkey thumbed a switch.

"Dunsfold Control, Dunsfold Control, this is LTA *Everness*."

"Roger, *Everness*, this is Dunsfold."

"Request flight plan Hackney Great Port–Bristol Great Port."

"Roger that; is Captain Annie going home for Christmas?" the air-traffic controller said. He had a cocky, knowing voice. Everett could hear cheering in the background. Captain Anastasia pulled down a microphone on its boom arm.

"No, Dunsfold. Repair docks."

"Don't they have repair docks in Hackney?" said the cheeky controller.

"Not as cheap," Captain Anastasia said. More laughter in the air-traffic control. On *Everness*'s bridge, the mood was serious and edgy.

"Okay, *Everness*, you are clear to proceed initial bearing two-sixty-eight degrees, twelve minutes, thirty seconds to Bristol Air

Traffic handover; standard western flyway altitude," the controller said. "By the way, Captain, I don't know how you did it, but whatever you did to *Arthur P*: fantabulosa, as you'd say."

"Thank you, Dunsfold. Out." Captain Anastasia clicked off the radio. "Make it so, Miss Sixsmyth. Two hundred metres. Mr. Sharkey, activate our radar beacon. We don't want to graze the paintwork of any of those fine, shiny passenger liners."

The lights of London wheeled before Everett as *Everness* turned on her axis. As she turned she gained altitude. Sen played the impellers as sweetly as a musical instrument. *Everness* came on to her heading; Sen pushed forward the thrust levers and the great ship. Two hundred metres was tower-top height, skyscraper-scraping height. Everett held his breath at the parade of winged Victories and Nemesises with swords and shields and blindfolded Justices with scales all crowned with the recent snow, domes and crosses and spires and globes, seemingly just beneath his feet. He could look down into the street and see the steely shine of the city—ahead was the floodlit dome of St. Paul's, dazzling under its cap of snow, now Fleet Street and the Strand bright with flickering Christmas neons. He could see the cars, the trains, the people pushing on through the late snow, the river darting with fast hydrofoils and hovercraft. Sen touched the controls and nudged *Everness* a hairsbreadth towards the elegant terraces and snow-white squares of Bloomsbury. Light beamed up through the glass dome of the British Library. Ahead, the Tyrone Tower rose like a steel hand, its buttresses and gargoyles and cornices lit ghost-blue by floodlights. A single shaft of light stabbed skywards from its summit.

"Take us in, Sen," Captain Anastasia whispered. "Easy does it. We are supposed to be crippled." Tottenham Court Road was a slash of neon; to the south, Soho a glowing knot of light. A few stray snowflakes blew across the great window and fell sparkling through the street glow; winter was closing in again. "Full stop, Miss Sixsmyth." Sen pulled all the levers back. They clicked into neutral.

Everness hung motionless half a kilometre east of the Tyrone Tower. "Mr. Sharkey, declare the emergency."

"Dunsfold, Dunsfold, LTA *Everness* declaring an emergency," Sharkey said into the microphone. "We have lost main power. We have no motive power."

"*Everness*, we read," said the Dunsfold air-traffic controller. It was the same man who had congratulated Captain Anastasia on her defeat of the Bromleys. He did not sound so chirpy now. "Are you drifting?"

"We can hold station," Sharkey said.

"Notify us of your position."

Sharkey read out a string of digits.

"Thank you, *Everness*. We have your radar beacon as well. Do you have an estimate?"

"Two hours to restore main motive power," Sharkey said.

"We will issue a standard navigation hazard warning to all air traffic. At least you picked a quiet night for it, *Everness*."

"We'll notify you when we restore power. Out."

Captain Anastasia waited for two breaths, then picked up the intercom.

"Mr. Mchynlyth, we're ready for you. Deploy the drone. Mr. Sharkey, on camera please."

The overhead screens lit, but Everett, in his favourite place by the glass, had the clearest view. The drone darted out from underneath *Everness*, hung a moment in the open air, then swivelled its fans and, under Mchynlyth's guidance, buzzed towards the Tyrone Tower. It was a little insect-like inspection drone, designed to go to those places on the outside of the ship unsafe for humans. There was no place that Mchynlyth considered unsafe, but he kept the drone because it was a clever, well-made piece of technology and he liked clever, well-made things. In design it was almost identical to the camera drone Everett had seen on the video clip Colette Harte had given him; jumping in from an aerial survey of E2: four fans, legs, and a processing core. Functional design was functional design, whatever the universe.

The drone towed a line, a nanocarbon filament thin as a hair, strong as diamond. When Mchynlyth had shown the reel to Everett he had warned him to keep his fingers away from it. "Take them right off, snick-snack," he said. "So clean you wouldn't even feel it." So fine it was invisible on the low-resolution cameras, but Everett thought he glimpsed a gleam of light, like sun catching a strand of spider silk, as the line crossed one of the floodlight beams. Now the monitors switched to the drone camera. Mchynlyth brought it in low and low to the twenty-second floor and dropped the grapnel at the end of the line around the shoulders of a severe-looking helmeted warrior woman standing beside a shield. He cast off.

"Mr. Sharkey, Mr. Singh, to the cargo deck."

Everett had never heard Captain Anastasia's voice so solemn. Now. The time was now. He wasn't ready. He had to prepare himself; he had to think himself into what he was going to do. No time. He had to be ready. There were words he had to say. There were good-byes; huge good-byes. He saw that Sen realised this too, that the time had come for them to be parted forever, that in a few moments he would walk off the bridge and be gone.

"Everett Singh!"

He had never seen a face so white, eyes so ice-pale.

"Sen . . ."

"I'm coming with you."

"Stay here!" Captain Anastasia thundered.

"I'm coming. I want to be with Everett." Her jacket was buttoned up, one glove already pulled on, her shush-bag slung across her shoulder.

"Stay with the ship."

"No!" She stepped away from the controls.

"*Everness* is yours, Miss Sixsmyth. You have the command."

The bag slipped from Sen's shoulder to the floor. She stepped back. As mother, Anastasia could not have stopped Sen. As captain, without even issuing a direct order, Sen could not disobey her. This was the ship. Her eyes looked as if the darkest thing in the world had reached through them and torn her heart out. Her lips were open in incomprehension.

"Mr. Singh." Captain Anastasia's grip on Everett's shoulder was iron as she pushed him onto the main catwalk. Almost, he thought to tear himself free, to break every one of her fingers, scream into her face. Almost he thought of looking back to Sen stunned, heart cracking on the empty bridge against the winking Christmas lights. That would have killed him inside. Anastasia Sixsmyth was right. All good-byes should be sudden. Then he saw the look on her face, her mouth tight, the corners of her eyes bright with moisture. It wasn't about him or Sen. It was about her keeping her daughter safe, the kid she'd rescued from the destruction of the *Fairchild*, keeping the promises she had made on that burning hulk. She understood that none of them might return to her.

Mchynlyth had lowered the cargo hatch a metre to allow the drone to slip out. The drop down was easy; the greater drop beyond, to the teeming traffic wheeling around Grafton Place, would have frozen Everett rigid only a few days ago. Since then he had run rooftops, leaped alleyways, swung from containment netting over sharp-edged steel, jumped across empty air to land on a ribbon of nanocarbon no wider than his outstretched arms. He landed easily. Mchynlyth had already rigged the zip-line harnesses to the fibre. They looked alarmingly as if they were hanging on nothing. Everett reached up to test the harness. Mchynlyth slapped his hand away.

"Don't touch the line!" He strapped Everett into the zip-line harness, then took the one behind. "Brake is here; harness release is here. Don't mix them up."

"Ready, Mr. Mchynlyth," Captain Anastasia said. She was directly ahead of Everett on the line. Sharkey would make the run first. Mchynlyth touched a remote. The cargo bay door opened fully.

Everett hung from the near-invisible line. In front of him the dark was filled with gusting snow. With his Confed war-yell, Sharkey launched himself into the night.

"Come on, Mr. Singh," Captain Anastasia said. She smiled at him over her shoulder, then raised a hand, and in a moment was a tiny doll-figure hurtling towards the Goth-scape of the Tyrone Tower. Everett touched the brake. In a breath he was out in the air. The cold, the speed took his breath away. Snow smeared in his face; he wiped it away with frozen fingers. Beneath him were the rooftops, the chimneys, the electricity pylons and terraces and gardens of Bloomsbury. Someone had decked out a balcony with Christmas lights; here a Christmas tree had been fastened into a flag-holder; in this roof garden a man and woman stood, drinks in hand, looking up at the falling snow. They did not notice the line-riders crossing the sky. The line riders were specks among swirling specks. He was high, he was invisible, he was invulnerable. Everett flew through sound. London was a symphony around him; the traffic rumble beneath him, the hooting of car horns, the sound of pop music from apartments, the clank and clack of trains, distant emergency sirens, the distant purr of *Everness*'s engines, the hiss of the line running through the diamond bearings on his harness, and now—coming in waves from far, and farther, and farthest—the bells of London Town, ringing out from the steeples and the spires and the belfries for Christmas. Everett glanced back. Behind, Mchynlyth rode the line. He looked as if he sat in thin air. He was grinning like a madman. Beyond him, flecked by snow, hung *Everness*. Her bridge twinkled with fairy-lights. Did he see a figure at the window? Everett snatched his attention away and looked ahead. The Tyrone Tower was coming up fast, a jagged wall of buttresses and cornices and long concrete finials and spires. Sharkey was already down on the twenty-second-floor balcony Everett had identified from his spy mission. Captain Anastasia came to a stop and dropped to the balcony below. Which was the brake, which was the release? Everett hit a button.

Overhead the bearings shrilled as the brakes dug in. He came to a halt, swinging gently, looking up into the stern face of the stone guardian angel.

"Out of the way, ya bassa!" a voice shouted behind him. Everett hit the release and dropped to the balcony as Mchynlyth's boots whistled in over his head. In moments all four of the rescue mission were crowded together on the narrow balcony. Disturbed pigeons flew up, wings clattering.

"You did remember to bring . . . the youknowwhat?" Mchynlyth said.

Everett slapped his backpack. Sharkey had already picked the window lock. They stepped through into the half-built elevator lobby Everett had seen on Sen's spy-camera. The images on Dr. Quantum could not convey the smell of dust, concrete, plaster, wood.

"Lead on, Mr. Singh," Captain Anastasia said. Everett called up his graphic of the Tyrone Tower and zoomed in on the twenty-second floor. He held the tablet up and compared the photograph with the reality.

"Through these plastic sheets," Everett said. He had set up Dr. Quantum so that the map reoriented at every turn of the corridor.

"Do you think there'll be guards?" Mchynlyth asked. He rested his hand on a pant pocket that bulged with the unmistakable outline of a thumper-gun.

"I didn't see any," Everett said. Captain Anastasia raised an eyebrow. "I mean, Sen didn't see any." But he did see Sharkey pull his coattails close around him, and that they moved heavily and stiffly, as if rigid steel barrels were stowed there. "Right here. This is the corridor." The only difference between picture and reality was the chambermaid's trolley. "Last door on the left." And now he was here. On the twenty-second floor, in the corridor, only a door between him and his dad. Yet again, it had been so sudden, with too much happening for Everett to be ready, to feel ready.

Captain Anastasia rapped on the door with a knuckle.

"Dr. Singh?"

No answer.

"'Behold, I stand at the door, and knock: if any man hear my voice, and open the door, I will come in to him,'" Sharkey said.

"Button it, Mr. Sharkey." Captain Anastasia rapped again. "Dr. Singh. I am Captain Anastasia Sixsmyth of the LTA *Everness*. I have your son here with me; Everett." She nodded to Everett.

"Dad?" Everett touched his cheek to the door. "Dad? Can you hear me? It's me, Everett. Are you in there?" No answer. Not a sound of movement from inside. What if he weren't there? What if he'd been taken away somewhere else while Everett shopped for Christmas dinners and escaped over rooftops and fought Bromleys and made rescue plans? What if he'd left it too long? They might have taken him to another, more secret and secure place; they might have taken his dad off this world entirely.

Captain Anastasia rapped the door again.

"Dr. Singh, I'd advise you to stand back. Mr. Mchynlyth, take it down."

"Ma'am." From another of his many pockets, Sharkey took a tool. He handled it carefully, as if it were a small and delicate but very venomous snake. He squatted down at the door lock. Everett could not make out what the device was; it looked very simple, two flat paddles the length of his little finger, as thick as a sheet of paper. Both tapered at one end to a fine point. Mchynlyth pushed both paddles into the crack between the door and the frame just above the lock, one above the other. The lower he pushed all the way until it vanished. He took a hook from another pocket and fiddled around under the lock, muttering under his breath, until he caught the paddle and pulled it out, underneath the deadbolt.

"Stand back," he said, took a paddle in each hand, and pulled firmly towards himself. The door swung gently inwards. Mchynlyth held up a paddle. The second one swung below it, suspended on an invisible line. Nanofibre, Everett realised. "And that's why you keep yer fingers away," Mchynlyth said. The lock bolt had been cut clean through.

Captain Anastasia pushed the door open. This was the first of a suite of rooms. The room was dark; Everett had a sense of sofas, chairs, work desks, a comptator station. A bicycle stood in a trainer rig. A Milani full-carbon Shimano headset road bicycle. A bicycle Everett had last seen going into the back of an Audi on the Mall. A door led to a more brightly lit room beyond. A figure stood in the doorway, silhouetted against the light. It carried a table lamp in its hands like a weapon.

"Dad?" Everett said.

The figure raised a hand. Lights blazed on, blinding the rescue party. Everett blinked his vision clear. A short man, brown skin, brown eyes; slightly built, trim, not running to upper body fat like many middle-aged Indian men. He wore Canterbury track-bottoms and a T-shirt. His feet were bare, as if he had just got out of bed and pulled on what came to hand. Him. Him oh so him, completely him, utterly him, absolutely him. Then all thought ended and Everett rushed to his dad.

Tejendra raised the table lamp like a club.

"Stop there. I don't know who you are."

"It's me. Everett. *Everett.*"

"Yes. Maybe. But are you my Everett? My son?"

There is not one you, Tejendra had said, on a fine summer night as they sat up on Parliament Hill, looking down over heat-hazy, lazy London. *There are many yous.*

"Of course I am!" Everett shouted.

"You would say that."

He had told Sen that he thought Charlotte Villiers and the fair-haired man in the good suit were the same person in parallel worlds. Charlotte and Charles. They would think nothing of bringing another Everett Singh from another plane to fool Tejendra. Back, way back on his home world, Everett had drunk cappuccino on a rain-swept Covent Garden piazza while Colette Harte told him about a plane, E4, that was identical in almost every way to E10—apart from politics, and something that had happened to the moon. There could be an Everett Singh on that world.

"Believe me!"

"Convince me."

Something only Dad and I know, Everett thought.

"We were going to the ICA to hear a talk on nanotechnology."

"They know that. They took me from there."

"White Hart Lane. Second of November. We beat Inter Milan 3 to 1. Gareth Bale scored a hat-trick."

"Half of London remembers that game."

"Vinny took a photograph of us. With pies."

There was a silence.

"I need more," Tejendra said.

"Cuisine nights!" Everett exclaimed. "You'd cook Thai."

"Yes."

"I'd cook Mexican."

"What did you cook?"

"Chilli. With . . ."

"With what?"

"Chocolate." *Chocolate in the chilli. Chilli in the chocolate.*

The lamp fell from Tejendra's hands.

"Son," he said simply. "I'm sorry. I had to be sure."

And Everett had no idea what to do, what to say. Maybe a hello. Maybe a good handshake. Maybe a cool line, like a character in a game. Maybe he should just punch him on the arm, *Hey Dad.* Then he went beyond knowing what to do and not knowing to what he felt. They hugged. They just hugged. They parted; they looked at each other. They hugged again. Everett crushed his dad to him, crushed him to him with all his strength, a never-letting-you-go hug. But it ended. It must always end, and it's embarrassing then. They stepped away from each other.

"You made it work," Tejendra said. "The data set."

"The Infundibulum," Everett said. "Tying your shoelaces."

Tejendra waggled his head, the old Punjabi gesture that meant yes/good/sort-of.

"I thought you'd get that."

"And if I hadn't?"

"You'd have worked it out another way. Your dad knows you. Can I see it?"

Everett set Dr. Quantum on the desk. He clicked open the Infundibulum icon. The screen filled with the slow-turning, glowing knot-work of the Panoply of all worlds. Tejendra leaned over it. The display lit his face green.

"Fractal seven-dimensional sealed knots," Tejendra said. There was a look in his eyes Everett had seen when Tejendra was explaining how the universe really worked to him. It didn't matter if Everett understood or not, what mattered was that Everett caught the light, felt some of the heat of his excitement. Science eyes: Tejendra was seeing the bigger universe, the way it all fit together: the wonder stuff. "Beautiful, beautiful work, Ev. Beautiful."

This was a scientist's beautiful. Beauty was at the heart of physics: the laws of reality, the mathematics that explained them so precisely, were always simple, elegant, beautiful. True. Everett's heart swelled. There was no higher praise.

"Gentlemen, I don't mean to hurry you," Captain Anastasia said.

Tejendra did not look up.

"Dad, we have to get out of here," Everett said. "We have to get up to the gates." Still, it was not over. He had to get up to the gate level. He had to power up a Heisenberg Gate and open it. He had to go through to Roding Road, step out of nothingness on Christmas Eve in his own living room, while Tejendra held the gate open. He had to bring them back, and go through the gate a final time, to a world far away, a place they would never be found.

"Dad!"

Tejendra snapped out of his fascination.

"Yes, let's go. I have the operating codes—I need them for the work they think I'm doing." Still he hesitated. He picked up Dr. Quantum. "Everett, Captain, you gentlemen; whatever happens, don't let her have this. Charlotte Villiers. She would become more powerful than you can possibly imagine. There is a group inside the Plenitude; they call themselves the Order. They're politicians, diplomats, big businesspeople, media folk, military, some scientists, some religious. They want the Infundibulum. That's why they took me and tried to get me to re-create my work here. It would give them control over the Plenitude, control over the whole Panoply. They could project their power anywhere in the multiverse. There is something out there, something they stumbled across, something they must keep secret from us, but it's big and it's coming. They say they need the Infundibulum to give us the edge, to keep us secure. They always say that; it's to keep us safe, keep us secure. For our own good. Whatever happens, Ev, she must not have the Infundibulum."

Tejendra handed the tablet to Everett.

The windows exploded inwards. Everett covered his head as glass showered around him. Figures in black swung through the shattered bedroom windows on lines and dropped to the floor. In the same instant more dark figures burst through the open doorway. Laser beams danced through the air. Mchynlyth dived, rolled, came up with his thumper drawn. Sharkey, only a heartbeat behind, went for his shotguns. His hands froze halfway to his holsters. A laser-sight drew a red dot at the centre of his forehead.

"'As the fishes that are taken in an evil net, and as the birds that are caught in the snare; so are the sons of men snared in an evil time," he said. He slowly raised his hands. The soldiers moved quickly to encircle Tejendra and the *Everness* crew in a ring of gun muzzles and red laser light. Their weapons were black; their uniforms were black; they wore black soft caps on their heads. One of them, a woman with a blonde ponytail under her black cap, seemed familiar to Everett. Then he remembered where he had seen her before: one of the guards at the Channel Tunnel gate facility back on his Earth.

"Sharpies," Mchynlyth said. "I hate sharpies." Captain Anastasia did not speak at all.

The circle of soldiers parted. Two figures entered the suite. The first was a short, badly moving man in a shapeless coat and unpolished shoes: Paul McCabe. The second was Charlotte Villiers. She wore a wasp-waisted suit with a ruffle at one shoulder. Her small, severe hat had a short veil over her face. She looked like death in heels.

"At ease, soldiers."

The SWAT team put up their weapons but stayed alert, ready for action.

"Everett, Everett, Everett," Paul McCabe said. The tone of false sorrow in his voice made Everett want to punch him. "If only you'd been honest with me, if only you'd trusted me from the start. None of this is necessary. I'll take you home. Come on."

"Silence, McCabe," Charlotte Villiers snapped. "I could explain to you that your father grossly misrepresents us, Everett. Yes, of course we heard everything. Our world is threatened, your world is threatened, all our worlds are threatened. We are honest. We are good. We are right. But ultimately, why should I bother? I have all the power here. It is necessary that I have the device. Give it to me."

"No," Everett said. He clutched Dr. Quantum tightly to his chest.

"Oh, Mr. Singh, please. This is not the movies. Sergeant." The SWAT team raised their guns. "Start with the woman. Then the American who is so fond of the Bible. He can find out the truth of the words he quotes." The guns clicked round onto Captain Anastasia. "Mr. Singh?"

"She'll do it, Everett," Paul McCabe said.

"Dad?" Everett said.

"Ev, give it to her."

"But you said . . ."

"She can take it from us any time she wants. Give it to her."

Everett set Dr. Quantum down on the floor and pushed it towards Charlotte Villiers.

"Sense has prevailed. Thank you." Charlotte Villiers opened her little clutch bag. Suddenly, the jumpgun was in her hand. "Now, I've had quite enough of the Singh family." She levelled it at Everett and Tejendra. "Good-bye."

Everett went sprawling as Tejendra pushed him away as hard as he could. There was a flash of light. Tejendra was gone.

Charlotte Villiers gave a little animal shriek of anger, like a street cat facing off over a kill, and brought the jumpgun to bear on Everett. There was a sound like a mechanical cough. The jumpgun flew from Charlotte Villiers's fingers. She cried out in pain and grasped her wrist. A thumper bag lay on the ground next to the jumpgun. In the centre of the smashed window Sen hung in a drop-line harness, thumper in her hand. Laser beams danced in the air as every SWAT-team gun came to bear on her. She gave a little squeak. In the moment of distraction Sharkey pulled out his shotguns, Mchynlyth raised his thumper, and Everett rolled, grabbed the jumpgun. Everett aimed the jumpgun at Charlotte Villiers.

"Bring him back."

"You know I can't do that."

The SWAT team swung their laser sights onto the *Everness* crew. It was a standoff.

"I'll shoot."

"And? I will live elsewhere, but you will all die. And we shall have the device. Your equation does not balance."

Tejendra was gone. Tejendra was *gone.*

Everett scooped up Dr. Quantum and turned the jumpgun on it.

"It's gone forever. You'll never find it."

"Now Everett, I need you to know that I do not condone . . . ," Paul McCabe began.

"Shut up, you buffoon," Charlotte Villiers snapped.

"I'll do it," Everett said.

"I believe you would, Everett," Charlotte Villiers said.

"I've drop lines here!" Sen shouted from the window. She reeled the thumper bag back into her weapon. "Come on!"

"Tell them to put down their guns," Everett said. He picked up Dr. Quantum and held it out at arm's length, the jumpgun pointed at it.

"As he says, Sergeant," Charlotte Villiers said. "You have rewritten the terms of the equation, young man."

Sharkey covered Everett with his shotguns as Captain Anastasia pushed him to the waiting drop line. The jumpgun was cumbersome and impossibly heavy in Everett's hand, as if it had taken into it all the wrong it had ever dealt out. He kept it trained on Dr. Quantum. The sheer adrenaline burn, the goalkeeper reflex, that let him dive to safety, see the spinning jumpgun, scoop it up and aim it all without conscious thought, all by pure physical instinct, was fading. The shakes, the fear were creeping over him. He had made the save of his life. No, he hadn't saved anything. He hadn't saved what mattered. Tejendra was gone. His dad was gone. His dad had been there for a moment, and that moment had been real, so real that it made all the other incredible things real. And in a flash of light, he was gone. Gone where no one could ever find him. He was dead to Everett. And nothing was real now.

"Hand here, foot there," Captain Anastasia said. "You know how to do it, Everett. You know how to do it."

She fastened him onto the line beneath Sen. Everett kept the jumpgun trained on Dr. Quantum though every muscle and sinew screamed with pain.

"Everett," Paul McCabe said, "I'm so sorry." His voice sounded to Everett like a yappy little dog, the kind you want to kick. For him there was only one person in the room. He met Charlotte Villiers eye to eye. Her eyes were cold and they were pale and they were blue as the Atlantic and they held not one atom of pity. He saw respect there, and therefore hate. No one had ever bested her before, and for that she would be his undying enemy. She would hunt him to the edge of the multiverse to correct that error.

"Miss Sixsmyth, I expressly said that you were to remain with the ship," Captain Anastasia bellowed as she strapped in.

"You also expressly said that I's had command," Sen said.

"Yes I did. And you took command. Smartly done, Miss Sixsmyth."

"Love you, Ma." Sen grinned. "Going up fast in three, two . . ." She hit the wrist control. Everett was jerked out of the window and into the air so hard he almost dropped the jumpgun. Flying. He was flying up through the cold black night, through the flurrying snow. He looked up. Above him, seeming poised on the pinnacle of the Tyrone Tower, lit up by the tower's floodlights, was *Everness*. Below was the black Gothic façade of the tower, yellow light pouring from the shattered twenty-second floor apartment.

"Dad!" he screamed down into the dark. "Dad! Dad! Dad!"

28

Sen dropped into her seat behind the thrust controls. Sharkey took his position at the communications desk. The monitors showed a distorted close-up of Mchynlyth down on the engineering deck, grinning into the camera, both thumbs up. Captain Anastasia bent over a comptator, tapping keys.

"Your heading, Miss Sixsmyth."

"Yes, ma'am," Sen said. She tapped the bearing that had just appeared on her screen and slid it into the navigation comptator.

"Ahead full."

Sen pushed the thrust levers to the furthest extent of their travel. *Everness* trembled as the impellers bit deep into the air. Mchynlyth had taken an engine from the starboard side and—in a thrilling operation involving ropes, slings, and abseiling—fixed it to one of the engine mounts in the port side damaged in the fight against the *Arthur P. Everness* was flying on six of her eight impellers, but she was trim and balanced, and Mchynlyth had spares in the engineering bay that he boasted he could rig in an hour each, if the ship needed to run. The story about refitting in Bristol had been a fiction to allow them to tack in across central London, within zip-line distance of the Tyrone Tower.

"Take us up into the cloud. Radar off, and observe radio silence, Mr. Sharkey. We go to dark running."

"We will be flying blind, forgive me my insouciance, ma'am," Sharkey said.

"Noted, Mr. Sharkey, and forgiven. All exterior cameras on monitors, please. Let's keep our eyes open. Sen, bona speed for the coast of Deutschland."

"'And if the blind lead the blind, both shall fall into the ditch,'"

Sharkey muttered as Sen turned to the lift levers and drew them slowly up. Wisps of cloud, flecked with snow, fringed the upper edge of the window; then *Everness* vanished into grey blankness.

"Mr. Singh."

What was that? Sounds, voices, people moved around Everett like the snow in the cloud through which *Everness* flew. Nothing was real; nothing was solid. He knew he was on the bridge of the airship, that he was fleeing across a winter cityscape to the open sea, and beyond it Deutschland and safety, flying low and dark to avoid detection, but he had no idea how he had got there from hurtling up the drop line into the London night. He knew that the figures moving through the dazed numbness in his head were people he knew and cared about, trying to save their lives and their ship. He knew it, but he could not connect to it. He could not make it feel real. He should not be with these people. He should be with his dad, with Mum and Victory-Rose. Again and again his memory went back to the room on the twenty-second floor, to Charlotte Villiers, feet apart, the jumpgun clutched in both hands, the strange little emission-head—not like any gun muzzle at all—pointed at him. He could see the curl on her red red lips as she squeezed the firing stud. He could see hotel room carpet—so new it still had fluff-balls, but still ugly as all hotel carpet is ugly—loom up as Tejendra sent him sprawling towards it. He could see the flash of light as the jump-gate opened. What he could not see was the moment Tejendra went from *there* to *not there*. Not there. Never there. Never would be there again. Flicked out to some random world in the ten to the eighty of the Panoply. That sound again. His name. Captain Anastasia calling his name.

"Captain?"

"I'd like to see that weapon you took." She beckoned Everett to the empty flight engineer station. Mchynlyth liked to be close and dirty with his machinery. It kept him a safe distance from Captain Anastasia.

Everett set the jumpgun on the desk. He wiped his fingers on the hem of his shorts. He imagined that it left a film of oil on his fingers that he would never quite get out, stained down to the skin cells like a tattoo. He never wanted to touch it again. Captain Anastasia carefully picked the jumpgun up with her fingertips. She studied it with distaste. It was small, squat, chubby, but it sat in the hand as if it changed shape to fit the contours of the individual palm and fingers. There were two thumb-wheel controls on the top, a trigger contact on the handle, and a data port in the rear. None were marked; none gave any sign as to how they operated. The barrel was a short, thick cylinder that ended in a small concave dish.

"Unhallowed thing. Mr. Singh—Everett—I need your help. I need to know everything about this device. Can you do that for me?" She looked Everett full in the eye, daring him to look away, daring him to push her away into something foggy and blurred and unreal. "Will you do that for me?"

Then the floor tilted. Engines screamed. *Everness* pitched nose-up. Everett reeled towards the open door. He grabbed the edge of the desk and clung on. The jumpgun slid. Captain Anastasia lunged across the engineering station and grabbed it with both hands. The nose pitched higher. Loose debris avalanched across the floor. Everett saw Sen hauling back on the control yoke with all her strength. The ship shuddered. Every switch, every screen, every dial and magnifier rattled. Everett hung on to the desk for his life. Through the great window he saw the snow-covered back of an airship. It filled the glass. Still *Everness* climbed, metre by metre, trying to clear the airship crossing its flight path. There was a sound like the steel jaws of the wolf that ate the sun closing. The ship shook to its very atoms. Then Sen pushed the yoke forwards. Captain Anastasia fought her way to the intercom, handhold by handhold.

"What was that?" she said.

"Iberian Skylines 2202 *Infanta Isabel*, on route Madrid–London," Sharkey said. "Close enough to read El Capitano's shoulder tags."

"It just came up out of nowhere," Sen said. Her face was whiter than pale. Her voice was thin as winter.

Captain Anastasia thumbed open the intercom. "Mr. Mchynlyth, status?"

On the monitor, Mchynlyth threw up his hands in resignation.

"Ach, between Bromleys and the sharpies and the Plenitude, the Goodwin Sands and the Tyrone Tower, what's a couple of centimetres off the rudder? We'll live; we'll fly."

"Captain." Every head turned to Sharkey's communication post. No one had ever heard him call Anastasia by her title. "They know we're here now. The Iberian put out a near-miss report."

Captain Anastasia grimaced. She pressed her hands to the glass and looked out into the fog and snow.

"We're not even over the Smoke Ring."

"Captain, Dunsfold ATC is demanding we identify ourselves and file a flight plan," Sharkey said.

"Ignore them, Mr. Sharkey. Maintain speed and heading, Sen. If they know where we are, then there's no point us fighting on through this murk. Take us up and out of it."

Sen answered at the helm. The cloud and snow broke around *Everness*'s prow like waves as she lifted out of the snow cloud into the clear air. A half-moon lay on the eastern edge of the world, lazing on a silvered blanket of clouds. The sky was brilliant with stars, each as sharp as a spear-point. Through the numbness, the shock, the unreality, Everett felt the sky touch him, call him out. It was the oldest mystery, the wonder on which all of science floated: the stars. He went to the window. The airship seemed to race over the endless landscape of moon-silvered cloud. Everett looked up at the constellations. He knew their forms, he knew their names; the gods and monsters and heroes that held truths more huge and marvellous than any legend. Moonshine lit his face. He became aware that Captain Anastasia was watching him.

Sharkey cupped an earphone to his head and held up a hand: silence in the bridge.

"I'm getting chatter on Frequency Two Eight."

Nervous glances flew across the bridge.

"What's Frequency Two Eight?" Everett whispered to Sen.

"The militaries talk on it," she said.

"Well, since they can see us we might as well have a look at them," Captain Anastasia said. "Full radar sweep, Mr. Sharkey, but don't overdo it. We want to preserve a certain air of mystery."

She bent over a monitor. The magnified display lit her face green. Like Tejendra's face when he looked into the Infundibulum, Everett thought. And then he looked at the stars and made a promise to them. I will find him. Through all the planes and all the worlds, I will find him. I have the Infundibulum. The Panoply is mine. And he is the man who built the Heisenberg Gate. Whatever world he's in, if the resources and the knowledge are there, he can build another one. You haven't beaten us, Charlotte Villiers.

"Captain, ma'am . . . ," Everett said.

Captain Anastasia held up her hand. *Quiet.*

"Two contacts?" she said, frowning at the screen.

"That's how I reckon it, ma'am," Sharkey said. "On our heading. Small and fast and on our tail."

"We'd better have Mr. Mchynlyth up here," Captain Anastasia said. "He can put that time in His Majesty's Navy to good use."

Mchynlyth was piped up from engineering.

"Mchynlyth was in the navy?" Everett asked Sen.

"Engineer on the *Royal Oak*," Sen said.

What's the Royal Oak*?* Everett wanted to ask, but he was learning that of airships and their ways and their crews there was no end of questions.

Mchynlyth on the bridge looked as out of place as a tiara on a pig. "Aye," he said, adjusting the magnifier lens and squinting into the green glow. "Two naval cutters, sure as eggs is eggs. There's no mistaking that signature."

"We've outrun cutters before," Captain Anastasia said.

"We've outrun old Deutscher customs scows on the Baltic

patrol," Mchynlyth said. "Those'll be Navy Class 22s; the nippiest wee buggers this side of the Atlantic."

"If we rigged the spare engines?"

"It'll be two and a half hours before they run us down instead of two."

Captain Anastasia returned to her charting table. Everett had felt *Everness* quiver a few minutes ago as she crossed the invisible thermal of the Smoke Ring, the chimneys that powered London hidden down beneath the snow cloud. He made calculations in his head. They would be out over the snow-covered flatlands of East Anglia, east by northeast. The coastline could only be minutes away, and the sea and German airspace. He saw Captain Anastasia make the same calculations and reach her own conclusions.

"Take us up, Miss Sixsmyth. Ten thousand metres."

"Ma? Ma'am?"

"Ten thousand metres, Miss Sixsmyth."

"That's the top limit of our operational envelope," Mchynlyth said. "If we over-pressure . . ."

"I'm aware of that, Mr. Mchynlyth. I'm also aware that Sheerness Automated Weather Station is reporting a southerly deflection of the polar jet stream down to 51 degrees north. If we can get onto that air current, it'll give us an extra eighty knots and we can surf her right into the throat of Deutscher Bight."

"An extra eighty knots," Mchynlyth said. "And we're flat-out as it is."

"Do you concur, Mr. Mchynlyth?"

"We've the structural integrity of a fart in a hurricane."

"Do you concur?"

"I concur, ma'am."

"Take her to the ceiling, Miss Sixsmyth."

"'Pride goeth before destruction, and a haughty spirit before a fall,'" Sharkey muttered.

Everness obeyed Sen swiftly and sweetly. She shied and bucked in the turbulence as she entered the fast-moving stream of high-altitude air. The cloud layer was so far below it looked to Everett like a landscape in its own right, a nation made of night. He could see three hundred miles in every direction. Those red-and-green sparks moving across the cloud-scape were the riding lights of airships. He stood among the stars. Everett became aware that Sen was beside him.

"Hey, how, who . . ."

"Autopilot. So, it's bijou bumpy, but the machine can handle that without Sen. Everett Singh, I's made you something."

Everett felt her press a soft square of card into his hand: a trump from the Everness tarot, facedown in his palm.

"The deck, well, it's a living thing like? So it needs to grow, coz if a thing stops growing it starts dying. So every once in a while it tells me it needs to be able to talk about a new person or a new adventure or a new start or a new possibility, so I makes it a new card."

"This is my card?" Everett curled his hand to look at the card's face. Sen touched him quickly and lightly.

"No, Everett Singh. You turns it when you needs it."

He slid the card into one of the side pockets of his shorts.

"We're being hailed," Sharkey announced. "One of the Navy cutters."

"On screens, please," Captain Anastasia said. Everyone pulled magnifiers over the tiny display tubes. The screens crackled with static that cleared to show an airship bridge. Pilot, navigation, engineering, and command posts were crewed by smart-haircutted men in sky-blue military jackets and round berets with red pompoms. The captain was distinguished by his peaked hat and a lot of gold braid.

"LTA *Everness*, this is HMAS *Indefatigable*," the captain said. "I am Captain Davenport. I wish to speak to your commanding officer."

Captain Anastasia pulled down an intercom on its boom-arm and pressed the transmit button.

"I am Captain Anastasia Sixsmyth of *Everness*. What's your business?"

"Captain Sixsmyth, descend to one thousand metres, stop all engines, and prepare to be boarded."

"The two cutters have entered the jet stream and are closing with us," Sharkey said.

"So noted," Captain Anastasia said. She thumbed the talk button again. "*Indefatigable*, we are a registered merchant ship on a commercial flight to Berlin."

"You have not filed a flight plan, you are in violation of air traffic control regulations, and we have it on authority that you are in illegal possession of a piece of technology that poses a security threat to this realm," Captain Davenport said. He was a smart but pudgy-faced middle-aged man, hair neatly slicked, with the prim but disappointed look of a commander who knew that a naval cutter was the highest he would ever rise in the air service. This was the most action he would ever see.

"On what authority?"

Charlotte Villiers stepped between Captain Davenport and the lens. She smiled. The wide-angle lens made her lips look huge and vampire-red and devouring.

"My authority. Hello, Captain Sixsmyth. Everett. Happy Christmas. I really would advise you to follow Captain Davenport's orders. You are in possession of Plenitude property, and it is incumbent on me, as plenipotentiary, to safeguard it. I am in one of the fastest and most modern military airships. You are in a crippled cargo barge that, frankly, has seen better days. I have two squads of royal marines at my disposal. You have, well, we can see what you have. Children, Captain, children. Do the sensible thing. This need not be painful. Oh yes. In case you're entertaining notions of a last-minute brilliant idea or a daring escape, you might want to make another sweep with your radar."

Charlotte Villiers reached up and turned off the camera.

"Mother and Mary and sweet Saint Pio," Sharkey said softly. The screens lit up with a radar display: tracking down from the north, cutting in towards the coast of Norfolk, was a monster radar contact: a behemoth airship escorted by six smaller ones. Mchynlyth dialled up the magnification on the lens until he could clearly read the ident number on the radar contact.

"RAN 101," Mchynlyth said, squinting. "That's her, all right. Me old mucker the *Royal Oak*. She must have been patrolling the Norwegian coast, keeping an eye on those perfidious Tsarists."

"What's the *Royal Oak*?" Everett asked.

Mchynlyth spun a brass trackball on the main comptator, tapped some metal keys.

"This is."

The illustration that appeared on the screen showed an airship hanging in the air above the mighty berths and polls and locks and channels of east London docks. It made them look like garden ponds, the ships unloading in them like little clockwork toys, the kind you got for the bath that worked once and never again. Everett knew he was looking at a monster. This made clouds look small. This was a flying city.

"If that picture's true; it—she—must be five, six hundred metres long."

"That picture disnae do her justice. Two thousand Imperial feet, nose to tail," Mchynlyth said proudly. "And an honour to serve on every one of them. And those wee flecks on the radar around her, those wee flies? Those are corvettes, each of them the size of our airbag here."

Thirty impeller pods. Multiple command decks and flying bridges. Gun blisters and missile racks. On each side, three wings, each wing carrying aircraft—aeroplanes—perched on launch rails like perching pterodactyls, wings folded around their glass cockpits, propellers furled.

"Those fighters'll catch us before we get even close to Deutscher airspace. They can shoot us clean out of the sky and there's not a flyin' thing we can do about it."

Everett frowned. High-speed cutters loaded with marines closing behind him, the Royal Air Navy's most powerful carrier with six escort ships each the size of *Everness* closing to intercept from the north. All this firepower. They could turn *Everness* to wisps of ash, blowing on the wind. But it didn't make sense.

"Captain Anastasia, can I have the jumpgun?"

She held it out at arm's length. It still felt oily and dirty and wrong down to its atoms to Everett, but he laid it on Mchynlyth's engineering bench and looked at it. Looked hard at it. Looked close at it. Looked long at it. Looked at every tiny notch and line and knurl of it. The controls were simple. The right wheel controlled the aperture: when he turned it, the little screen showed a fan-shaped display, lighting up higher and further to show the width of the jump effect. The other seemed to control recharge—the shorter the recharge time, the less wide the area of effect. The options for the jumpgun were lots of quick, small shots, or a few big, wide-angle ones. The charge meter read full. A panel on the bottom of the butt opened to show an oblong charge pack. Everett could make nothing of it. He slid it back into its housing. It locked with a smooth click. There was a safety ring around the trigger; you pressed and turned it to lock, and the trigger button sprang out and lit up. Everett quickly turned the safety lock back. The docking port. He lifted the gun close to his eyes. There were metal contacts in there. It looked very very like a USB port. The shape of the socket and the arrangement of the contacts were different, but Everett did not doubt that if he asked, Mchynlyth could work up an operating USB cable. The gun was intended to be connected to something computational. There was information inside it. Information about what?

Patterns, coincidences, intentions began to fall into place.

"Captain . . . ," he said.

Then everyone on *Everness*'s bridge ducked as two small, white, incredibly fast objects shot out from under the hull, scorched across the window, and hung in midair ahead of the ship, holding station in the rocking, rolling jet-stream.

"Get a light on those, Mr. Sharkey," Captain Anastasia ordered.

Spotlights stabbed out from under the great window and illuminated the hovering objects. They were two remote drones, holding precise position side by side, ten metres apart. The control was perfect; they precisely matched *Everness*'s velocity.

"So, the wee lady Villiers is taking a personal hand in it," Mchynlyth said.

"Explain please, Mr. Mchynlyth."

"You'll not have seen those. They're not standard issue—not yet. I know what they are because there's old navy ratings drink down the Knight. Snipships, Captain. What you can't see is that between them there's a nanocarbon fibre. Like the one I opened up that lock with, but a lot stronger. I think you get the picture. They'll lop off our impeller pods one at a time snippity snappety and then slice us up like Polska sausage."

"Captain, a word with you," Sharkey said.

"Speak, Mr. Sharkey," Captain Anastasia said. The snipships held position in perfect formation.

"Ma'am, with your permission, in your ready room."

"Impossible, Mr. Sharkey."

"What I need to say, well, it ain't for, shall we say, public consumption."

"Not possible, Mr. Sharkey. Whatever it is, say it here and say it quick. We are running out of options."

"Very well, ma'am." Sharkey turned his chair into the centre of the flight deck. "I did give you the opportunity—let all here be witness to that. Give him to her. The boy. Give him to the Villiers woman. She can take that comptator thing he's been lugging around any time she wants. We're in no position to stop her. Give her what she wants. That way, we might be able to save the ship. We might be able to fly the trade routes like we always have. We might be something other than rebels and renegades and vile offenders. We might have a life better than being hunted like dirty thieving magpies down the rest of our days. Give her the boy, Captain. Save the ship." Sharkey looked at every face in turn. He held Everett's look the longest. Everett's eyes were very still. "I'll call them myself."

And Sen vaulted over the flight station, snatched a screwdriver from engineering, and in three heartbeats had the blade pressed to the corner of Sharkey's left eye. His hands hovered over the handles of his shotguns.

"You never ever ever say that," she said in a voice like winter. She leaned over him as close as a kiss. "You never ever ever do that. You never ever ever think that, you dirty bad faithless man. This is *Everness*. This is us. All of us. We's family. Everett's family. Family's all we got."

"Sen, return to your post!" Captain Anastasia thundered. Sen slowly drew the screwdriver away from Sharkey's eye, but she never took her eyes off his. "Miss Sixsmyth, your station! Speed, heading, and altitude are unchanged. Mr. Sharkey, maintain radio silence."

"*Royal Oak* has launched fighters," Mchynlyth said, bent close to the radar screen.

"Why?" Everett shouted. All the disconnected, flocking, wheeling thoughts and doubts and suspicions turned as one, became one understanding. "Why? I still have the jumpgun. I can blow the Infundibulum into some random universe. If Charlotte Villiers attacks me, she loses. So why does she threaten us? Unless—unless she thinks I won't do it. Why would she think that? Because there's something she knows that she thinks I know too. Something that makes the Infundibulum as valuable to me as it is to her. What is it?"

"Captain, those fighters will be on us in three minutes," Mchynlyth said.

"So noted, Mr. Mchynlyth. Continue, Mr. Singh."

Everett held up the jumpgun in his right hand, Dr. Quantum in his left.

"Is it that this has never existed before? This plus this? Jumpgun plus Infundibulum? There's a computer socket in the jumpgun—it's designed to get information out of it. Maybe you can put information into it as well. It's like a little Heisenberg Gate you can carry in your pocket. But I can programme Heisenberg Gates. It's how I got here. I can make them take me anywhere. And now I'm asking, so what information can you get out of it? It sends you to a random world. That's a quantum effect. Quantum effects are random. But they're not meaningless. Listen to me, listen to me: there's a thing in physics called quantum entanglement. Two particles, once they're in the same quantum state—entangled—they remain connected no matter how far you separate them. You could send one to the end of the universe, and whatever you did to the particle here on Earth, it would be reflected in that other particle, instantly. And it's the same for that particle, whatever happens to it, no matter how far away, the particle here on earth responds instantly. They're entangled. Could it be, this gun opens a random gate, but the entanglement leaves a trace inside the gun, if only we could find it? Maybe it never was a weapon at all; maybe it was some kind of exploration device, like for mapping the Panoply? Open a window into another universe, then read the coordinates. Because, if it is, if it can do that, then there'll be some trace, some record inside, of where it sent my dad. And I think it can do that, and that's why Charlotte Villiers thinks that I won't destroy the Infundibulum. I need them both. I need the information from the jumpgun to find that trace, and I need the Infundibulum to be able to control the gun."

Everness had flown to the edge of the night. Dawn was a line of yellow light on the eastern horizon, shading to star-spattered indigo in the vault of the sky. The cloud layer was an unbroken carpet of black and purple. The fighters came out of the dawn light, three of them, howling in on twin propeller engines, as lean and mean and hungry as sky-sharks. They ripped in low and fast down the length of *Everness*'s spine, turned, and came back for another pass. Cannon unfolded from the wings; missile racks slid from the gull-white bellies.

"This is what I've been saying," Sharkey said. "Give it to her! Give it to Charlotte Villiers. That way, everyone wins."

"Silence, Mr. Sharkey," Captain Anastasia said. "No, everyone does not win. Everett does not win. We've seen once before what Charlotte Villiers would do when she has the jumpgun and the Infundibulum. She is stronger now because she believes Mr. Singh has no choice but to surrender to her. I do not believe in no-win scenarios. Mr. Singh: this weapon, it's designed to be programmed?"

"Yes."

"You can make it work?"

"Yes. I think so. Yes, I know it. It'll take a bit of time."

"I can give you time. Jump us out of here."

Sharkey was on his feet.

"Are you out of your mind?"

"Jump us out of here, Mr. Singh," Captain Anastasia said. "All of us." The fighters raked *Everness* again, tail to nose, and turned out in the breaking dawn. The two snipships moved apart from each other. And in the heart of the sun-glow lay a black flaw, the carrier *Royal Oak* and her escorts.

"Ma?" Sen said in a very small voice.

"Mr. Singh?"

Everett rolled the click-wheel all the way to maximum aperture.

"I think it should get the whole ship in."

"Oh, that's reassuring," Mchynlyth said.

Everett offered the jumpgun to Captain Anastasia. She shook her head.

"No, Mr. Singh. The decision must stand with you."

"They're coming," Mchynlyth said.

Everett turned the jumpgun on himself. He closed his eyes. No. He had to see it, see the Heisenberg Gate open before him. Where would they go? No one could know. He opened his eyes and looked into the black metal concavity of the jumpgun muzzle.

"Snipship contact in three, two . . ." Mchynlyth said.

Everett pulled the trigger. The world went white. Then it went away.

29

The world came back. And it was white.

It still didn't hurt a bit.

"We're still here!" Mchynlyth said.

"That, I rather think, is a moot point, sir," Sharkey said.

"Radar and radio, Mr. Sharkey," Captain Anastasia said. "I want to know where we are. Mr. Mchynlyth, status report at your earliest convenience. I want to know if everything made it through. I was expecting something a little more . . . dramatic. Mr. Singh, is you all right?"

The jumpgun fell from Everett's fingers. It clattered on the decking and lay dead and cold as ice.

"Nothing on radar, nothing on radio," Sharkey said. "We are alone."

"And intact," Mchynlyth said, clicking through the closed-circuit cameras, internal and external. "Pretty much."

"All engines stop," Captain Anastasia ordered. Sen slapped all the levers back to their zero position. The gentle but constant vibration of the impellers stopped. "Now, where the hell are we?"

The crew of *Everness* lined up in front of the great window.

"That's what I call a white Christmas," Mchynlyth said.

"'By the breath of God frost is given: and the breadth of the waters is straitened,'" Sharkey said.

Dawn was spilling over a world of ice. Horizon to horizon the sea-ice extended, pressure ridges and cracks and faults casting long purple shadows in the low light. Even from altitude Everett could see snow-devils and storms of glittering ice-dust swirl across the frozen sea and drift in the lee of the pressure ridge. Ice, endless ice. He could feel the bottomless cold through the tough glass.

Everett felt Sen's hand slip into his. Her fingers were warm; they were life and contact and people. He'd looked into the blank muzzle of the jumpgun and seen cold and destruction and randomness.

"We have work to do," Captain Anastasia said. "But first, Mr. Singh, I believe we have well-hung pheasants and Ridley Road's finest manjarry in the galley. In your best time; rattle us up a fantabulosa Christmas dinner. We're going to celebrate."

"Aye, ma'am."

"Only when you're ready, Everett."

The fingers of Everett's free hand traced the outline of the Everness tarot Sen had made for him. He slipped the card out and turned it faceup. Like many of Sen's trumps, it was a collage, pieces snipped from a bizarre mix of magazines and newspaper carefully arranged and pasted. A male figure in a military-style jacket and baggy shorts stepped from a blank white doorway. The figure's arms were stretched out on either side: in one upturned hand he held a globe, in the other a spiral galaxy. In the background, low on the hand-drawn horizon, was a tiny cut-out airship. In the blank space at the bottom Sen had written the card's name in her clumsy, loopy handwriting.

Planesrunner.

PALARI

Palari (polari, parlare) is a real secret language that has grown up in parallel with English. Its roots go back to seventeenth-century Thieves Cant in London—a secret thieves' language. It's passed through market traders and barrow-mongers, fairground showmen, the theatre, the Punch and Judy Show, and gay subculture. Palari ("the chat"—from the Italian *parlare*, "to talk") contains words from many sources and languages: Italian, French, *lingua franca* (an old common trading language spoken across the Mediterranean), Yiddish, Romani, and even some Gaelic. It's taken in words from Cockney rhyming slang—"plates" for *feet*, from "plates of meat" = "feet"; and London back-slang—"eek" is short for "ecaf," which is "face" backwards.

Many words from palari/polari have entered London English.

In Earth 3, palari is the private language of the Airish. In our world, polari still survives as a secret gay language.

GLOSSARY OF PALARI:

ajax: nearby (from adjacent?)
alamo: hot for her/him
amriya: a personal vow, promise, or restriction that cannot be broken (from Romani)
aunt nell: listen, hear
aunt nells: ears
barney: a fight
batts: shoes
bijou: small/little (means "jewel" in French)

blag: pick up/beg as a favour/get without paying
bod: body
bona: good
bona nochy: goodnight (from Italian—*buona notte*)
bonaroo: wonderful, excellent
buvare: a drink (from Italian *bere* or old-fashioned Italian *bevere* or Lingua Franca *bevire*)
capello: hat (from Italian *cappello*)
carsey/khazi: toilet.
charper: to search (from Italian *chiappare*, to catch)
chavvie: child
chicken: young male/boy
clobber: clothes
cod: naff, vile
cove: friend
dally/dolly: sweet, kind.
Dinari: money (perhaps from Italian *denaro*)
dish: ass, bum, arse
dona: woman (from Italian *donna* or Lingua Franca *dona*) a term of respect
dorcas: term of endearment, "one who cares." The Dorcas Society was a ladies' church association of the nineteenth century, which made clothes for the poor.
doss: bed
drag: clothes, especially women's clothes (from Romani *indraka*, a skirt)
ecaf/eek: face (back-slang). *Eek* is an abbreviation of *ecaf*.
fantabulosa: fabulous/wonderful
feely: child/young/girl
fruit/fruity: in Hackney Great Port, a term of mild abuse
gelt: money (Yiddish)
kris: an Airish duel of honour (from Romani)
lacoddy: body

lallies: legs
latty: room or cabin on an airship
lilly: police (Lilly Law)
luppers: fingers (Yiddish *lapa*, a paw)
manjarry: food (from Italian *mangiare* or Lingua Franca *mangiaria*)
measures: money
meese: plain, ugly, despicable (from Yiddish *meeiskeit*: loathsome, despicable, abominable)
meshigener: nutty, crazy, mental (from Yiddish)
metzas: money (Italian *mezzi*: means, wherewithal)
naff: awful, dull, tasteless
nante: not, no, none (Italian: *niente*)
ogle: look, admire
omi: man/guy
omi-palone: effeminate man or homosexual
onk: nose
palare pipe: telephone ("talk pipe")
palliass: mattress or place to sleep.
polone: woman/girl
riah: hair (back-slang)
scarper: to run off (from Italian *scappare*, to escape or run away)
sharpy: policeman (from "charpering omi")
sharpy palone: policewoman
shush: steal
shush-bag: hold-all/backpack
slap: makeup
so: to be part of the in-crowd/Airish (e.g. "Is he so?")
strides: trousers
tober: road
todd: alone (from rhyming slang *Todd Sloanne*—alone)
troll: to walk about looking for business or some kind of opportunity
varda: to see/look at (from Italian dialect *vardare* = *guardare*—look at)

yews: eyes (from French *yeux*)
zhoosh: style, make a show of, mince (Romani: *zhouzho*—clean, neat)
zhooshy: flashy, showy

ABOUT THE AUTHOR

IAN MCDONALD has written thirteen science fiction novels and has lost count of the number of stories. He's been nominated for every major science fiction award, and even won some. Ian also works in television, in programme development—all those reality shows have to come from somewhere—and has written for screen as well as print. He lives in Northern Ireland, just outside Belfast, and loves to travel. *Planesrunner* is the first part of the *Everness* series.

Quiz #: 180844
BL: 5.5
13 pts